Rudolf Virchow
Four Lives
in One

Leslie Dunn

ISBN-13: 978-0972699891

DEDICATION

To my father who was my first hero, and
my son and daughter who taught me to live in the moment,
who are and were the greatest gifts from God.

Special thanks to Charité Hospital for their hospitality and tour.

Cover image can be found at:
http://commons.wikimedia.org/wiki/File:Rudolf_Virchow.jpg

CONTENTS

Rudolf Virchow

1839 – Approx. age 18

1860 – Age 39

1862 – age 41

1882 – Age 61

1890 – age 69

1896 – Age 75

Virchow's wife, Rose Mayer

Rose and Rudolf, 1851

Benno Reinhardt, 1819 – 1852, best friend of Rudolf and cofounder of Virchow Archiv who died at age 32 from tuberculosis.

1849 (L-R) Scherer, Virchow (banished from Berlin), Rotterau, Kölliker, Rinecker

1891 – Age 70

1890

1890

Photo taken by author

Buried at Old St. Matthews Cemetery, Berlin, Germany

Of note, Rudolf's wife, Rose, and a daughter, Hanna, are buried with him. Directly across from their graves lie Rose's father and Rudolf's father-in-law, Carl Mayer.

Photo taken by author.

Preface

In the 1970's singer Don McLean wrote a bittersweet song about Vincent Van Gogh. Van Gogh was just another artist of his time who acquired posthumous fame. McLean captured Van Gogh's essence in one eloquent line: "This world was never meant for one as beautiful as you." Asked why he wrote the song, McLean stated simply that he had to.

Rudolf Virchow, M.D. experienced an opposite effect from Van Gogh. Virchow (pronounced "Firko") grew to international fame during his life, 1821-1902, but faded into obscurity over the years. Threads of him scattered yet remain current throughout the world – a publication he began more than one hundred and fifty years ago continues, the meritorious annual Virchow scholarship carries on, streets, buildings, stamps and statues bear his name. Upon his death, the German nation declared that with Virchow's passing, the country lost not one man but four.

I first became aware of Virchow's name learning anatomical sites in the brain (Virchow-Robin space) when I worked in Radiology. Next, I heard his name in a college class of Anatomy and Physiology as one who named most of the common tumors and set the current standard for autopsies. By the time I heard of him in Principles of Disease, a class for medical coding, my interest was piqued sufficiently that I wondered, "Who is this man?" The more I researched his astonishing life, the more I wondered why so many had not heard of him. As my respect and admiration grew I couldn't comprehend that Virchow didn't have a place on the bookshelf, not about his accomplishments, but about who he was.

While enmeshed in researching Virchow he naturally found his way into my conversations. The passion with which I spoke of him caused some to wonder if I channeled him. Although I don't believe in such things I wish that it was true. Some days I could do with a dose of his courage. When asked why I wrote the book, like McLean with Van Gogh, I had no choice –my life would be incomplete had I not written it.

I respectfully leave it to more scholarly writers to provide biographical writings of Virchow. With deep humbleness I wrote this great man's book, most of which is based on Rudolf's letters to his father fleshed out and brought to life. After the death of his father which of course ended the letters, the rest of the book is a series of anecdotes written by others and, prolific writer that he was, his personal and professional writings. So rich was his life that eight folders, one for each decade of his life, kept things barely manageable during researching and writing his book.

Please note that italicized text throughout the book represents either direct quotes of Virchow's or another person from history. Portions of the book were written based on references by Virchow - for example, Schmidt initially was an ardent supporter of Virchow and then turned against him. It was a turning point. In another example, Dr. Virchow fought on the barricades and talked other doctors into it, too. Upon research, mention of his involvement exists more as a footnote than a critical moment in his life. That he cared enough to put his life on the line on behalf of the working class deserves much more than a passing note. Since little is made of Virchow's bravery, the scene exists from scant references and brought to life through research.

If you know the terms leukemia, embolism, thrombosis, socialized medicine and Informed Consent, if you've heard of

Helen of Troy and Neanderthal man and take for granted that meat you purchase passed inspection, your life has been touched by Virchow. At his insistence, a school of nursing in Berlin started and his work began the road to current day chemotherapy. As surely as a flood changes the course of a river so did Rudolf Virchow change the course of our lives. He was a short man with raven black eyes with titles and nicknames, "Father of Pathology, "Pope of Medicine," or simply, "Dr. V." He was to medicine what Galileo was to astronomy. He was a nineteenth century Ralph Nader to the common working man. He was Daniel to the goliath Otto Bismarck. He was a cool and grounded counterbalance to the romantic and flighty Heinrich Schliemann. Offered the great German honor of adding "von" to his name he declined. He believed that it would distance him from the common man on whose behalf he fought until his death.

It is not overstating to say Virchow revolutionized medicine. Before the age of thirty he ended two centuries of romantic beliefs, the theory of Four Humours, ushering in medicine as we know it today. He courageously and with great calm withstood insults and sharp criticism, even the revoking of his medical privileges at Charité and banished from Berlin. Later in his life when he discovered that white grains in pork were not a natural entity of the meat as was believed but rather larvae of worms, he held public speeches in the streets of Berlin which eventually instituted inspections of meat. Regrettably it would be sixty years before the United Stated followed suit.

He believed it is a physician's duty to enter the arena of politics stating that physicians are "natural attorneys of the poor." Always one to practice what he preached, he remained a dominant figure in politics for most of his life. Of what good are medicines only, he reasoned, for a population living in conditions that incited disease and illnesses. When presented with a populace afflicted with a single diagnosis, such as typhus, Virchow advocated relentlessly for not only medical treatment but also for education, wealth and democracy. Physicians, he believed, would influence legislation that best enhances the health, wealth and education of the working man, hence the term "medico-political."

While my admiration is more than a little for his accomplishments, what stirs my soul was Virchow's almost supernatural zeal and energy he sustained for over fifty years to benefit those without a voice. When his world crashed around him because of his beliefs, he compromised, but when next able to get back into politics he did so with fearless enthusiasm. Through the force of his intelligence, network of friends and powerful persuasion he used the power he eventually attained not to benefit himself but always to benefit others.

Virchow belongs not to one country, nor to any specialized field. He was a citizen of the world. With deep humbleness it is my hope that I portrayed his essence including his triumphs and his downfalls. It is also my hope that the reader agrees that it is finally time to bestow much belated recognition to this unique and amazing man, and allow him to remind us that one person can make a difference.

Leslie Dunn

Rudolf Virchow

"What we do for ourselves dies with us. What we do for others and the world, remains and is immortal"

Mason Albert Pike

Rudolf Virchow

POLICE BARGE INTO WEDDING

The minister patted Rudolf and Rose's shoulders. "We must do this quickly," he whispered. He placed a hand on each of their heads and from the depths of his soul administered the briefest of a matrimonial ceremony. Friends and family closed their eyes as the minister prayed for the newlywed's marriage and for their protection. He finished with a murmured, "Amen."

"Now go in peace, love, and God's eternal blessings on your marriage," he said. Like a shepherd leading innocents to their slaughter the minister walked Rudolf and Rose down the aisle of the church. The young couple's glowering, enraged fathers stood shoulder to shoulder at the door stopping the menacing intruders who were trying to force their way past the newlywed's fathers.

From the doorway the police captain's voice boomed throughout the silenced church: "RUDOLF VIRCHOW – YOU ARE TO LEAVE BERLIN IMMEDIATELY!"

KING OF THE BAD BOYS

"RUDOLF CARL VIRCHOW!" Headmaster Horst roared.

At the sound of the headmaster's voice, four seven-year-olds hiding behind a shed -- Goring, Hager, Brewing and Virchow -- crouched down and stiffened. As Horst stepped around the corner, the boys gaped at the red-faced Goliath. Their bodies shrunk like leaves in a fire.

Virchow forcefully ground a cigar's lit end into the dirt. Before Horst could stop him, Virchow popped the nubbin into his mouth and swallowed. Horst and the other three boys winced involuntarily.

Horst stared down at the eight widened eyes, ignoring what must be going on in young Virchow's stomach. "Did you really think you could hide the odor of that cigar?" he bellowed. "Where did you get it this time, Virchow?"

"My father tossed it into the yard, sir," he said, his voice shaking.

"And so you picked it up and brought it to school and share it with your *FRIENDS*?"

Some students gathered outside the school. One little girl said to another, "Sounds like Goring is in trouble again."

"Goring *and* Hager *and* Brewing *and* Virchow," said her friend.

"Oh, oh."

Goring spoke up. "He didn't bring the cigar this time, Headmaster Horst. I did."

The other three little jaws dropped open, then snapped shut.

Mr. Horst's whole head twisted to one side like a dog on the hunt, his eyes transfixed on Goring.

Then Brewing chirped in, "No, sir, it was me."

Looking at Brewing, Headmaster Horst said in a low voice, "Oh, I see."

Malevolently his gaze dragged from one boy to the next. He bent down and wagged his finger close to each of their noses. "You are all going to defend Virchow, are you? Hmmmm?" Then rasped, "How would you like to share in his punishment?"

Before they could respond, he stretched tall and barked, "VIRCHOW, STAND!"

Brushing the dirt from his brown checkered pants, Rudolf stood up. He rubbed his stomach to ease the growing, rising nausea.

Horst seized Virchow by one ear. "Come with me," he growled, dragging Rudolf along the dirt path. "There is a place waiting for you at the back of the classroom. And since this is the second time for this disgusting nonsense, you will spend two days with your

face to the wall AND I expect a visit from your father tomorrow."
To the other three he said, "All of you return to the classroom -
NOW."

Almost to the classroom, with his pinched ear on fire between
the headmaster's fingers, Rudolf torqued his head sideways and
launched the cigar at the headmaster's shoe.

Rudolf Ludwig Karl Virchow born October 13, 1821, in the
small town of Schievelbein, Pomerania now the city Koszalin in
northwest Poland was the only son of Carl and Johanna Virchow.

Carl Virchow's varied interests reflected in his multiple
vocations - the town treasurer as well as a farmer and butcher. He
maintained a rental library and was an amateur botanist. His
impractical, philosophical nature clashed with his wife's lifelong
aspirations for the comfort and security of wealth. Carl's
pocketbook opened far too wide for a handsome new cow, yet crop
insurance cost too many thalers. This short in stature, self-serving
man with sky blue eyes, whose hair color was known only to his
wife due to his constant wigs, nonetheless, was a scholarly
eccentric. He bore a passion with the education of Rudolf, his only
child, that some deemed an obsession.

Johanna Virchow, Rudolf's mother, with a stout figure and
shorter than her husband, was not a pretty woman. Brunette with
almost black-brown eyes that Rudolf inherited, she was raised in a
deeply religious home. She and Rudolf shared a near idolatrous
relationship.

Because of his father's multiple occupations, Rudolf grew up in
a poor home yet rich in intellectual inclinations. As an adult
recollecting his youth, he said his first memory was that of looking

at pictures of flowers and trees in his father's books. Even the gifted, though, are not angels.

Headmaster Horse said, "Mr. Virchow, I apologize for calling you away from your work..."

Mr. Horst glanced at Mr. Virchow's wig. Yet another expensive one, he noted. Heavily lidded blue eyes directly gazed at him. Large, low set ears seemed to form parenthesis in which was centered the man's bulbous nose. A mere opening beneath that nose passed for lips. Horst sensed no tenderness.

"That's all right, Mr. Horst. I apologize for my son's behavior yesterday. His mother and I had turns with him last night."

Horst noted Mr. Virchow's fine clothes with lots of buttons, an ivory handled walking stick and rings on eight fingers that suggested a higher social status than that of a farmer. "Rudolf is a very bright student – one of the brightest I've ever seen."

Mr. Virchow believed the headmaster spoke from the heart. He relaxed a little.

"He also has become quite the leader," Mr. Horst added.

"Oh?"

"Did you know that others refer to him as the 'King?'"

"The what?" Mr. Virchow erupted into laughter, tapping his walking stick on the floor. His tiny son. Who recited bedtime stories verbatim, who asked questions relentlessly about everything. "King? Of what, Mr. Horst? Of the bad boys?" He swiped at his eyes with the back of his hand while he struggled to get himself under control.

"This is not funny, Mr. Virchow."

Virchow pulled a silk embroidered handkerchief from his pocket and dabbed his eyes. "Sir, I regret laughing and I assure you that I do not find this funny. It drew an absurd picture in my mind, that's all."

Although he didn't say it, Horst agreed but kept his voice firm, his face serious. "As you know, Mr. Virchow, this is not the first time Rudolf has gotten himself into trouble. But from his high intellectual development and curious nature, I have the impression that although he is accepted by this lot of ruffians, he is not truly comfortable in their presence."

"Then why do you think he goes along with them?"

"If you want my opinion, it appears to me that as the brightest one in the bunch, he holds a place of honor among them. They look up to him."

"Then perhaps he needs a place of honor among the good students, instead," Rudolf's father said.

The headmaster stroked his beard thoughtfully. "Yes, I think he does."

"Mr. Horst, would Rudolf's class be interested in lessons in botany?"

"I don't know, Mr. Virchow. What did you have in mind?

"I have had an interest in botany for a number of years and have passed that interest on to my son. Perhaps the teacher would allow Rudolf to teach other students what he's learned, or perhaps during science class, the teacher might consider allowing Rudolf to demonstrate his knowledge?"

"Let me talk to his teacher and I'll let you know."

Taught by the headmaster, Rudolf advanced to the highest grade and first in his class. Also at that time, the rector gave him private lessons in Latin and French, although the rector's knowledge was too limited for Mr. Virchow's liking. Mr. Virchow persuaded the Protestant minister in town, Mr. Benekendorff, to set up a private school. Under Benekendorff's private tutorage, Rudolf received a quality education in religion, history and continued Latin.

Two years later, Mr. Benekendorff closed the school and Rudolf returned to the school of headmaster Horst and rector. The rector charged nine-year-old Rudolf with the responsibility to teach other students Latin. As an adult, one of Virchow's greatest roles was that of a teacher but not so in his youth. Rudolf's persistent father persuaded another minister, Mr. Gantzkow, to give his son and a few other students private lessons. By the age of eleven, Rudolf demonstrated superior abilities in multiple fields including history, foreign languages (Greek, Latin, and French) and science.

In 1832, Mr. Ganztkow gallantly attempted for six months to teach the boys, but the disparity among his pupils made him decide to close his school. Yet again persistent on his son's behalf, Mr. Virchow asked Mr. Gantzkow for private lessons for Rudolf. This time, Mr. Virchow's persistence paid off. For the next two years under Mr. Gantzkow's tutorage Rudolf's education soared in history and biology and he gained a higher proficiency in foreign languages as well. Thus began a lifelong study of foreign languages eventually enabling Virchow to introduce words now commonplace to the field of medicine.

Rudolf Virchow

On May 1, 1835 at almost fourteen years old, when poor children's education ended and employment began, a reluctant Rudolf and his friend, Johann Schroder who also showed outstanding academic abilities, moved from Schivelbein to Koslin, Germany to attend the Gymnasium, or high school. Although initially homesick, the excitement of the larger town spawned Virchow's love of travel. Stimulating courses fed his craving for knowledge, and praise from some of his teachers encouraged him to seek the same from other teachers. Although math proved especially difficult, Rudolf's teachers bumped him ever higher in the school's hierarchy from his entry level last place.

But again, his rogue side flared and got him into trouble.

His frivolous conduct rolled Rudolf's status downhill as he offended first one teacher then more until he found himself in last place in high school, a most undignified, shameful and intolerable place for him. Utilizing his mother's theological lessons of purifying his thoughts and sentiments, Rudolf reeled himself within bounds. By the age of sixteen he successfully completed the required school-leaving examination, his behavior so completely turned around that on his confirmation day, Easter 1837, Rudolf was given the privilege of reading the confession of faith on behalf of those being confirmed.

In an essay written during his last year at the Gymnasium, Rudolf described his reasons for choosing the field of medicine as a career: *"First, it must be a pleasure to study the human body, the most miraculous masterpiece of nature and to learn about the smallest vessel and the smallest fiber. But second and most important, the medical profession gives the opportunity to alleviate the troubles of the body, to ease the pain, to console a person who is in distress, and to lighten the hour of death of many a sufferer."*

PEPIN AT MILITARY MEDICAL FACILITY

On scholarships, both Rudolf and his childhood friend, "young Schroeder" became "Pepins" at the Military Medical Facility of the Friedrich-Wilhelms-Institute and together they traveled the one hundred forty-seven miles by carriage from Schivelbein to Berlin. Considered the finest medical facility in Germany, military-run Charité' Hospital's faculty consisted of both civilian and military doctors. Associated with the University of Berlin, the student body was also comprised of both military and civilian students.

Scholarship students such as Rudolf and Schroeder, future Prussian military doctors, received free tuition at the University and Charité as well as room and board. Rudolf quickly learned that the medical residents were divided into two categories: those whose parents could afford the institution's fee and the have-nots.

After graduation physician fellowship recipients were expected to join the military unless the state believed, or was convinced by influential persons, that the physician's abilities would benefit the state in another capacity, such as research. Few exceptional physicians were relieved of their obligation to the military. Less than three years after becoming a doctor of medicine and surgery, Rudolf was one of the few.

Upon arrival at the school Rudolf's uncle, Ludwig Hesse, a builder involved in the construction of Charité, accompanied Rudolf touring the school and meeting new professors and administrators. Through the years, Uncle Hesse underpinned Rudolf's eventual success in small but important roles as Rudolf was the only and beloved son of Johanna, Hesse's sister.

After a brief time of settling in, Virchow wrote home about things of which his father would be interested – Rudolf's roommates (Hoffman from Suhl, *"bad tempered"* and Fouquet from Wetzlar, *"in many respects an oddity,"*) a list of his expenses and descriptions of the facility and military doctors - the Surgeon Generals (Generalarzts) of which there were four, the House Medical Officers (Hausstabsarzts) and Staff Physicians (Stabsarzts).

A physician with the rank of major in the medical corps (Oberstabsarzt) Grimm, only thirty-six years old, especially impressed Virchow. He wrote to his father of Grimm's highly distinguished and elegant manner, light blond hair and blue eyes, and how Grimm's fluent and coherent speech contrasted with what he believed that of the clumsy and abrupt speech of Grimm's superior, Surgeon General (Generalarzt), Wiebel. Though initially critical of Surgeon General Wiebel, (*"especially when wearing plain clothes, he looks not unlike a Pomeranian tenant farmer"* and *"what he says is extremely trivial and not at all befitting his position..."*), Virchow eventually grew fond of Wiebel and even amused by Wiebel's mannerisms. He wrote to his father of the old Surgeon General falling asleep during a conference and Wiebel revealing during his own birthday party in December that rather his birthday was in summer.

Rudolf then described his grueling Monday through Saturday class schedule: Seven to eight a.m. Monday through Saturday, Anatomy; Wednesday and Thursday eight to nine a.m. History of Prussia; Monday through Thursday nine to 10 a.m. Splanchology; Monday through Saturday eleven to noon, Chemistry; Monday and Tuesday noon to one p.m. Osteology; Thursday and Friday one to two p.m. Medical Methodology; Monday through Saturday two to three p.m. Anatomy taught by his favorite teacher, Dr. Müller; Tuesday, Wednesday and Thursday three to four p.m. Anatomy of Sensory Organs, again by Dr. Müller; Friday and Saturday three to four p.m. Physics; and Monday through Friday from four to six p.m. Logic and Psychology ("a terribly boring class"). In summary, ten classes spanning eleven hours, six days a week. Sundays, off. That translates to a thirty-hour credit semester. Currently, fifteen are considered full-time.

Near Christmas of 1839, only three months into medical school the strain of little rest, heavy class schedules, constant worries about finances and homesickness thinned the ranks. Of this eighteen-year old Rudolf wrote to his father:

Berlin

Thursday, December 5, 1839

(Completed Friday, December 13, 1839)

Leslie Dunn

Dear Father,

I was delighted to receive your letter. Let me tell you that it does not matter if you omit "pupil of the royal, etc." from the address; nobody sending a letter to this place would write it on the envelope.

As regards our relationship with other students, it is in fact fairly good and up till now I have had no cause for complaint. No student, unless he is by nature a snob and somewhat warped, will hesitate to associate with a Pepin. Other people, however, seem to hold us in lower esteem than the students.

I must admit that all these people are extremely polite if you are well-mannered and courteous to them and give them no cause for complaint. Unfortunately, however, I have landed in a section that for the most part consists of terrible people. They take great delight in skipping lessons, playing cards, drinking beer and so on. Even my roommate, Hoffmann, is one of those who almost regularly skip two or three lessons every day.

One Stabsarzt usually comes in to inspect each course. This incommodes the fellows and they stay at home; then most of my dear colleagues who are waiting at the entrance to the auditorium quickly sneak away. For instance, in the class in Logic it generally happens that of four sections, i.e. of 36 pupils, only six pupils are present. Several times a Stabsarzt arrived only to find a great majority skipping lessons; and each time the entire section received a severe reprimand. Last Sunday our Hoffmann, too, was confined to quarters.

Finally, in response to your question regarding the dissection of cadavers, we are presently dealing with the science of muscles (mycology). Of course, fresh specimens alone are used for this as it would impossible to demonstrate the muscles of a corpse that is old, dried up, or preserved in alcohol. Sometimes there are heads, sometimes arms or legs, a severed trunk, a part of a back with one leg or a part of a chest with one arm – in short all possible variations.

The trouble is that corpses are in short supply. Of 150 students who are supposed to dissect, only seventy can be kept occupied in a week, and very often eight to fifteen may be found working on one body. At present we have anatomy lessons daily from seven to eight in the morning, and here we use the same specimens that the professor used for his lecture the day before. In these lessons the teaching Stabsarzt calls on a pupil and asks him to demonstrate the specimen. Now if the muscles happen to lie deep, under two or three layers of muscle, naturally he will have to fold them back in order the show the ones in question.

Recently it so happened that Müller delivered his lecture on the muscles of one head for a whole week, and since the weather was warm at the time the thing stank horribly. During a lesson, the Stabsarzt once called on me to show him a muscle that lay far back in the opening of the throat. It goes without saying that I had to turn the head, or rather the skull, upside down, and then push my hand through the throat into the cavity of the pharynx. You can imagine what a horrible smell came from the throat.

Recently, however, we had an even worse smell. Müller took up the muscles of the back and those of the abdomen, and for this he used a whole body whose legs had been cut off from the middle of the thigh. He taught on this from Tuesday until Saturday, and

14

on Monday we had a review. The look of the specimen was now a beautiful sight to see; the neck was torn in tatters, the chest laid open, the abdomen dangling in pieces and the intestines were bulging out! Even the Stabsarzt, who was explaining the theory of ruptures on the half-rotten abdomen, struggled for breath several times. I cannot say that I had a feeling of dread at the sight of all this; it is only the smell that disturbs me, for it is unbearable. Since it is unavoidable, I put up with it. You need not worry about the matter.

I have a mass of work on hand. Whenever possible, at six p.m. I go to see my friends nearby, and then I study til eleven at night. It goes on like this every day without a stop from six in the morning until eleven at night, except on Sunday, and you can imagine how the days and weeks fly past. In the process you get so tired that in the evening you find yourself yearning for the hard bed – on which, having slept in half lethargy, you wake up in the morning almost as tired as before.

As far as our meals are concerned, by and large I am quite content with the situation. Of the three and a half thaler that the King pays the restaurant manager, he receives only two and a half thaler for each of us. Actually we have withdrawals and expenditure for each and every trifle. Every month, 2 ½ thaler are deducted to buy equipment for my future career as surgeon at the Charité. Lately, all of us who were newly admitted have to pay one thaler each into the furniture account of the Charité! We have to buy blankets for the beds and even those who have received woolen blankets from the Institute have to buy a bedspread.

15

All these things say little for the beginning, and Hoffmann is finding it difficult to get used to them. He wants to leave and is pulling every string to do so. Young Schroeder, who is also attending a great number of classes, constantly feels unwell, and because, as I presume, he wants to wean himself from eating, is becoming an absolute skeleton. Recently, to his great delight, old Generalarzt Wiebel, First Surgeon General, promised Young Schroeder a monthly allowance of five thaler. It will then certainly be easier for him to subsist, something that seems to have been very difficult for him so far.

I still do not know whether I shall send you a good Christmas present or whether you even want one so if you do not receive anything, please forgive me. In case I should chance upon something good that you might appreciate one of these days, then you will probably obtain it after the event – I won't be talked out of that.

As for me, have no worries. All that is I need is your love, and I hope that I shall win it in the end. After Christmas I must really buy myself a pair of trousers. For these I may have to make a demand upon your kindness. The other clothes will do for the time being, but at Easter I shall have to treat myself to a new coat. I do not have a hat yet, and I shall purchase one either just before Christmas or wait till later. Whenever I need one, I borrow it from a friend. Toward the spring, there will probably be a new and fixed mode in hats, and if I buy one I would like to have a felt hat, and one in fashion.

Young Schroeder, who is shipping a chest, will send my letters with it. I am enclosing a street map of Berlin, which costs 1 silver groschen. Please obtain the enclosed letter at the post office in Koslin; you need not pay postage.

I miss my skates badly. Should it be possible for you to send them along later on, I would be very pleased. I am quite well and I hope both of you are also. Please give my kindest regards to everybody, especially to Mother, to whom I express my hearty thanks for the delicious preserves. Farewell!

Your most loving son,
Rudolf Virchow

GRADUATION, MORGUE FIRST ASSIGNMENT

For four years, Mr. Virchow financed or found scholarships for Rudolf's education but aggrieved his son with accusations of Rudolf being "cold-hearted, a dreamer and egotistical." His father responded to Rudolf's essays declaring that that they "had a lot of big words." This sniping from his father who ensured, either through payment or persuasion, that Rudolf's education relegated his son to a higher calling. To his credit, Rudolf absorbed the criticism without retaliation. Despite Rudolf's reassurance, his father frequently requested of Rudolf declarations of love which his son tried to satisfy. Impossible, though, for a man who would eventually be described by two words: Icy enthusiasm.

For nearly seven years, Rudolf frequently acknowledged his deep gratitude to his father for the financial support, although the tardy receipt of the support was a frequent source of anxiety for Rudolf. Humorously, Rudolf's struggle to keep his tailor bill under control vexed him all through medical school. Although he could not help it that he was poor, like his father he took pride in his appearance.

Rudolf's brilliance, self-respect and reverent admiration for a few influential superiors set him apart. The future "Pope of Medicine," as Virchow would be called later in life, did not believe in overturning time-honored methods of medicine although by utilizing the highest level of methodology of his time, Virchow eventually revolutionized medicine for all time. Virchow passionately applied the studies of his favorite teacher, Johann Müller, conjoined with beliefs of his other paragon, eighteenth century Giovanni Morgagni, a twilight pathologist who emphasized performance of research with "great detail and thoroughness," leaving nothing to guesswork. Three factors -- a brilliant and restless mind, an education at the finest university and application of Morgagni's beliefs at Müller's knee -- shaped the foundation of Virchow's life as a doctor.

Occasional respites at his uncles' homes (maternal and paternal) and that of friends refreshed and centered him. During his second year of medical school, at age twenty one, Rudolf took a five week traveling camping vacation during which he crossed the bridge from youth to man. This vacation became his epiphany coalescing Virchow's views on humanity, politics and his place in the world:

Koswig

Saturday, September 24, 1842

My dear Father,

Here I am again, at last. After more than five weeks, full of joy and sorrow, full of abundance and privations, I am again approaching my starting point and I consider my first duty the pleasant business of telling you that hundreds of miles will

*separate us no more. My fondness for traveling is completely
satisfied for the time being.*

*After having been exhausted at the start by terrible drought,
later by wandering in a fine drizzle of rain for days on end and
restlessly hurrying onward day after day as if I were driven by
an evil spirit, I am now satisfied with the performance of my legs
and the work of my chest. Of course in the morning I would strike
out full of pleasure and expectation for the fresh mountain air,
which blew about me virtually throughout my travels, in the
evening, however, I often felt a strong longing for home, when I
saw everybody hurrying home after having finished their daily
work, or when we were hurrying late in the evening through a
small town and could see people gathered together for their
evening meal in their peaceful dwellings, whereas we did not
even know where we were going to lie down to rest for the night.
Anyway, that is all over now! The privations of the journey
combined with all its pleasures are linked together to form a most
beautiful garland of memories. I saw much, very much. Many a
valuable experience has been added to my hitherto rather small
store, and confidence in my strength is rooted in an awareness
that I am able to deal with people in a pleasant manner. I have
had occasion to meet many people; I traveled with people of the
most various ranks and nations; everywhere I associated with
the folk and tried to comprehend its peculiar traits – I was never
rejected or treated indifferently. What I appreciate most is the
knowledge that I am not insensitive to any aspect of life; that
every phenomenon of eternal nature and the human spirit
appeals to me in its full intensity and touches my heart. I was*

especially attracted by everything of general significance, by all that is great and universal, and I realize more than ever that in the innermost depths of my heart I hate the narrow minded and particularist interests which, especially in Pomerania, have destroyed every larger spiritual movement. My patriotism has become more animated, but it is not that dead and passive love of the fatherland which halts in mad pride after its achievements, and looks down upon other peoples with arrogance. It has rather become purified; it has respect for a foreign nationality, even for Austria. The urge to do something and not sit idle while great events of our day are taking place has become stronger, but not so strong as to make me blind to our fine, already existing institutions.

But enough of such general phrases, which you again perhaps may interpret for me as pride and arrogance, or as stubborn persistence in reprehensible things? I just wanted to convey to you a general impression of my tour, since I do not have time now to write about it in detail. I was here three days, in Halle five, in Leipzig one, and in Dresden four. Then I walked for two days with students from Halle and some foreigners through Saxon Switzerland, where by day and night I watched the huge forest fire, about which you must have read.

On September 1, I was in Teplitz; then I traveled to Prague, where I stayed for two days, and spent the following two days in Carlsbad. From Teplitz, till the end of my tour I traveled with Wolff, a student at Halle from Perleberg, in whose company I enjoyed everything twice as much. From Carlsbad we went on foot to Maria Kulm, the famous place of pilgrimage, where thousands of devout Catholics were just then celebrating the birth of Mary; from there to Frazenbad and Eger. On September 8, we crossed the Bavarian border, visited Wunsiedel and Bayreuth, where Jean Paul was born and lived, made a visit to his widow, and then hastened to Suhl via Culmbach, Coburg and Hildburghausen, where I paid a visit to Hoffmann's parents. Thereupon, we passed through a part of Thuringia, and from Rudolstadt to Halle we wandered through the lovely valley of the Saale. On the 14th we reached Jena, where my fellow traveler left me. I stayed there with a friend for five days. On the 20th we parted and I arrived here the day before yesterday. I intend to go to Berlin today and to Freienwalde tomorrow. I again had to borrow some money, which was obligingly offered to me by Adelung, otherwise it would have been impossible to undertake this journey, and I hope to be able to pay him back myself. Now farewell; I have already gone on for too long.

Your most loving son,
Rudolf Virchow

Each graduating medical student presented his thesis and dissertation. On October 20, 1843, Rudolf dedicated his required papers to Oberstabsarzt Grimm in thanks for Grimm's encouragement over the previous four years. On the next day, one week after his twenty-second birthday, Rudolf Virchow uttered the ancient Physician's Oath as a Doctor of Medicine and Surgery, seated himself in the doctor's chair and closed the ceremony with a prayer.

Charité placed Rudolf, as it did all newly graduated physicians, in charge of a ward under the directorship of a higher staff physician. Virchow's first assignment was where all life sustaining decisions that preceded his patients' final state failed. Rudolf was assigned to the lowly morgue, or 'death house,' his supervisor, Medizinalrat Ludwig Friorep. Of note, a year after charge of a ward, military physicians were assigned active duty, their rank inferior to that of a sergeant. Despite this bleak prospect, the *"mere empty formality"* of attaining his degree had *"the greatest significance"* in Rudolf's life.

To celebrate the occasion, after he paid off the remainder of his tailor's bill, Rudolf *"had a tailcoat made in a fanciful style that would doubtless upset Schivelbein folk, but corresponds perfectly to the dictates of the fashion magazines."* Dressed in his new coat, he self-sponsored a party in a rural spot a quarter of a mile from town with nine of his closest friends who *"clouded their minds with the wine"* sent by Mr. Virchow for the festive occasion. The party returned to Charité at three a.m. At a *"solemn breakfast"* the next morning at Charité they consumed the remaining wine. For the rest of the day, they drank champagne chased by punch prepared from drops of the remaining wine. *"Thus ended the day,"* Rudolf wrote to his father.

Five days later, standing in the ward completing his final rotation before beginning his morgue duties, Virchow faced one of his superiors and said, "Stabsarzt Klatten, it's the evening of the 26th. Although I appreciate your offer to bring in help from the Institute, the 1st is just around the corner. I only have five more days to get through."

"Virchow," Klatten argued, "your colleague is spitting up blood, a sure sign of tuberculosis. There is no chance that at any time during the next five days will he recover. You already had a full load with the Women's Internal Ward. Between it and the Men's Division, there are over one hundred and fifty patients. Too much! What time do you get up in the morning?

"At 4:30."

"And what time do you go to bed?"

"11:30."

"So on five hours of sleep you tend to over one hundred and fifty patients and give me a daily detailed account of each and every one of them."

Klatten's fatherly concern touched Rudolf's heart, and he smiled fondly at the white-haired doctor. "Stabsarzt Klatten, I appreciate your concern. Five days ago I became a doctor and I am still benefiting from the elation. As long as patient care doesn't suffer and the required paperwork is kept current, I don't need help," Virchow stated. "I know I couldn't keep up this pace for very long but for only five more days..."

"Second Woman...," a woman sang out from her bed at Virchow.

Klatten feigned disapproval with a lowered chin, his jowls sagging.

"I don't encourage that, you know," Virchow said slightly defensive. He nodded his head in the direction of the woman and squared his shoulders.

"But you don't mind it, either," Klatten said with a lift of his chin and a wink. "It's all right to be liked by patients, Virchow. I've heard you explain things to them and as much as my esteemed colleagues might argue against that, it truly seems to calm the patients and makes your job a little easier. I heard that the lunatics..."

Demonstrating what would become his lifelong practice of remembering that no matter what the diagnosis or his status, his and the other doctor's patients were first and foremost human beings. "'...melancholics...,'" Rudolf interrupted.

"Excuse me, the *melancholics* flocked to say farewell to you when you ended that rotation. Weren't you the one who wanted to avoid that clinic?"

Rudolf agreed. *"A month into it, and even into my second month, I thought it impossible to win over that distrustful and suspicious bunch. Then I had to do a third month and the tide changed."* He shrugged and continued in his intellectual manner of which the older doctor had become respectful and genuinely admired. *"There is a lot of religious mania among them, but surprisingly some of the most interesting personalities in Charité."*

"Maybe you are thinking about changing your field from surgeon to psychiatry?" Klatten fished.

Rudolf responded immediately. "No, sir."

Klatten switched the subject. "Are you eating all right?"

"English style," Virchow quipped and patted his belly. *"At eight in the morning I have a large slice of roast beef with a beer then an abundant lunch."* With a half serious look, he added, "I think it's made this impossible strain possible."

"The roast beef or the beer?" Klatten relented. "All right, then. But if you change your mind and need assistance, please let me know."

"Second Woman," the woman called out louder.

Rudolf looked at Klatten and shook his head with amusement.

"Would you like to come over for dinner on Wednesday night? I'd like to have my family meet you."

Rudy smiled ruefully. "How about after the first of the month?"

EARNS NEW ROLE, CREATES NEW TERMS

Six months later during the spring of 1844, four years before the German revolution, changes occurred among the senior personnel of the military medical services at Charité. Of special importance, the death of second Surgeon General Buttner opened a lower level Surgeon General position for which the elegant, blonde haired, blue eyed now forty-five year old Grimm was chosen. A new Upper Staff Physician (Obertstabsarzt), Eck, also was chosen. Both of these men, Grimm and Eck, eventually served as influential men in Rudolf's career. Of the two, Grimm remained steadfast in his support of Virchow. Also discussions began about reforming medical services in general and the position of military surgeons; in particular, Virchow's position. Still, Virchow's two- to three-year career plan included joining the cavalry with an immediate hope of earning extra income in private practice. Socially, there was time for little more than student meetings at which political issues were increasingly discussed.

By summer, Rudolf committed his father to silence and extracted a reluctant promise that his father no longer uses his *"influence anywhere"* on Rudolf's behalf. He confided to his father that Charité's closed Admission Office would not be reopened. Instead the plan called to convert the office space into a new Chemistry and Microscopy lab for which there was great need. The plan inspired great competition among the nineteen surgeons as to who would manage the new lab. By fall, the schism reached its highest levels as military physicians of Charité feuded with civilian physicians as to which faction would manage the lab.

"Herr Schonlein, it's not that I object to your calling me names," Generalarzt Grimm with sarcasm by word, not tone, said as he and Schonlein faced off in the nearly completed lab. "But, on behalf of the military, I am prepared to take this as high as necessary."

Schonlein loudly retaliated. "Since I am the King's physician-in-ordinary, why don't I take it there for you?" He glared at Grimm. The laborers surrounding them stopped talking. This was going to be a good story around dinner tables that night.

"Better yet, Grimm," Schonlein continued, "ever since I joked with the king that beer is healthier when taken with his doctor, we've taken a few beers for his health." He jabbed his elbow in Grimm's side. "That would be the best time to tell him the way the new lab should be run, and by whom."

Grimm saw the older man's angry determination to win this battle yet knew he had the winning hand. Changing tactics, Grimm said, "There are many qualified candidates to manage the lab. Why are you so stubborn about Remak and Heintz?"

Schonlein snorted. "Stubborn? I'm not stubborn. You are the one that is stubborn. Those two have been working for me for no pay. Remak especially would make the best candidate for the new lab." He puffed out his chest. "I trained him myself."

"No doubt, the best training at Charité," said Grimm.

"No doubt," Schonlein snapped back. "And I suppose you have a better candidate in mind?"

"Yes, I do," Grimm said.

Schonlein crossed his arms, stuck his bearded chin into the air and affected a pose of looking down his nose at the much younger Grimm. Massaging his neck as though to assist the word's utterance, he growled, "Virchow."

Grimm said, "Yes."

Schonlein snorted again, louder, then roared. "He's only twenty-three years old! What can he possibly know about medicine, let alone running a lab? He's barely off his mother's tit!"

"For some time has done chemical work in Prof. Lindes lab and microscopy work under Johann Müller."

Schonlein bushy eyebrows rose at the mention of Müller's name and his shoulders drooped slightly. Due to Müller's genius and magnetic teaching style, he attracted students at a considerable boost to the school's revenue. He received what he asked of Charité.

Unknown to Schonlein, Grimm primed Virchow four months prior to accept the position if offered. Grimm went in for the kill. "Schmidt himself has interceded on Virchow's behalf with Minister Eichhorn and since even the King is reluctant to prevail over medical management decisions here at Charité... I'm sorry,

Schonlein. Your men, I agree, deserve to be in a salaried positions. Perhaps," he delivered the final blow, "they will consider working for young Virchow?"

"GET BACK TO WORK!" Schonlein yelled at the workmen.

(Added note: And so began a long conflict with Remak.)

In their favorite tavern, Seeger's, on a frigid November evening Reinhardt, Fouquet and Virchow leaned back in their chairs. With legs crossed, their pointy toed, shiny boots drifted back and forth as they sipped steins of beer.

Nearby, with the back of his chair leaning against the wall near the fireplace, a patron snored. Close to him, two gentlemen stood at a right angle to one another in debate. One held his glass high in the air by its stem as he looked at his stout-figured partner. The stout man, who held onto the back of an empty chair for support, stared straight ahead out the window as though ignoring his debater. At the back of the room, on a bar covered with a thick slab of white marble as wide as the room and two feet deep, sat plates of heavily salted rolls sprinkled with caraway seeds. A bartender held his chin up to peer through his spectacles as he filled a glass of wine. Rudolf mused that the bartender looked as serious as a researcher filling a beaker. Behind him, a wide doorway framed with burnished carved wood led to the shelved alcohol storage area.

"Can you believe its almost Volkstrauertag (Memorial) Day," Reinhardt said to the other two, "and that the year's almost over?"

Their sodden overcoats dripped melting snow on hooks near the fireplace. The scents of drying wool blended with burning cedar logs and cigars filled the cozy room. Reinhardt and Fouquet both wore their hair parted far on the left side and brushed forward. Although Virchow preferred stylish clothing, he kept hair Virchow, Reinhardt's new moustache added at least three more years to his appearance.

"Are you going home for Christmas, Rudolf?" Fouquet asked.

"No, not this year. I've already written to my parents and told them. And asked them for money."

All three had reduced pencils to nubs writing home for money over the past two years. Reinhardt said, "Do you know that it takes us a month to earn what railroad workers earn in one day? Maybe we should trade in our stethoscopes for a sledgehammer."

"I don't think so," said Rudolf.

Reinhardt wouldn't let it go. "A journeyman carpenter who is not even a full-fledged carpenter earns sixteen silver groschen a day to my five."

"You love medicine, you love medicine," Rudolf chanted.

Reinhardt rolled his eyes and shrugged. "Yes, yes..."

Rudolf resolved, "When I finally have a decent salary, I will send money home for as long as my parents live."

The other two shook their heads in agreement.

"You are welcome to come home with me for Christmas, Rudolf," Fouquet said returning to the original subject.

"I truly appreciate that, friend, but I'm working on something that can't wait."

"Not even for Christmas?" Reinhardt chided.

Rudolf looked at his friend penitently, his voice softened. "Of course I will take the day off but..."

"It's that...what was it that you called it, Virchow?" Fouquet said.

"Embolism," Rudolf said.

"Ja," Fouquet said.

Reinhardt cut in. "Embolism? What is 'embolism,' Virchow?"

"Tell him, Virchow."

Four men playing cards at a table nearby looked up.

Reinhardt looked at Virchow with a, "go ahead and amuse me," kind of look.

Rudolf lowered his voice. "Four days ago on November 11, a patient, Eulalia Zach, age 54, died the day after surgical removal of a pelvic tumor. Her surgeon wrote the cause of death as "Inflammation of the Veins." At autopsy, I found no inflammation. However, I did find a clot in the pulmonary artery just above the heart leading into the lungs."

"Hmmm..." Reinhardt murmured.

"The clot was situated at the *branch* of the artery here..." he spread his left thumb and index and pointed at the base where the fingers were webbed. "It was not in the main artery itself which made me suspect that the clot traveled upstream from somewhere else in the body."

"So you kept looking, of course?" Reinhardt prodded.

"Of course. I traversed the artery down through the pelvis then down the leg where I located the 'parent' clot. I removed it from the vein in the leg and found that its end and the clot's end in the branch of the pulmonary artery fit perfectly together like two pieces of a puzzle."

"And so you created a *new* medical word, Virchow?" Reinhardt said.

"Not *a* new medical word – *two* new terms, my doctor friend," he said. "'Thrombus' from the Greek, 'thrombos' or clot: a fibrin plug, a coagulation of blood formed within a blood vessel that remains attached to its place of origin. 'Embolus' – Greek for 'stopper' -- is a broken off piece of thrombus that travels through the blood stream like a runaway engine of a steam train. The cause of this patient's death was not 'Inflammation of the Veins,' but *pulmonary embolism*," he said. "I hereby claim *thrombosis* and *embolism* for pathology."

Like what occurred in Virchow's life, what he established would in time became commonplace. These medical terms, as well as others, are now known to doctors and many laymen.

The three friends smiled, raised their glasses in a toast to what they sensed was Virchow's epoch discovery.

Fouquet said, "Soon we will be attending classes taught by Virchow instead of Müller."

Rudolf retorted, "Perhaps classes of Virchow *and* Müller."

In time, that prophetic statement came true.

"What about the Chemistry and Microscopy lab?" Reinhardt asked. "Has a final decision been made yet about who will run it?" All three knew the military physicians had chosen Virchow.

"Minister Eichhorn and Schonlein hold to their candidates while the rest of the directing physicians of Charité and the medical staff hold to me. Jungken, under whose teachings I wrote my dissertation, especially wants me to be in charge. Since he has been keeping me busy in that direction, my guess is that it is more or less official, especially since I've acquired chemistry equipment and already doing research. Friorep does more of the work in the morgue so that I have more time for running the new lab. He's also made a couple suggestions of subjects for me to study – phlebitis for one, English for another."

Reinhardt shook his head. "Latin, French, Greek...why English, too?"

"Why phlebitis?" Fouquet quizzed.

"Who should I answer first?" Rudolf asked good-naturedly.

"Me," Reinhardt said.

"Me," Fouquet said.

Rudolf turned his face first toward Reinhardt, "Because of the English medical advances," then turned to Fouquet, "because phlebitis seems to originate a cascade of events that eventually cause death, and the links need to be studied. Enough business talk. One more round, then time to leave."

Leslie Dunn

MEDICO-POLITICAL SPEECHES BEGIN

Five months later Virchow, the new Chemistry and Microscopy Lab Director, was chosen as orator during festivities at the Friedrich-Wilhelm Institute. It would be the first of many speeches that harpooned Virchow's name into the medical field of his time.

On May 3, 1845, Virchow stood behind the wooden rostrum, leaned on it and gave a speech that defined the youthful brash genius as a member, if not leader, of the new generation of German physicians.

Despite that the speech had been reviewed and approved by the new Oberstabsarzt Eck, Virchow anticipated opposition from the guests especially the older physicians. To his surprise, the elders approved. Some younger ones did not. Perhaps reluctance to follow the footsteps of one of their own, especially one of the youngest of their own, his words provoked jealousy among some of his peers.

In a voice fortified with conviction, Virchow spoke of his visions for medical progress. He asserted progress must come from three sources: Clinical observations rather than educated guesses, animal experimentation to study drug effects and microscopic as opposed to the macroscopic (visual) study of disease. He introduced his new medical terms – thrombosis and embolism. Next, he described living matter in three ways that would eventually usher out the two thousand year old reigning theory of Four Humours.

Rudolf asserted that living matter is the sum of physical and chemical action, that living matter is the expression of cellular activity and that the *smallest unit of life is the cell.* That these facts are now understood, even taken for granted, testifies to Virchow's visionary genius. It is not overstating that Rudolf's speech, as well as others of like mind, heralded the birth of modern medicine.

Becoming a giant in one field was too confining for a man of Virchow's unrelenting drive, unquenchable passion and genius. Virchow switched gears barreling into another arena where he would eventually spend a considerable amount of his time and energy: Politics on behalf of the common man.

During his speech's political agenda, Virchow advocated abandoning the military hierarchy at the Friedrich-Wilhelm Institute, concluding that the institute itself should be closed due to the strain and poor conditions of the doctors. Thus he spoke of the institution to which he was indebted for his education and livelihood. Virchow's sense of responsibility on behalf of others made his speech eloquent and forthright. In time he would learn of the price of his compassion. With this speech young Virchow charged into medical and political arenas from which, for the next sixty years, he never retreated.

Leslie Dunn

Friday, May 9, 1845

Dear Father,

This time it is you who make me wait for a letter; it seems that you wish to pay me back in my own coin. Meanwhile, Friedrich-Wilhelm festivities were celebrated on May 3 and I delivered my speech. I believe I have already written to you that it contained a formal declaration of medical faith with not altogether ineffective attacks upon opponents of the modern school. Eck had read through the speech beforehand with uncommon generosity, leaving untouched virtually everything that I would have struck out in the work of another had I been in his position. He was critical only of my overall stance and emphasis on certain points; it often sounded, he said, as if I were a member of the French Academy. You know this old fault. Nonetheless, the impression it made on the military physicians present – and the audience was entirely composed of such people – did not appear unfavorable. Many of them expressed their approval afterwards. Neither of the two Generalstabsarzte, Wiebel and Lohmayer, was present. Wiebel, who has been ill for some time, invited me two days later to read the speech to him. I met Lohmayer in his anteroom and he held out his hand to me and said: "I have read your excellent speech with the greatest pleasures." Wiebel, who was very communicative and held me for more than two hours, asked about my relationship with your brother and then remarked that we were both making our family quite "famous!" – to which I remarked that our objective was service and not fame, etc. Things thus seem to be going well so *far. Nothing has been yet decided about publishing the speech, but Eck seems disinclined to sponsor the publication of views which he otherwise supports.*

My next efforts will be directed toward obtaining private quarters in the Charité and permission from the medical staff to complete the teaching examination in the winter. As I wrote you recently, honorable efforts are underway to relieve me of my military obligations so that I may perform research and become an instructor.

This affair has again a pecuniary side, which I regretfully must take up with you yet again. Among other things, there are two reasons for my wanting to take the state examinations as soon as possible. First, once I have successfully completed the examinations, there will be no further obstacle to my writing what and how I wish to write; second, I will be able to conduct private courses, which are in great demand and for which I have sufficient material. In either case I can recover at least part of the money. Completing my examinations will, moreover, make my position more secure. The question thus boils down to whether you can place of sum of 80 thaler at my disposal around November, if I obtain permission to take the examinations. As things stand, I believe I could manage comfortably with this sum. I have considered the matter carefully, since I would gladly have wished to spare you such an expense; but all things taken into account, this course seems to me the best.

With my fondest regards, dear Father, and a hearty farewell.

Your Rudolf

Two months after his speech, it sat ill with Virchow that, through Eck, not a word had yet been published, a common practice of the time. It especially distressed him in that Minister of Culture Eck commended the speech both before and after its presentation. While Eck encouraged and supported Virchow's views, no doubt Eck fell under criticism for permitting the radical a public forum.

While in the tavern, a traveler overheard Rudolf and his friends talk of Charité. Interrupting the group, the traveler, who was also a doctor, remarked that things were once said to be very bad at the Charité but that now someone very good at dissections was there. Laughing, the group introduced the 'very good' dissector Virchow to the stranger. After the traveling doctor recovered from Rudolf's startling young age, he told them Virchow's name was becoming known in Halle, Prague and Vienna. Although flattered, the news strengthened Virchow's resolve that in order that his medical discoveries and political convictions be disseminated accurately and distantly, he must attain the authority to self-publish. Uncensored.

Coincidentally, the German states requested during this time that Rudolf's Uncle Virchow equip the army based on the Prussian model that was devised by his uncle. Yet, like Rudolf, the meager pay shamed and irritated his uncle.

Recognition this early in his career flattered Rudolf yet highlighted the void of experience in the field; he of so little knowledge regarded as an authority! It alternately amazed and dismayed him. It also deeply frustrated Rudolf that pathologic anatomy, disease processes of the body, had not been systematically studied. He determined to approach this unmapped territory with guarded analysis, meticulous documentation and an open mind. Had it not been for the grand acceptance of his initial findings, the combined frustrations of his unpublished speech, shallow pay and the ocean of work he faced might have paralyzed him.

In August of that same year, Rudolf was chosen as one of the guest speakers at the Fifty Year Anniversary Celebration of the Institute, the same institute against which he railed in a speech only three months prior. A newspaper reported the distinguished military attendees as well as the leading medical notables of Berlin, students of several institutes, university professors and senior officials. Uncle Virchow, by honor of his promotion in the Prussian troops, was also in attendance.

Virchow's bold speech again included references to his medical discoveries and the new medical terms he created – thrombosis and embolism.

In 1845, the same year as his speeches, one medical discovery established by multiple doctors in several cities and countries would *not* be a part of Virchow's upcoming speech. However, that discovery would ultimately engage him, other doctors and colleagues in a dispute that would last for nearly fifteen years.

Months previous, alone in the autopsy room, Virchow's brow furrowed. He had gotten used to the putrefying odor of the corpses long ago, as used to the odor as a human being could get. Otherwise, the summer heat simmered odors would have expelled him from the room hours ago. Engrossed in the appearance of the deceased's blood stream the words, "white blood" repeated themselves over and over in his thoughts. His deceased patient was a fifty-year old woman with limbs so swollen and tight that they looked as though they were made of white porcelain and not of flesh. She had suffered profuse bleeding from her nose and her spleen measured about a foot in length, almost twice the normal size. But the blood that filled her arteries and veins was almost snow white with only tinges of red.

Scanning the reports and books on his shelf, Virchow pulled the latest article written by Vienna's famous pathologist, Rokitansky. Virchow felt certain that the case Rokitansky described either matched or closely matched Virchow's current autopsy. Sitting at his desk and scanning through the table of contents, Virchow found the page and skimmed until he found the famous pathologist's graphical details about the case of 'pyemia' (loosely – blood pus or poisoning). Virchow looked again at the blood of the woman – pyemia or white blood?

Virchow made a decision, one that would rankle the medical profession. This and Rokitansky's case were identical. What was wrong was Rokitansky's conclusion. Stepping to the wash basin, Virchow rinsed his hands, dried them thoroughly, then sitting at his desk he began to write, *"Weisses Blut..."* ("White Blood") with as much concern for detail as the great Rokitansky. Virchow described the colors of the dead woman's blood: instead of a predominance of red with traces of white, the woman's blood was predominantly white with traces of red. He gave a minute description of the microscopic appearance of non-nucleated granular cells and horseshoe-shaped granulated cells. He stated his belief that neither his nor Rokitansky's cases should be classified as 'pyemia.'

The word for this 'white blood' disease would not be published by Virchow until 1847. Whose name would be associated with the new medical term would be the subject of public dispute between doctors from Germany and Scotland for many years to come.

Virchow's speech would not mention the white blood disease. He did, however, include the medical terms he created, thrombosis and embolism, as well as his newest findings regarding phlebitis that contradicted literally everything previously accepted about the condition. During his speech yet again he asserted a patient's right to information about their diagnosis and care. This belief of Virchow's, and his insistence on its practice, eventually set the groundwork for what is now known as Informed Consent.

The size and importance of this second audience resulted in reactions to the extreme. Some effusively glorified his speech while others were enraged and damned it. Unarguably, though, this second speech layered on the first three months prior endowed twenty-four year old Virchow increased fame.

Charité

Wednesday, August 27, 1845

Dear Father,

August 2 went very well. Mine was a difficult task, that of speaking in between two such experienced orators as Histiographer Preuss and Oberstabsarzt Eck. Nevertheless, I made my theme as provocative as possible, and the views I expressed on phlebitis were absolutely new so they had to be heard.

In the evening, there was a great feast at Kroll's house, not to speak of an unlimited supply of beverages. Here I had the opportunity of speaking to members of the audience and receiving their judgments. The old military physicians were profoundly shocked at the new wisdom. That life was to be given such a mechanical interpretation seemed to them quite revolutionary – or at any rate quite un-Prussian. There must be a kind of halo roundabout, which affects our vision and prevents us from seeing things clearly. Privy Councilor Busch, director of the obstetrical clinic, remarked: "Well now, have you heard? It seems we know nothing at all!" In contrast, I had the pleasure of being defended by a very eminent scholar whose views are entirely free from prejudice – Privy Councilor and Regimental Surgeon Betschler, director of the obstetrical clinic, not of Charité, but of Breslau. He defended with great energy and biting eloquence my ideas against the followers of obscurantism, or those whose policy is of withholding knowledge from the general public. Ideler, the director of our lunatic asylum at the Charité who is always ridiculing me on account of my 'newfangled ideas,' conceded that my line of thought, followed strictly, must lead to significant results, even if it is not the only correct one. The ramifications of this discussion occupied us from 10 to 12 at night. The day was doubly fruitful for me; first, because of the recognition I received, which is always flattering and so difficult to achieve, especially at the beginning of a career; second, because it became clear to me on this occasion that people were duller than I had previously supposed. Not a single deductive leap is permitted; every conclusion must inexorably follow from fixed premises; the only way lies in defining one's own premises, not those of another. A day like this comes only once; I could never have made up for it if I had let it pass unused. Opportunity must be seized by the forelock.

Would it not be possible for you to provide me with 40 thaler for the time being? The other half can wait until the new year. Please do not take this letter amiss because I have only talked about myself. I wish you good health and prosperity.

Your Rudolf

In December of that year, Rudolf's superior, Medizinalrat Friorep, Director of the Morgue, confided in Rudolf the two reasons for his plans to retire from Charité: entering into the publishing field and accepting the position as Physician-in-Ordinary of the Grand Duke. Recognizing Virchow as a serious contender in the field of medicine, Friorep urged Rudolf to apply for the position as Director of the Morgue. If chosen it would place Rudolf, two years post-graduation, in charge of both the Chemistry Microscopic Lab and Morgue with full access to the most advanced research and equipment. Rudolf encountered no shortage of diseased bodies on which to perform investigations -- a gruesome, yet serendipitous combination for the intense and charged young researcher.

It must be noted that Rudolf's apprenticeship at his father's side as a butcher desensitized him to the presence of dead flesh yet his mother's theological teachings endowed Virchow with a reverence for living things.

Virchow's article regarding the "white blood disease" published near the time of his speeches coincided with three reports of the same disease by others: David Craigie, 1845; John Hughes Bennett, 1845; and John Fuller, 1846. Of these three, Virchow most admired Bennett's careful study and description of the diseased cells yet agreed with Bennett *only to a point*. Bennett, like Virchow, noted that the condition was not a disease of the blood but Bennett asserted that the excess cells in the blood were derived from a pus-forming 'blastema' (a mass of living substance capable of growth and differentiation). Virchow believed, instead, that the cells were related to the colorless cells normally found in blood. With that, Virchow claimed a place in pathology for the colorless blood corpuscle he termed, "leukocytes."

With the battlefield heating up and players identified, it would be another seven years before the simmering argument would erupt into the 1853 professional journals.

As the last official act of the nearly dissolved governing body of the hospital, it forwarded to Germany's Minister of Culture the name of Rudolf Virchow as Director of the Morgue. By early summer 1846, Virchow's added responsibilities provided him, at age 25, with complete financial independence from his parents.

After successfully passing the grueling and lengthy state examinations for teaching, Virchow delivered his first lecture on pathologic anatomy to a class of eight students. The extra compensation for teaching ratcheted up Rudolf's salary finally relieving his parents of their financial burden. For the rest of their lives, true to his word, they benefited from his gratitude.

Leslie Dunn

CARL VON ROKITANSKY AND
THEORY OF FOUR HUMOURS

In December of 1846, in Vienna, three hundred and twenty-six miles from Berlin, Rokitansky's dissection laboratory resembled an old weathered shed that served as both a corpse and dissection room. Jars lined the shelves as well as books and papers in progress of Rokitansky's growing pathologic collection. Despite Rokitansky's having performed over twenty-two thousand autopsies in twenty years and publication of his findings about disease and its effects on the body, Vienna General Hospital, as well as medicine in general, had yet to recognize the importance of the field of pathology. His students, however, fully realized Rokitansky's genius.

An unassuming, humble and even-tempered man, Rokitansky's muttonchops threaded throughout with gray extended down to the corners of his mouth, his chin clean shaven. His hair line receded to the center of his scalp and with his spectacles he was a pleasant appearing man. He easily carried on conversations while his scalpel whittled away on the dead, exposing and explaining the source of disease that ended the patient's life. Unlike his lecture hall voice that was weak and monotone, in his dissection laboratory his voice rose and fell as his sorted through muscles, pushed aside intestines and cut free a diseased heart.

"This patient died of bacterial endocarditis," he announced to the eight students gathered around the autopsy table. "In other words, an infection of the heart. You will notice the bacterial lesions," he said pointing to the lesions infiltrating the pericardium or outside covering of the heart. He lifted the specimen free from the corpse. "I have one in the jar in the heart section on the shelf," he nodded in its direction. "This one would be just as excellent as a specimen for display."

"Where did the infection begin?" asked a student. He, as well as the others, kept their knee-length black overcoats buttoned against the drafty December chill in the tiny building. Although the coals contributed some warmth, the chill served to damper the odors in the room so no one complained for more coal.

"Krasen Lehre," Rokitansky replied. "In other words, the crasis teaches. To answer your question – in the blood, of course."

"Humoural pathology," another student mumbled instructing the student who asked the question.

"Yes," said Rokitansky. "Crases – bodily fluids and how they are mixed in the body. This patient's disease was in the blood humour that embraces all the organs." Holding the pale, lifeless heart in his hand, he reviewed the most fundamental and current beliefs of medicine of his time. "Four basic humours – blood, yellow bile...what are the other two?"

"Phlegm and black bile," the students said together by rote.

"If the patient's skin is hot and dry, which humour dominates?"

"Yellow bile," they responded.

"The associated personality type?"

"Anger," one said.

"Violent," said another.

"You are both correct," Rokitansky said. "And if the skin is cold and moist? And its element?

"The humour of phlegm," said one.

"Element of water," finished another bored student. He whispered to another, "When is he going to get back to the heart?" He got a slight kick to the shin.

Rokitansky ignored the comment and continued with the review. "The element of earth – its humour, clinical manifestation and personality type?" He looked at the student directly across from him. "You."

"The humour of black bile proven by cold and dry skin in depressed, melancholic patients." Then added to impress the great teacher, "Melan, meaning 'black.'"

"Very good. Are we missing any humour?"

"Blood," said the same student. "Warm and moist skin, element air, with a personality type such as yours, great doctor."

The other students looked at each with amusement. The speaker often tried to bolster poor grades with flattery.

Not one to succumb to sweet talking students, Rokitansky replied, "Thank you for that observation, doctor. At the moment, though, I feel under the dominance of cool water."

The seven other students chuckled, pleased that the flattery failed.

"Gentlemen, as you know, the humoural doctrine has withstood the test of time beginning with Hippocrates over two thousand years ago and supported by Galen in the second century. Since that time, the doctrine consistently has been improved, its application restores health and explains what otherwise could not be explained of the mysteries of the connection between the human body and soul. I have viewed thousands of diseased bodies in their minutest detail..."

The eight students nodded in respectful agreement.

"...and as much as I have discovered, there is still far more left to discover," he said with a wisdom born from years of learning. "Humoral pathology is simply a requirement for common practical sense."

Leslie Dunn

VIRCHOW ARCHIV, MEETING AT MAYER'S

By May of 1847, although political thunder rumbled throughout Germany, the life of Rudolf Virchow was pleasantly eventful. An order of the King officially relieved Virchow of his military obligations and on January 1, the Ministry granted him the position of Charité 'prosectorship,' (anatomist) at a salary of three hundred thaler a year. In order that he be exclusively available to the Institute, he was assigned private quarters in Charité hospital with free heat, more than what was offered to his predecessor, Friorep.

Finally achieving the freedom to publish whatever he chose without editing by a superior, Rudolf and his long term friend, Benno Reinhardt, launched a successful publication, *Archivs of Pathologic Anatomy and Physiology, and Clinical Medicine.* Impressively the publication continues to the present time, known since 1903 as *Virchow's Archiv.* Rudolf sent home a copy of the first issue with a note to his father *"to especially look through the pages of the first article, by me, 'On Standpoints,'* and on *"the second plate... you will see all that we see through the microscope; it is a paper on cancer of which the illustrations are a part."* We know, then that from this letter's content that Rudolf's father was aware of his son's medical genius and that Rudolf's political beliefs went beyond the safety of popular convention.

On a balmy evening in late June, 1847, Virchow, Reinhardt and visiting professor Rudolf Albert Kölliker of Würzburg, Germany walked to the home of Dr. Carl Mayer. An invitation had been offered in honor of Dr. Kölliker's visit.

Kölliker, originally of Zurich, recently moved to Würzburg as a newly appointed Professor of Anatomy and Physiology. He had done a residency at Charité and, like Virchow, was profoundly influenced by Johann Mueller. In town to attend a speech presented by Virchow of whom he heard a great deal recently, he decided to stay a few days and watch Virchow work.

Although Kölliker towered over Virchow, when watching Virchow in the lecture room he hadn't noticed Virchow's petite size. As opposed to Rudolf's unstylish short hair, Kölliker's dark brown hair was collar length with a little flip of the ends, parted deeply on the left side and pomaded to a smooth sheen. His thin eyebrows and smallish eyes were offset by his thick moustache. In Reinhardt and Virchow, Kölliker found intellectual partners whose quick, biting comebacks he enjoyed immensely.

Nearly dinner hour, dressed in top hats, summer daytime jackets and carrying walking canes the three young doctors walked the nearly vacant Friedrichstrasse street. Passing by their favorite tavern, Seegers, Reinhardt playfully tugged Rudolf's arm in a mock attempt in that direction.

An officer passed. As a gentleman and his wife walked past he lifted his hat in greeting at the three doctors while his wife stared straight ahead out from under her bonnet, her gloved hand resting in the crook of her husband's elbow. In the shadowed courtyard of a nearby building stood two gentleman deep in discussion, one in knee high boots, the other in shiny pointy toed leather shoes, both with their hands clasped behind their backs. Another gentleman on horseback traversed the courtyard. Other than these few, the street at the early evening hour was as peaceful and quiet as a church.

"Here we are," said Virchow as he led them through the vine covered trellis of the home he'd visited for over a year.

The door opened and Frau Mayer who had been watching them approach waved them inside. Stepping to her side, Dr. Mayer greeted them. As the three men stepped inside, Dr. Mayer introduced Kölliker to his children.

"These fine companions will join us for dinner," Mayer said. "My daughters Rose, Lisette and Barbara and my son, Max." He indicated each in turn, the children smiled politely at the tall stranger. "Virchow and Reinhardt, please show our guest to my study," he said. "I'll be there in a moment."

Passing through the living room, Kölliker glanced in the heavily gilded mirror hanging above the fireplace and smoothed his hair.

"For which daughter do you preen?" Reinhardt teased.

"They are only children," Kölliker said with a gruff voice.

Reinhardt looked at Virchow with a mischievous grin and said to Kölliker, "Barbara, perhaps? Forget Rose whom I think has an eye on Rudolf."

Rudolf elbowed Reinhardt's side.

"These are not children," Reinhardt continued. "They are beautiful young, intelligent women."

"Humph," Kölliker's reply.

Entering Mayer's study Rudolf sighed and relaxed. The wallpaper with its burgundy roses and curling deep green vines against a soft springtime green perfectly set off a serene, almost romantic background.

Three seven shelved bookcases huddled next to each other, covering an entire wall. That they could support the solid rows of books attested to their high quality. On the top of the bookcases, high above their heads, sat framed portraits of the King and other members of the royalty. A fanciful snow white column sat in the corner with no useful purpose other than beauty. A stand such as one used for holding a musician's score sat at the far end of a floral covered couch. On this stand lay a newspaper, a string down the middle to keep the reader's page open.

Neat, high stacks of paper hid the top of the desk and on a couple stacks sat decorative paperweights. The room perfectly reflected Mayer's love of beauty and his organized intellectual pursuits.

Mayer entered carrying a tray with a bottle and wine glasses, his wife close behind. The children could be heard laughing in the background, one of them playing the piano.

"Dinner will be ready in about a half hour," Frau Mayer said. "If anyone is too hungry to wait, I can bring in a couple rolls."

As each one of them shrugged his shoulders and assured her they were fine, they stared at the silver tray carried by her husband.

"Cookies?" she persisted.

"No, thank you," they said looking at her briefly their attention returning to the silver tray.

"How about some grapes?" She smiled sweetly.

Despite being the newest person in the house, Kölliker glanced up at her, catching on to her little joke. "I'd like some jellied goose."

The others glanced up at Kölliker, then at Frau Mayer. They smiled at the gentle woman they had come to love so dearly.

"You've had your fun, wife," Mayer interrupted. "Now back to the kitchen, you wench."

She giggled. "I like him," she said to her husband looking at Kölliker. "These other two," she said waving her hand at Virchow and Reinhardt, "need to learn to be less serious."

Virchow and Reinhardt grinned.

Newly initiated into the Mayer house Kölliker smiled as he, too, relaxed.

"Now for what you three really want..." Mayer placed the tray on the desk, "good conversation."

The three of them groaned, walked to the tray and helped themselves to a drink.

"Come sit down," Mayer said after they filled their glasses.

As two of them settled on the couch and one on a chair, Mayer asked, "Kölliker, you were a student at Charité, weren't you?"

"Yes, sir. Then I studied medicine at Zurich, where I was born, and Bonn. I qualified myself as a Privatdocent in Zurich in 1843 at the age of twenty-six."

Mayer counted quickly. "Then you are now the age of thirty?"

"Correct."

"And of what are you a private teacher?

"I was appointed a Professor of Anatomy and Physiology two years ago and just recently accepted a position in Würzburg."

Mayer grew quiet for a moment. "Würzburg is attracting fine professors," he said cautiously.

Kölliker glanced at Virchow and then said to Mayer, "I'll take that as a compliment, Mayer."

"As you should," he responded with kindness.

After a light rap on the door, it opened. Barbara, Max and Rose looked inquisitively at their father.

Mayer said, "If it's all right with the three of you, I think these other three would like to join us."

Looking at each other, Virchow, Reinhardt and Kölliker politely nodded their heads.

"Good. Then let's take up our glasses and move to the larger sitting room, if you gentlemen don't mind," Mayer said.

As the seven of them moved to the sitting room closer to the kitchen, Frau Mayer called out, "Just a few more minutes and supper will be ready. Herr Kölliker, are you sure you don't want a potato?"

Mayer called back to his fun loving wife, "He's fine," while their children giggled.

As they were resettling in the family room, Rose said to Rudolf, "How is that terrible toothache of yours?"

"It's kind of you to ask," he said. "I thought I'd have to buy tools and yank it myself. Hefty doses of Echinacea helped along with self-administered ether," he joked.

Aware of the new numbing agent at Charité, her eyes widened as she recoiled.

"That was a joke," he quickly reassured her. "I was joking," he repeated remembering too late that nonmedical people could not always ascertain when a physician joked.

"Rudolf Virchow," she chided, "that was a poor joke."

Embarrassed, he took her hand in his and brought it to his lips. "Will you please forgive me, young Fräulein?" He looked up at her with his head bent over her hand, his dark eyes wide and appealing.

At fifteen and a delicate beauty that frequently caught male attention, no man ever caused the sensation she felt in response to the touch of Rudolf's lips. She stared at him, her mouth in a small 'o'. She snatched her hand from him. "For your punishment, Rudolf, you will have to sit as f-a-r away from me as possible at dinner," she said. "M-m-mother needs me in the k-kitchen," she said abruptly, then left. Rudolf stared after her for a moment uncertain what to make of her hasty exit.

"A great majority of the Landtag," Max said hoping to provoke a meaty conversation, "according to the newspaper, is against the present government."

Mayer quickly interjected, "Kölliker, discussions involving the government are often debated in this home. Since you are removed at Würzburg, I hope this doesn't bore you."

"The government reaches Würzburg, also," Kölliker said flatly. "I think it can only benefit me to hear what is being said in mighty Berlin."

Rudolf said, "Max, newspaper reports do not accurately describe the near violent discussions of the Landtag, although reports about the dissension *are* accurate. Strong feelings regarding the accuracy of the royal address report of the Treasury, specifically the loan for the East Prussian Railroad, are underplayed in newspapers thanks to hardworking censors."

Reinhardt spoke up. "It is highly doubtful that during the nine year construction of the railroad that the money allotted will stay in the railroad coffer."

"And not used for other purposes by the government?" Barbara asked.

"Ja, Fräulein," her father said validating her guess.

Kölliker looked at Barbara in surprise. "I'm not used to hearing a female voice during a political discussion."

"Then you must visit the home of the Mayer's again," she said coyly.

He lifted his glass in her direction and smiled at the flirty fourteen year old, then sipped from his drink. Carl Mayer's face darkened.

"Rudolf," Mayer said abruptly changing the subject, "tell us quickly what you are up to."

Rose perched to attention in her chair.

"Reinhardt, you tell him," Rudolf said charitably.

Reinhardt cleared his throat, feigning a great orator. "We are nearly complete with the second issue of Archiv. Rudolf has reported much progress in it with his experimentation on dogs regarding thrombosis and fibrin as well as results of our combined studies with the microscope."

Mayer looked at Kölliker and winked. "Würzburg had better keep their thoughts away from these two," he said waving a finger at Virchow and Reinhardt. "They have a future right where they are."

VIEW ON HUMANITY CHANGES FOREVER

The year was 1848, the springtime of the European Revolutions. Three interrelated crises contributed to the Italian, French, Austrian and German revolutions – years of poor harvests resulting in severe food shortages, what would now be called a recession, and the industrial revolution.

Newspaper type was set by hand, a tedious process that limited the size of the paper to six to eight pages, the publishing schedule to once or twice a week and the press run to a few hundred copies. European newspapers required government approval to publish and also begrudgingly betrothed editors to a government-sponsored censor. Articles disliked by the censor did not see print. In protest, editors risked their license to print by leaving blank spaces where the censors deleted text. This at least allowed the people to see how much tatting and cutting the censors provided with their news. Tavern and café owners bought small quantities of newspapers for patrons so those who could not afford a newspaper kept informed of the spreading revolution.

Leslie Dunn

Germany at that time consisted of a confederation of autonomous states – Brandenburg where Berlin is located, Prussia and Austria (the two mightiest states), Schleswig, Saxony, Holstein, Silesia and the Grand Duchy of Baden – thirty-nine separate states each sharing one cultural heritage, each desiring unification. The earliest beginnings of the dream of unification of the Vaterland (Fatherland) began in 1817 with Burschenschaften (student associations) at universities. These Burschenschaften chose black representing gunpowder, red for blood, and gold for fire to symbolize a unified Germany. In medieval times, these colors represented the Deutsches Reich and later the volunteer infantry that fought in wars against Napoleon. Black, red and gold – colors of revolution.

Fifteen years later, on May 27, 1832, approximately thirty thousand people gathered at the Hambacher Fest in Palfz in the Kingdom of Bavaria. They demanded a liberal, unified Germany, freedom of the press, lifting of feudal burdens and religious tolerance. Predictably, a series of arrests followed as well as new laws suppressing liberals. The monarchy continued to maintain a political caste system, and oppression worsened in the years to come.

Within a little more than a decade, crop failures severely reduced available food sources for a majority of the population. Even farmers struggled to put food on their own tables. In June 1844 the Prussian army silenced an uprising of weavers in Silesia - the weavers were told to "eat grass."

Rudolf Virchow

The Industrial Age bloomed coincidental to this period. Lured by employment opportunities, the starving and, therefore, easily exploited population streamed to the cities for jobs in the flourishing textile, iron-making, milling and brewing industries.

Within thirty-five years the population more than doubled and the price of land rose fifty times in value. Romantic marriages gave way to marriages of financial necessity and society saw an increase in both abortion and infanticide as parents murdered newborns so that their other children might live. Two families crowded into tiny apartments yet still went hungry.

By the middle of the century, Berlin lauded a reputation of 'most modern of European cities.' In this most modern city, crime rates soared and seven percent of the female population denigrated themselves into prostitution. Soon, however, malnutrition, sexually transmitted diseases and utter hopelessness affected the majority of overcrowded and overworked German citizens. As the industrialization progressed, the civil population devolved. Despondent workers labored on products they were unable to afford and families working as many as fifteen hours a day were still unable to earn enough to support themselves.

The monarch's apathy must end; it was time for the people to stand together. But how? Meetings and committees required government licensing and most applications were denied. Censors muzzled newspapers. As a result, people gathered under the guise of 'banquets' where denouncing the government was the main course.

In February, one month before the Berlin revolution, French banquets exploded into well planned battle as barricaded citizens fought against their own soldiers and police. King Louis-Philippe fled the city. Unlike Berlin, though, the French civilians organized before their barricade fighting which fortified their victory. Immediately after King Louis-Philippe's flight, the victorious people proclaimed a provisional republic headed by members from the two newspaper staffs.

While the Parisians fought, in Berlin that same February, Johann Albrecht Friedrich Eichhorn, Minister of Culture of the Prussian government, requested that twenty-six year old Dr. Rudolf Virchow travel to Silesia, the town that four years prior its citizens were told to eat grass. Virchow was to determine the method of contagion and prevent spreading of the disease, typhus, before it spread to Berlin.

Shortly before he left Virchow wrote to his father:

Berlin

Sunday, February 20, 1848

"Dear Father,

The wish that I mentioned in my last letter was soon fulfilled. I wrote to you that I would like to see the epidemic in Upper Silesia, and now I have been accorded the great privilege to do so. Minister Eichhorn, unable to find time to busy himself with a scientific study of the disease, has entrusted me with the task of studying more precisely its nature and origin. I will be leaving very soon. The journey will perhaps be over in two to three weeks.

I have three thalers (dollars) as my daily allowance, and so I think I can manage. Give my regards to Mother; I have so little time that I cannot write more. Farewell."

Your most loving son,

Rudolf

While Rudolf stayed in Upper Silesia, he lodged at the palace of Count Hochberg. He dined on fresh vegetables, spicy sausages, and exquisite wines. The palatial accommodations, however, magnified the contrast between living conditions of the monarchy and its townspeople.

The contrast seared Virchow's conscience.

At the clinic for fourteen days, he witnessed families subsisting on potatoes, vodka, milk and sauerkraut. He heard talk of a population lectured by the Catholic church to *"leave it to celestial providence to free his body occasionally by rain of the crusts of dirt; vermin of all kinds, especially lice, permanent guests on his body."* Rudolf wondered, what good were the German-speaking teachers in this Polish village? Wasn't this a town much like the one of his birth?

France's victory in February soon ignited the fuse on Germany's powder keg. Not far away in Upper Silesia, Virchow's soul burst into flames. It would be a fire that burned in his soul until his last breath.

Upper Silesia

Thursday, February 24, 1848

"Dear Father,

Since yesterday, we have been in the midst of the affected area. The misery is endless and one sees here quite clearly what can become of masses ground down by the Prussian bureaucracy. This animal servility is frightful. The country is, for the most part, quite like some regions in Pomerania; mostly fertile soil, at times sand, rarely earth closely mixed with coarse gravel. The towns look passable, but the villages are very wretched. The rooms of the houses are very small, animals and humans sharing the same accommodation with windows not meant to be opened; the stove and the beds occupy most of the room. The people, however, are horrible, pitiable figures, moving barefoot in the snow, feet swollen, and faces pale, eyes dull. They kiss your arm, the hem of your coat, your knee, all in one breath. Enough, it is horrible.

It is certain that the famine and typhus did not appear separately, but that the latter spread on such a scale only because of the famine. The extent of the epidemic is terrible: the number of orphans in the villages of both Rybnik and Pless is officially estimated to be about 3,000. Large rooms have been arranged to accommodate them. Staying in these well-aired and heated rooms on an adequate diet, they are so satisfied that not only do they not mourn the loss of their parents but are even happy about it.

Everyone gets a daily ration of half a kilogram of flour, and some salt. If this continues for six months, they will obviously ruin their stomachs and die. In this district of 59,000 inhabitants, 20,000 will have to be fed for six months. The government has taken no further steps, apart from supplying flour. The effectiveness of the monks-hospitalers, however much as it may be praised in the newspapers, has been relatively insignificant. There are still many villages without a physician; not until the government sends four times as many physicians as there are at present can we talk of adequate treatment. That this misery could never have reached such proportions had sensible preventive measures been taken, and that the government, especially Finance Minister von Bodelschwingh, due to his disbelief and stubbornness, has sacrificed as many people as would be lost in a minor war is absolutely certain. And yet the government does nothing more than send flour and here and there a physician, and use up a lot of paper in writing. It is horrible, disgusting.

    Farewell and many greetings to Mother."

        Your Rudolf

Germany's dual desires – overturning the government *and* unification – mandated even greater organization than that needed by the French. Sadly and singularly, the raging population of Germany had no organization and no leaders. Suffering had grown to such a profound degree that the people could think of nothing but ending it. With no defined leaders and nothing to set in place once the government was overthrown, the deficits eventually unraveled the promise of victory.

The term 'Fatherland' held different meanings, depending on which side of the throne one sat. To the people of the thirty-nine German states, the land was Father and they the citizens of Fatherland. In Prussia, King Friedrich Wilhelm IV defined himself as Father of Land that was his birthright. King Wilhelm believed in the divine right of the throne needed no more defining than the rights of a natural father, refusing to grant a constitution because he "would not allow a sheet of paper to come between him and his people."

Through the people's persistence, though, Wilhelm decided, against the counsel of his ministers and generals, to listen to his people; rather than continue to resist the movement, he would lead it. However, his disgraceful language in his ordinance to the press and his deployment of large numbers of troops caused barricades to sprout like thorns on Berlin streets near the palace. More troops were deployed. In a short time, the people formed committees for citizen's protection and although arms dealers had been required to surrender their supplies, enough demonstrators had rifles and pistols to concern King Wilhelm.

In a final act the People of the Rhinelands delivered an ultimatum on Saturday, March 18, 1848 to the King - if he did not fulfill all their demands by evening the Rhinelands would join the south German states and leave Prussia, King Wilhelm's seat of strength.

Rudolf Virchow

TO THE BARRICADES!

In February 1848, Rudolf returned to Berlin from his assignment in Upper Silesia. Saturated with despair over the Silesian's abysmal living conditions, he reported to Charité Hospital.

Less than thirty days later, civil unrest in Germany cascaded into revolution. Rudolf burst through the door of elder C. L. Schleich, M.D. "Schleich, have you any weapons?"

"Only this old gun and a rusty saber."

"Out with them!" young Rudolf ordered.

Racing down the hall, Rudolf's voice echoed throughout Charité: "TO THE BARRICADES!" Medical colleagues and students responded to Virchow's persuasive battle cry joining in the German revolt against the king.

Rudolf sat down, leaned his back against the wooden barricade and stretched his cramped legs. He glanced at the pistol in his hand, his fingers blackened from gunpowder. Sounds of battle boomed throughout Berlin, its army charging against its citizens on this night of revolution. The smell of cannon-erupted dirt wafted on the night breeze while explosive flares lit the sky red as dawn. Rudolf rubbed his sweaty palms against his pants. For Dr. Virchow, this gun was yet another way of fighting for people's lives.

"I need more gunpowder," Rudolf whispered to his co-publisher of *Virchow Archivs*, Benno.

"Have you any left?" Reinhardt said.

"Enough for a couple more shots. What about you?"

"I've got more than that, but not much," Reinhardt said.

Other doctors with guns in hand crouched near, each resisting the almost instinctive training to respond to moans that surrounded them. Not far from them, a defiant inscription on the palace door read, "Property of the Entire Nation."

Despite the pistol in hand, booming cannons and rioting Berlin, Rudolf could still see, smell and hear the typhus-stricken victims dying in Upper Silesia, each breath a struggle as pneumonia drowned the patients in their own fluids, their feverish faces bloated from kidney failure. During those fourteen days in Upper Silesia, Rudolf's clinical interest dissolved into sadness then plummeted into despair. Neither he nor any doctor could stop typhus from ravaging the famine-weakened population, he concluded. Social conditions resulting from the monarchy's apathy rendered a physician impotent. *"If medicine were to fulfill her great task,"* Virchow later wrote, *"then she must enter the political and social life; therefore, medicine must be viewed as a social science."* For physicians to truly be effective, they must concern themselves with the social state of their patients.

After returning from Upper Silesia, Rudolf brooded over Eichhorn's required report of his trip. Without apology, Virchow laid blame for the outbreak on social conditions and the government. Typhus, he concluded, was an invincible enemy. King Frederick William IV was not.

Virchow gripped his pistol. The battle moved randomly and surely throughout the city.

"What time is it?" Reinhardt asked.

"Nearly 11," Rudolf said.

"We've been fighting for almost six hours," Reinhardt said. "Have you got anything in your pocket..."

"I've got a tube," Rudolf said. A tube was an instrument for removing bowel content from the body.

"...to eat, I was going to say before I was interrupted, Doctor. I want something to go in my mouth, not up my..."

"You two seem to be enjoying yourselves." It was Johann Schroeder, M.D. "What's there to smile about? There is nothing amusing on this night." Although swayed by Rudolf's passion to join the ranks of fighting doctors for the people's cause, Schroeder's desire for a warm bath, bed, and safety eroded his normal good nature. Born in 1821, the same year as Rudolf, raised in the same town of Schivelbein in Eastern Pomerania, Germany, it was he that traveled to Berlin with Rudolf to study medicine in 1839, nine years earlier. His tone softened, "How much longer do you think this will go on, Rudolf?" Schroeder asked.

Rudolf's brown eyes flickered between the faces of his two friends. "Young Schroeder," Rudolf lapsed to the kin-like nickname, "it will not end until the King gives the people what they need. Decent wages, freedom to worship, public speech, medical care and most of all, a constitution."

Schroeder witnessed the burning, intense gaze in his friend's dark eyes before, heard the quiet monotone, and for a moment looked as though he could not believe they were the same age. Rudolf's passion on behalf of the poor persuaded him and the other doctors to share Rudolf's convictions on this night do the unthinkable – arm themselves to kill. No one had seen Rudolf angry, and although he stood just over five feet tall, no one wanted to, either.

"Schroeder, see if you can find us something to eat from one of the others," Reinhardt said. "Or do you have something?"

Schroeder reached inside his jacket and pulled out a chunk of dark rye bread. He shrugged. "It's all I've got." He broke it in half and handed it to them.

Rudolf crammed the bread into the front pocket of his jacket wondering where he could find water and soap to wash his hands.

They heard, "Fire!" then the slurping, sucking, whistling sound of a cannonball arcing through the air. Instinctively they fell to their bellies, faces buried behind the wooden barricade that hours before had been a wooden cart. They felt the boom in their chest and then dirt rained on them. Uncovering their faces they saw a dark, puffy column of smoke backlit by fires erupting from a hole where the cannonball landed.

"That was t-t-t-oo..." Reinhardt stammered.

"...close." Rudolf finished.

Conviction nearly gone, Schroeder said, "Rudolf, we aren't going to do our patients any good if we are dead."

"And we aren't going to do them any good unless we win this fight," Rudolf shot back. "Schroeder, you've been down the line. Has anyone been hurt?" He worried about the others he persuaded to fight.

"Fouquet got cut on a splintered board that bled a lot, but he's fine."

Rudolf cautiously lifted himself to his feet, sprinkling dirt from his hair. He said, "I've got to get more gunpowder." He reached inside his pocket and pulled out the now crushed piece of bread. "Wish I would've eaten this beforeit got smashed." He crammed the bread into his mouth and then spit it out when he crunched dirt. He looked at his filthy hands. "I'll be right back."

"You're going out there for more gun powder? It's not worth dying for, Rudolf," Schroeder said.

"I've got to get more," he said.

Schroeder looked at Reinhardt and they both looked at Rudolf. He was going.

"Be careful, my friend," Schroeder said.

"Stay together," Rudolf warned.

He crouched and ran through the rioting in the narrow streets, dodged ankle-snapping holes in the cobblestone created by the cannonballs, splintered wood, crumbled stones, carriages afire, silenced bodies. Deafening, tumultuous rioting filled the streets of Berlin on this night of revolution, March 18, 1848. In response to the King's order for the army to clear the crowds, citizens erected barricades in the streets with astonishing speed using anything that could be stacked -- carriages, vendor carts, even ripping up the stones of the streets. Barricades served two purposes - halting progression of the armed troops and citizen protection.

A couple blocks away tucked safely in a narrow alleyway Rudolf saw a light glowing in a tent. He hoped that among the first aid equipment they had some ammunition.

"Is there some water, please?" Rudolf asked one of the women.

She glanced up and nodded, then ladled water from a barrel. He shook his head 'no' and stuck out his cupped hands. She looked puzzled. "You want to drink it from your hands?"

"Will you please pour it on my hands and is there any soap?"

She rolled her eyes. "We are in the middle of a battle and you want to wash your hands?"

Her soft voice and mild mocking tone lifted Rudolf's spirits. "Yes."

She poured water into his hands and handed him soap. How soft his hands looked. "Are you a doctor?"

He nodded.

"And you are here fighting?"

He nodded again.

"Which one are you?" she asked. She perched the ladle for his rinse.

"Virchow."

With widened eyes, she looked from his soapy hands to his face, and peered intently at him in the candlelight. Unlike the current fashion, he was clean-shaven and his brown eyes gazed at her with a dispassionate, half-opened tired look. Only the slightly receding hairline and darkened circles around his eyes gave any indication of age to an otherwise boyish face. "Virchow?"

He nodded.

"V-I-R-C-H-O-W?" she spelled.

He smirked.

"Do you have an older brother who is a doctor?"

"No, I am an only child."

"Is your father a doctor then?"

Rudolf imagined his impetuous, moody father in the role of doctor, a picture as incompatible as a stone mason performing last rites. "No, my father is far from a doctor. He is home in the village of my birth, Schivelbein."

"Your name is known to me, but you are... so *young*," she said.

It did not surprise him; he had heard it before.

From a colleague the insinuation annoyed him, as though intelligence and passion belonged only to elders, but with the King's army in retreat, he raised his chin slightly, proudly. *"Not too young to know that I can make a difference. It is going to take the highest educated and most influential voices to help those without a voice. Medicine is a social science, and politics nothing but medicine on a grand scale."*

For a moment, there was no gunfire, no yelling in the streets - only the sound of firm belief in his voice. She looked as if her fear of the battle calmed for a moment.

In the dim light, Rudolf noticed a little sparkle in her eyes. "What is your name?" he asked.

"Anna. I'm a nurse in the eye clinic." She noticed he stopped scrubbing. "Ready for your rinse, Dr. Virchow?"

"Yes, please," Rudolf said.

She poured the water and watched as the bubbles streamed to the ground.

He said, "Since my face is unfamiliar to you and I did a rotation through the eye clinic as a resident, you, then, must be new to Charité?

"Yes."

"Perhaps I will see you at the hospital. In a strictly professional manner," he said smiling. He thought of Dr. Carl Mayer's daughter, Rose, of whom he'd grown fond. "I came for gunpowder. I'm out and my friends are low. Is there any here?"

She nodded in the direction of the bag in the corner. "Help yourself."

As he walked toward the corner, she said, "Why don't you go back to Charité and rest for a few hours?"

"I can't," he said. He hesitated then repeated, "I can't," and returned to the street and his friends.

In a letter home, Rudolf describes the event:

Sunday, March 19, 1848

"...The King was already so weak that he was unable to offer any opposition to these vehement demands; he yielded; a declaration in a high-flown style appeared, which you will read, and there was general rejoicing. Everyone gathered in front of the palace cheered and called; the King appeared. He agreed to relaxation of censorship, held out the prospect of a new constitution, and

made other concessions, and everyone shouted hurrah. The citizens had only one other wish - that the military be withdrawn from Berlin.

The King found this too much. He asked General Mollendorf to ensure quiet; the Prince of Prussia gave orders to clear the square in front of the palace. Suddenly, drawn sabers of dragoons (a military unit comprised of heavily armed and mounted troops) dispersed the unsuspecting people. In one of the King's declarations touching on this incident, which you will read in the newspapers, stands the lie that the dragoons charged with their sabers unsheathed; this is a direct lie.

For the first time since the beginning of German history has it happened that a king fired at his subjects with cannons; small-arms fire was not enough—no, grapeshot and grenades were hurled at the people. The fighting raged simultaneously at three points: near the palace, in Konigsstadt and in Friedrichsstadt. Shot after shot sounded for twelve hours, and at 4 o'clock in the morning, no more than four of the people's barricades had been taken. On the other side of the barricade behind which I was stationed, there was the king's regiment from Stettin firing on us with two cannons; in our barricade, there were only twelve rifles yet the military were thrown back for more than two hours.

The colonel, Count Schulenburg, is dead, one major is fatally wounded, three or four officers and nineteen other ranks have died. By morning, the King's regiment had expended all its ammunition, yet the troops had managed to take only four or five barricades. The Berliners fought like lions; so many heroic deeds accomplished that one cannot speak of them individually. Let me assure you that I am completely uninjured.

That was the state of affairs, when at about 4 a.m., General Mollendorf was captured in Konigsstadt where a very strong-willed man, Urban (a newspaper editor) was in command. The general was brought to the guardhouse, where he signed an order to the Kaiser Franz and Alexander regiments directing them to cease fire and withdraw to their barracks. At the same time, the King was given to understand that if another shot were fired at the citizens, the General would immediately be executed. From that moment on the firing stopped, and this morning saw the removal of the Minister, the amnesty, the summoning of the Landtag, Federal State Parliament.

The King is now so hard pressed that at about 10 a.m., when the folk brought coaches bearing the dead bodies of the citizens killed in front of the palace, he and the queen were forced to appear on the balcony and view them under the maledictions of the people. The protestors shouted, "Take your hat off," and the king complied. On March 21, he paraded through the streets of Berlin wearing black, red, and golden sashes.

But concessions did not suffice. A partially armed deputation from the barricades of Konigsstadt, headed by editor Urban, made its appearance in front of the palace at about 11 a.m. and gave the King its ultimatum to decree a general amnesty and general arming of the citizenry by 4 p.m.; meanwhile the barricades were maintained and renewed in the direction of the palace. Around 4 p.m. there also began the distribution of weapons to the citizens from the arsenal; the military left its

77

posts, withdrew to the barracks and is now for the most part outside of the city. The citizens have occupied all posts, including those in the palace. Thus far we have come with this King.

In Charité there are 52 wounded and 11 dead civilians, 24 dead lie in the Werder church, and in the palace, etc. – 256 civilians perished in all. The damage done to the buildings, especially by cannon fire, is very substantial; the streets look frightful, and wagons can only pass through a very small part of the city. Atrocities on the part of the people are unknown, whereas the soldiers have done the most brutal things. Specifically, when the combatants were chased into houses, the soldiers slaughtered them like bandits.

We will be meeting tomorrow at Councilor Mayer's place. He, too, is a doctor at Charité but one of great standing and of strong intent. A general arming of all householders with carbines and a gun-club has already been decided upon. You can rest assured, moreover, that I will not uselessly sacrifice myself, either physically or in respect of my position.

I think that you, knowing your son, will not expect him to be shamefully unconcerned when the most sacred and honorable rights of citizens of the state have to be upheld. Please calm mother, do not allow her to distress herself too greatly on my account.

Your Rudolf

AFTERMATH OF BATTLE, ENTERS POLITICS

Two days after the battle, twenty patients assigned to Rudolf lined the ward at Charité, ten headboards against the north wall, ten on the south. The wood framed beds had charts neatly clipped to each footboard. The twenty feet ceiling and twelve feet wide arched doorway at the other end of the room contributed to an airy sense despite the lack of windows. Nurses kept sheets firmly tucked around the narrow mattresses and rarely left their patients, such that patients complained to Rudolf *"feeling as watched and oppressed as devout Christians are by the devil."* Of the four nurses assigned to Rudolf, three were male and one female.

His usual 6 a.m. examinations began a half hour early today due to the large number of wounded barricade fighters. Twice daily rounds, the unofficial meeting attended by the doctors and nurses to update each other of patient statuses, began at 7 a.m. and again at 7 p.m.

"Good morning, Dr. V," Rudolf heard throughout the room. Unlike many of his dour peers, Rudolf smiled, enjoying the affectionate nicknames he acquired during his rotations as a resident in various wards. His nickname while on internship at women's internal medicine -- "Second Woman," at the melancholics and epileptics ward -- "Little Doctor." Now a staff physician at Charité, even his father's letters arrived addressed to "Dr. V."

"Halstaf, how are you? And you, Schwartz?" Rudolf called each man by name as he passed among his patients not yet glancing at their charts.

By habit, he headed for the back of the room for two reasons: to assess the supply table set up by the nurses and to perform patient examinations from the back of the room to the front so, when finished, he could simply exit. Dr. Virchow answered patient's questions yet he also learned that allowing too much time led to some questions for which there were no answers.

Dr. Virchow reached the supply table at the far end of the room and walked slowly past it. The sounds of his steps echoed through the now quiet room. He knew all eyes were on him.

On the table lay many of the medical supplies and pieces of equipment common in Virchow's time. A clear glass fishbowl contained five or six leeches for bloodletting. The leeches were slick, glossy black, each as long and thick as a man's index finger. Rudolf noted the extra supply of wound wraps handmade by the nurses necessitated by the high number of bayonet and munition wounds. Six pewter bowls with scored concentric rings denoting ounce measurements for bloodletting lay stacked inside each other. Next to these bowls were lancets and multibladed scarificators – the scarificator the more effective bloodletter. Dr.

Virchow carried his own sets in his pocket, a gift from his Uncle Hesse.

From the Middle Ages through the 1800's, medicine adhered to the belief that there were four main body humours: blood, phlegm, black bile and yellow bile. Any suspected imbalance of a humour resulted in treatments, applications of medicines or herbs that cleansed the body of the impurity, i.e. vomiting, laxatives, bloodletting. This was, and had been, medicine for more than twenty centuries.

As distant as the methods are from today's medicine, there existed a bit of logic to the old theory. Bloodletting mimicked nature in that animals scratched on trees until they bled for relief of an infected body part. Women had monthly cycles that culminated in shedding of blood and the spontaneous spurting nosebleed - both of these unrelated processes were viewed as a therapeutic effort by the body to restore the blood humour balance.

From the supply table, Rudolf picked up the thermometer as well as the percussor used for thumping on the patient's chest to check for lung fluid levels and, with a nod to the nurses, he began examinations.

He reached for the chart on the first patient, Schwartz, and read what the nurse had noted from the previous night.

"Dr. V, we are so proud of you," the man said.

"Schwartz," Rudolf said, "you told me that yesterday."

"We are still so very proud," August said. "We had to fight. You and the other doctors did not."

"Yes, we did. And we will continue," Rudolf said.

"I don't know why you care so much, but we are grateful that you do."

Rudolf heard "yes" around him from other listeners and felt his throat tingle. He cleared his throat to stop his reaction before it escalated to tears. "The nurse's note says you did not sleep very well last night. Is this true?"

"The sounds. My ears still ring with the sounds of the cannons and guns," August said.

"And how is the cough?

August demonstrated. It sounded phlegmy, probably from lying still. Dissatisfied with the site of bright red blood on the wrap covering Schwartz's thigh wound, Dr. Virchow carefully unwrapped the bandage and examined the wound. It should have clotted by now. In August's chart Rudolf wrote to increase the dosage of Primrose, which would simultaneously benefit the sleeping problem and the wound. He prescribed Mullein for the cough.

For the next hour and a half, Dr. Virchow proceeded through the twenty patients, receiving thanks from each. His nurses stayed close by, handing him fresh bandages as he cleaned wounds and tended to the wounded men.

After rounds, Rudolf walked to the physician break room. The room was off limits to patients, and nursing staff entered only in the event of emergencies.

Benno usually shared breakfast with Rudolf. Normally Reinhardt practiced with Dr. Carl Mayer, a leading gynecologist, but today he volunteered for the call of extra duty to treat the wounded.

"How late did you stay, Rudolf? I left at 11:30 and you were still going on," Reinhardt said, referring to last night's meeting at the home of Dr. Carl Mayer, also a fellow revolutionist.

"Not much later. A little after midnight," Rudolf said.

"Did I miss anything?"

Rudolf smiled at his friend's enthusiasm. "The last bit of Frau Mayer's strudel."

"Which I'm sure you took care of."

"Of course. Someday I'll have a wife that can cook like that," Rudolf said.

"I'm concerned about the attorney, Waldeck – his behavior," Reinhardt said. "He's impetuous and loud. A man considering rising up to lead the people should be more refined and dignified. He throws his hands around so much when he is upset, people avoid sitting near him for fear of a slugging. Certainly, Mayor Grabow of Prenzlau seems to be the clear choice delegate. I know it is too soon to decide but we must organize quickly. "

"My Uncle Virchow, the Major, shares your concern about Waldeck but from a military perspective. He sees the man as undisciplined and fears he might not take orders. I see no problem with Waldeck. Eventually the circumstances in which he is being driven will shape his personality. I am more concerned about Reissner. We need men of the working class, the proletariat, not of the bourgeois. But his temperament outdoes Waldeck."

Reinhardt grew quiet for a moment. "Major Virchow is against the king?"

"He remains loyal to the king but many of his troops, including him, are on the side of the Town Council and are swayed to the rights of the people."

Reinhardt smiled. "Perhaps the fleeing of the King's brother and his banishment softened the troops' resolve. We must see to it, then, that Prince William remains banished."

"No doubt the French army and National Guard refusing to fight its citizens last month influenced them, too," Rudolf said.

"No doubt. Now that the people are somewhat armed enforcing the Prince's banishment will be far easier."

"I agree," Rudolf said.

Although Rudolf and Reinhardt talked softly young and older doctors, including Mayer and Schroeder, huddled around them, the growing circle noted especially by Jacob Donner, M.D.

Tall, slender, dark headed Donner stood far enough away so as not to mistakenly appear a part of the group, yet close enough to hear. Born to a physician who was also born to a physician, Donner believed the distinguished field of medicine to be one of the few noble distinctions of social class. Truly, only those weaned on medical terminology could fully comprehend the expected behavior and role of a physician.

Donner believed in a man's right to improve himself through effort, provided a man did not rise far from his beginnings. In Donner's opinion, Rudolf's efforts should have made him the most intelligent farmer in Schivelbein.

In order to graduate from the medical college of Friedrich-Wilhelms-Institut, the candidate must have permission to enroll for promotion, pass oral and written preliminary examinations called a 'tentamen,' and publish a dissertation and thesis with both the tentamen and thesis written in Latin. Required posting of the dissertation and thesis the day before oral presentation offer an opportunity for anyone to refute it, a challenge. It was additionally required that each candidate choose three students as opponents against whom the author defends his thesis. These three opponents were friends of the candidate but expected to heartily challenge the thesis. Compliance was high.

Rudolf chose Gustav Zimmerman, Albert Johow and Albert Fouquet. Donner, however, took exception to Rudolf's thesis and Rudolf had an unexpected fourth challenger. Rudolf's dissertation, "On Rheumatism, Especially of the Cornea," cited sixty-six references for development of his thesis utilizing physicians dating back to Hippocrates.

Rudolf researched corneal rheumatism from its earliest known beginnings. His comprehensive research as well as his lifelong study of Latin made short work of Donner's overnight study of the thesis. Humiliation deepened Donner's beliefs about Rudolf's inappropriate career choice.

As Rudolf sat encircled by the others in the Doctor's Lounge, Dr. Johannes Müller, 1801-1858, teacher of anatomy, neurological researcher and staff physician opened the door and scanned the room. His dark wispy curls flowed like restless currents in all directions around his temples and across the back of his head. His aristocratic nose had a slight dimple at the tip and his eyes were almost as blue as

Rudolf's father. Despite Müller's tendency to scowl and his habit of gripping his lips tightly, his students and colleagues knew his expression did not result from annoyance or anger but from deep thoughts, unless he and Dr. Friorep happened to share the same room. The feud between these two well loved and respected doctors was legendary at Charité. Müller profoundly affected medical science directly by his discoveries in the field of neurology, specifically sensory perception, and indirectly as one of the most inspirational teachers of medicine.

Müller beckoned to Rudolf.

"Excuse me," Rudolf said to the group and went into the hall with Müller.

Müller got right to the point. "One of my students is having trouble dealing with the stench of the cadavers. If Charité would better fund my class," Müller complained, "we would have a better supply of fresh ones."

Rudolf smirked, remembering well his days in Müller's anatomy class with six-day-old cadavers. After a warm weekend and returning to class on Monday for review, even Müller covered his face with a handkerchief.

"He's a bright student and I don't want to lose him. Do you think you can talk with him, give him a student's perspective – an idea on how not to turn green?"

Rudolf smiled. Of all the rigors of medical school, and there were many, the putrid odor of rotting human flesh tested students like nothing else and cured many of evening trips to the beer garden on the night before anatomy class.

"I'll be in my office after breakfast," Rudolf said.

"I'll send him up. His name is Klaus Hans Johann. Thank you, Rudolf."

Rudolf rejoined the small group as they discussed the meeting at the home of Dr. Carl Mayer in two nights on Thursday.

"Of course I'll be there," Rudolf said when Dr. Mayer asked. "I will be a little late, though. I am using part of my evenings to catch up on paperwork. Will your wife be serving dessert again?" he said winking at Reinhardt. The doctors laughed. Donner, with his back to the group, grimaced.

Reinhardt stood up and stretched. "Time to get back to work," he said.

Reinhardt and Rudolf left the room together. In the hall, Reinhardt asked, "What did Dr. Müller want?"

"To help a student," Rudolf said.

"With what?"

Rudolf pinched his nostrils. "The cadavers."

"Say no more," Reinhardt said. "Did he ask anything about the meeting?"

Rudy shook his head, "No. He shows no interest in being a part of medical or political reforms. And I suspect he does not approve of my involvement."

"That is unfortunate. An influential doctor like Müller could get ears to listen that are closed to us."

"The cause is so right, Reinhardt, and so necessary, we will be heard. We will just have to talk a little louder."

Rudolf normally enjoyed walking the streets of Berlin with its Trocadero architecture and its indescribable energy. On this evening, the sixth since the people's victorious revolution, the dawn of democracy heralded glimmering prosperity and quickened the city's pulse.

He headed for Mayer's house to attend the Friedrich-Wilhelmstadt 27th District Association meeting. Rudolf's heart beat with the energy of Berlin.

Charité

Friday, March 24, 1848

Dear Father,

The look of Berlin today, compared with what it was 14 days ago, is something truly fantastic. Everywhere life, everywhere arms, everywhere free and public speech. All Berlin is hung with German banners, and the streets have a colorful and lively appearance. People have been coming in crowds from all sides to see the place of the battle; whole delegations from towns and corporations appear in order to show how happy they are over these glorious victories. The Berliners themselves are naturally filled with the pride of victory and every street boy behaves as though he had encountered many soldiers.

What is something entirely new, and perhaps the most important thing in the affair, is that we have now won a feeling of self-esteem, self-respect and self-confidence. These traits are the foremost requirement for self-government, which constitutes the only form of state worthy of the people. Let us hope that we will not have to use the force of arms again to achieve self-government, for a second battle would surely be far bloodier than

the first. The army would be less dangerous in it than the armed
bourgeoisie would; it would be a real civil war.

> *Farewell and stay healthy.*
>
> > *Your,*
> >
> > *Rudolf*

Rudolf walked through the vine-covered trellis at the end of
the Dr. Mayer's sidewalk for the meeting. Frau Mayer warmly
greeted him at the door, a flour powdered apron wrapped around
her ample figure. The scent of cinnamon met his nose. She hugged
him affectionately, then grabbed the towel from her shoulder and
laughingly dusted him off. She truly loved this short boyish doctor
with snappy black eyes.

"Come in, come in, our future Herr of democracy," she said
half-teasing.

Her husband, Carl Mayer, M.D., gynecologist and instructor
of anatomy, held no special office at Charité, nonetheless he
retained a title of Privy Sanitary Councilor. Mayer had white hair
parted on the side and so thick that even combed back it provided
a snowy frame for his full face. His face reflected an inner glow
of self-assuredness, kindness, prosperity and happiness with life.
Others, disarmed by his pleasant appearance, soon realized the
intensity of Mayer's beliefs and his willingness to put those beliefs
into action. The Mayers' had seven children, five of whom were
girls. Though possessing no great fortune, the family enjoyed more
comforts than most Berliners, something for which the entire
family gave thanks.   Led by their father's example all the Mayers
enthusiastically shared opinions, and debates flowed like Frau

Mayer's coffee during dessert. The more educated and radical one's opinion, the better one suited the Mayers.

Rudy fit right in.

Petite sixteen-year-old Rose, Mayer's third daughter, rarely spoke during family debates but when she did she surprised others with her strong will, perception and intellect. Her sisters, Lisette and Barbara and brother Max proved formidable debaters. Rose's younger sister, Carol and older brother, August, rarely withstood debates but enjoyed the word fests.

"The town is still celebrating," Rose said smiling at Rudolf as she helped him remove his single-breasted black wool tailcoat with tight sleeves and wide lapels.

"Walking down the sidewalk, the town feels like it's a holiday," he said.

"Even 'Stern-Face,' the butcher is smiling," she giggled.

They walked into the living room where the mood contrasted sharply with Rose's lightheartedness. Reinhardt sat by the fire and faced the doorway. Rudolph Leubuscher, another doctor from Charité, stood next to Rudolf's good friend, Reinhardt. From his worn chair facing the fire, Mayer stretched to look at Rudolf. The leather chair squeaked. Rudolf noticed a newspaper rustling in his hands and reading glasses perched on the end of his nose. Fouquet stood quietly on the other side of the fireplace. A few of Mayer's neighbors and Mayer's family, including his wife, were present.

"Good evening to you all," Rudolf said pouring himself a glass of beer from the silver pitcher on the table near the door, wondering about the quietness of the room.

Mayer leveled his voice, "We were just discussing the lying-in-state of the citizens before the palace two days ago."

"Does anyone have a total number of deaths?" Reinhardt asked.

"At last count, 303," Mayer replied. "Of these, 183 coffins were placed before the New Church in the Gendarmenmarkt square. Listen to this," he said and then read aloud from the newspaper: *The Square seemed like a painting, the features of which no pen can describe. Interspersed among the black, surging masses were countless guild banners and the German colors black-red-gold which fluttered in the rays of the sun. Nevertheless, order and calm prevailed; yes, almost a profound silence, creating an impression that sanctified the occasion. No loud word was heard; each face expressed the deep seriousness of the occasion.'" Mayer stopped for a moment, wiped his eyes with the back of his hand, sniffed and then continued. "'In the background of this sea of humanity rose the gloomy scaffolding with its coffins. At two o'clock, the church bells began to ring; the chorale 'Jesus, my Joy and trust,' gave the signal that the procession would begin. The coffins, followed by the city magistrates, the rector and professors of the university in their gowns, writers and journalists behind a banner proclaiming "Freedom of the Press," delegations from other parts of Germany – some twenty thousand men and women -- moved past the palace, where the king once more saluted the dead, to a municipal park outside the city gates.'"* He closed and with reverence folded the paper.

A silence of sadness, honor, awe, and unity fell on the room.

Mayer spoke first. "All classes of German people fought, all classes died and all classes mourn. We are living history in these days, gentlemen." He reached for his glass and lifted it toward the fire. The others raised their glasses. "May God bless those who fought and died, and those who continue the battle for freedom and unification."

"Ja," they said in unison.

"The unification, though, is already being split because no one is in power," Reissner said in his blunt nature breaking the moment. Unlike the others in the room whose lives were insulated from the working poor, fearless Reissner's opinions counted for much on behalf of the proletariat at the meetings.

"What do you mean, Reissner?" Rudolf asked.

One of Mayer's neighbors, Wentzlaff, cut in, "No one is in control right now, neither the government nor the people and with no leadership there is division already."

One of the most popular men of the revolution, Benedikt Waldeck, the impetuous, loud, hand slinging attorney, attended their meetings spoke. "The King's order to clear the streets precipitated the fighting, not a command from a leader. Barricades were in retaliation to the King's order and meant to slow the troops."

Mayer's son, Max, said slowly, thoughtfully, "The people's show of strength and opposition to the monarchy initiated revolution. The people reacted to the King rather than being the initiators of the revolt."

Both his father and attorney Waldeck nodded.

Reissner cut in. "The bourg-eoi-sie," he stretched out the word with disdain, "now refer to the workers as 'rabble,' and the government is already using a tone very close to its tone before March 18. Nothing but a political trick..."

"And yet another display of German domination," Wentzlaff spat.

Schramm, another neighbor, said, "But the People's Party (Volkspartei) is alert, and it, too, is powerful. It will see to it that the people will get what has been solemnly promised to them and that the bourgeoisie who participated very little in the barricades will not benefit."

Reissner said, "When the rest of us were in the streets, most of the 'gentle coats' watched from their windows. One of them might even be recovering at Charité from standing too close to a window shattered by a rock I threw."

Reinhardt looked at Rudolf and raised an eyebrow, then they both looked at attorney Waldeck for his reaction to Reissner's admitted impulsive act of fury. While attorney Waldeck kept his expressionless eyes on Reissner, from her corner Rose watched the interplay between them.

Reissner continued, calmer. "In France, the National Guard and Parisian workmen stood ready at the time of the French barricades. Military and working men," he repeated for emphasis "Together they work hand in hand and maintain peace and order in Paris."

Rudolf said, "Berlin, on the other hand, was unprepared for a revolution. We had a largely unarmed population with no leaders."

Wentzlaff added, "Now we must quickly establish committees, organizations and leaders to write a constitution for unification."

Waldeck nodded, as did several others in the room, including Rudolf.

"What is the greatest agitation to the people, though," Reissner said, "is the summoning of the Landtag, the Federal State Parliament."

There was murmuring and nodding in agreement throughout the room.

"The Assembly of the Landtag must be prevented at any cost," Mayer stated firmly. "It refuses to recognize equal political rights of *all* citizens. The Landtag cannot continue to act as an intermediary with the king serving only the interests of the middle class and not of the working men."

"We must concentrate, then, on the upcoming elections to the National Assembly," said Mayer's eldest son, Max.

"I disagree," said neighbor Wentzlaff.

"Max is right," Waldeck said in support of young Mayer. "The Landtag has proven only partially effective against the king and these were men who were *not* elected. The National Assembly, on the other hand, will be comprised of representatives who will keep their seat providing they serve the *elected*. I have been asked to be its vice president."

Frau Mayer smiled at Waldeck, proud of his accomplishment.

"And what of the general arming of the people? Any word on that, Reissner?" Rudolf asked.

No one but her mother noticed the sudden blanching of Rose's face. Although feisty, Rose hated violence, more so it seemed to her mother when Rudolf was around. Frau Mayer excused herself to the kitchen.

The swarthy complexioned worker Reissner said, "Work is underway for the creation of a militia but so far it consists mainly of burghers, the prosperous middle class. Speeches and elections will go far and in these we must, and will, participate, but the poor workers and craftsmen must also be entitled to arms." As the others agreed, Reissner added, "Not that I believe in guns..."

Reinhardt and Rudolf again exchanged looks as Waldeck, as a signal of disagreement, loudly cleared his throat.

Frau Mayer returned with a tray filled with cake, plates and silverware, her dress softly sweeping the floor. Her husband's eyes crinkled at the corners with a small gentle smile that was just hers followed her every move. "Rudolf," Frau Mayer said softly, "you have many friends who admire you for your leadership, your passion, your energy. Although my husband would make a fine representative, your speaking abilities and credentials have been noticed by many. We need men like you, and Waldeck, to represent us. Would you consider running in the elections? Being one of our representatives?"

Rudolf answered without hesitation, "I would be honored."

Waldeck, Mayer, Reissner, Reinhardt and all the others raised their glass to toast.

Unnoticed in the corner, Rose smiled.

Rudolf would wield the weapons of words like razor sharp rapiers.

Rudolf Virchow

Charité
Monday, May 1, 1848

Dear Father,

I am using the first quiet evening to write you a few lines; it may, perhaps, turn out to be the last quiet evening in the coming two weeks, for the matter of the election has been keeping us constantly occupied. The election of delegates must have kept you busy today, too. Here the outcome has been extremely varied, especially as regards time, for there are voting constituencies where even at this moment voting is taking place. We, the 87th voting constituency, with 2971 souls and 990 primary voters, needed ten hours to finish with our ten electors, who will, however, be reduced to seven, as three were simultaneously chosen for the German and Prussian delegation. I also belong to the latter; in the first secret ballot, I won (obviously as an elector) an absolute majority for Berlin as well as for Frankfurt. My declaration of faith is very simple: democratic monarchy, i.e. a republic with a hereditary president.

Germany can no longer avoid becoming a republic; I am as strongly convinced of this as I am of my own existence. Either Germany becomes a republic, or it ceases to be Germany. This revolution is not merely political but essentially social. All our present political activity is only a way of bringing about social reform, a means of transforming the structure of society down to its foundations.

I am sure you will not be angry that I have told you what I think in plain words. I am now no longer a half man, but a whole man in that my medical credo is absorbed in my political and social credo. As a scientist, I can only be a republican, for the realization that the laws of nature, derived from the nature of the human being, can only be achieved in a republican state. But, as I said earlier, my concern is not with a democracy that has an elected president; rather I accept even a democratic hereditary king.

As soon as the election to the delegation is over we shall immediately proceed with medical reform and I hope it will be radical. Here, too, the pigtail must be lopped off and the democratic element taken into account. More next time. Please bear with my somewhat stormy and abrupt way of presentation. Kind regards. Farewell.

Your most loving son,

Rudolf

Twenty-six year old Rudolf's political involvements brought his mother to hysterics. Despite the miles between them she clearly saw the danger he was in, and she believed it unnecessary. During these times, Rudolf reminded his beloved mother to turn to friends for comfort, and if that failed, to draw on her faith. He appealed to her with his sense of the extreme injustice of the working poor and his worthy, though lofty, goal:

Charité

Tuesday, May 2, 1848

Rudolf Virchow

Dear Mother,

It was not possible for me to write earlier, for we had large or small meetings every day in the mornings and evenings concerned with preparations for the elections. Every day from nine in the morning until 12 or 2 in the night, I am on my feet. This will continue next week since we delegates must busy ourselves with the

preliminary preparations for the elections of representatives. There are also meetings for medical reform, to which I was delegated as a committee member; meetings of the general physicians where I am vice president; district meetings of the Friedrich-Wilhelmstadt; meetings for founding a new club; and finally public meetings to oppose the recall of Prince William of Prussia. In the meantime, I have to take the greatest pains to prepare my official report on typhus in Upper Silesia.

You say that you failed to understand what all this meant, and I wish to explain it to you. Now this is not so easy, but I will try to set forth the basic tenets of what we want. —The majority of human beings have long ceased to believe in the existence of hell; at present, they are beginning to consider even heaven highly doubtful. Hence, we wish that the poor and oppressed, which bear their sufferings on this side of the grave, would have a happier lot here on earth instead of waiting for heavenly joys. This improvement in the welfare of the poor or, which means the same thing, of the working classes, has not been possible under the existing constitution, for there the King's will alone is law, and the working classes (Klassen) had no means of asserting themselves. The privileged classes (Stande) always oppressed them. Therefore, we have overthrown the old constitution. The King should have no other will than the will of the people (Volk); there should be no privileged classes, in fact, no classes at all. Instead, everyone should have the same rights in the state, as is natural and reasonable; we want to form from now on a united people, composed of human beings, all with equal rights.

Our new constitution, which the representatives whom we will now elect are supposed to work out, will establish this requirement first of all. Once we have this constitution, the next step will be to educate the people more thoroughly, and there has to be an altogether different kind of public education. We hope to achieve this by excluding religion from the schools and by freeing the state from concern with the beliefs of the individual citizen; instead, useful things should be taught in schools. In order to ensure that the people keep this new constitution safe they will have to be armed, so that should the King or anybody else suddenly decide to diminish their liberties they may be in a position to defend their freedom with force. Now, if the people are educated and free, every individual will best appreciate his own interests and achieve what he lacks, and everybody will have the maximum possible happiness. This is the primary aim of our present endeavors.

Other than a slight hoarseness from much public speaking, I am perfectly well. Regardless of the outcome of the elections, I plan to resume teaching my class on Thursday following the elections. Write soon and tell me what the Schievelbeiners are doing. Farewell, and have no worries about me.

Your Rudolf

NEW CIVILIAN MORGUE DIRECTOR

Sun streamed through the front windows of the main hallway of Charité. Tapping his walking cane with each energetic step, Virchow headed out the building.

Nurse Anna rounded a corner from a room that opened onto the main hallway, nearly bumping into him.

He grabbed her arm to steady her. "Anna, how are you this morning? I'm sorry, I nearly knocked you over. I've seen you from time to time but I'm usually in a rush," Rudolf said, recalling his encounter with this nurse in the middle of the rioting of March 18.

"Dr. Virchow, I'm fine. And you?" Then, before he could answer, she said, "Judging from your coat and walking stick, I'd say you are in your usual rush." She smiled broadly.

Nurses passed by and took second glances, their footsteps echoing in the high ceiled hall. Large open windows lined the walls and the fragrance of the gardens surrounding this section of the hospital drifted inside. The three storied hospital now bedded fifteen hundred patients.

"I just finished teaching. Since I've switched my class time to seven o'clock in the morning, attendance has increased - even older faculty attends now and it pleases me to say most of them come with open minds. I'm leaving for the District meeting and later to speak at the machinist union meeting."

She shook her head back and forth. "I've heard you are involved with the things that are going on. Your schedule would put a teenager under," she teased. "I won't hold you back. Nice to see you again." She smiled again.

"Good day, Fräulein," he said.

"Rudolf!" they heard from down the long hallway followed by Reinhardt's brisk footsteps clapping on the floor. "Stop! I've been trying to catch up with you." He trotted up to them. "No easy task these days," he said looking appreciatively at the pretty nurse, then questioningly at his friend.

"Anna, this is my good friend, Dr. Reinhardt. Dr. Reinhardt, Anna Schilling, who is obviously a nurse."

"Nice to meet you," Reinhardt said earnestly.

"Nice to meet you, too," she said softly, her chin tucked, her blue eyes widened slightly.

Rudolf smiled at Reinhardt's tone and Anna's reaction. "Anna kindly poured water for me to wash my hands the night of the barricades and provided us with additional gun powder."

"Now I see why you risked your life," Reinhardt said.

Anna turned her head but not soon enough to hide the redness in her cheeks.

Rudolf cleared his throat. "Please excuse me, but I..."

"I'm sorry, Anna, but you must forgive me," Reinhardt said truly regretful. "It's difficult to find a minute with Virchow these days."

"I understand," Anna said. "I am not usually away from my patients this long and if I don't return, they will think I've left ill. If you will excuse me...good day, doctors."

She had taken only a couple steps when Reinhardt said, "I wish I had gone to wash my hands, too."

Rudolf laughed. "You'll just have to volunteer for duty in the eye clinic, if I remember correctly, and ask for a certain nurse to attend you."

"The eye clinic...I'll mark that down," he joked. "Now, the reason I've been trying to find you...I have an article for the Archiv on microscopes."

Rudy sucked in his breath. "Wonderful! We have not published much about their use. I constantly expound, 'Think microscopically!' in my class and frequently asked for more information."

Reinhardt paused for a moment and looked at Rudolf's face in the morning light. He noted the slight darkness circling his friend's eyes. "What are you doing for fun these days? When we were residents, we danced and drank too much and did silly things.

"I visited the Forster's in Freienwalde during Whitsuntide..."

"Rudolf, that was May...two months ago," Reinhardt scolded.

"You hardly have room to talk, my friend. I see your publications regularly, also, in addition to your research and work on the Archiv." Noting the caring expression on Reinhardt's face he relented his offense. He sighed. "The fire of revolution is slowly dying and we must keep it burning. There will be time enough to rest after writing of the constitution. Did you hear of the outcome of the arsenal affair last month?"

Reinhardt looked down, shook his head slowly, yes.

The newly created militia, although comprised mostly of the middle class, partially fulfilled arming of the people. The militia, however, did not include workers and poor craftsmen. The voting majority of the Berlin Assembly refused to agree on a Prussian constitution written to expressly recognize the achievements of the March revolutionaries, the 48'ers as they would be called. Upon hearing the result of the vote, the gathered crowd became unruly and was initially dispersed by the militia.

A company of the new militia shot at a group of workers who demanded arms and withdrawal of the military presence from the armory. Two persons were killed, several injured, and the outraged crowd built barricades. The crowd ransacked armament shops and eventually forced officers and soldiers who guarded the armory to retreat. But just as had happened on the night of the barricades the storming of the armory burst into action spontaneously with no clear leader. By late evening the crowd scattered.

The resultant arming of the proletariat alarmed hundreds of prosperous Berlin families who immediately fled the city. The monarchy, in retaliation, imprisoned workers responsible for the storming of the armory, strengthened its military presence in the city and created a special force to protect the armory.

"Everywhere, doctors are discussing 'Medical Reform,'" Reinhardt said.

"Wonderful. I'm not even interested if the talk is good or bad – that it is being discussed is what counts. It is meant to cause discussion, and so it is a success."

"You have generated some strong supporters, but also some have turned against you. Aren't you concerned, Rudolf, about your safety, about your standing at Charité?"

"Of course I am. These are dangerous times, Reinhardt, and I am in the forefront. But I've no wife and family here, although I am concerned about repercussions directed at my father and mother. A fellow advocate lives in Schivelbein and watches over my parents. I'm more than a little glad to pay his fee to keep guard over their safety. His name is Dehnel and he has been voted to the National Assembly."

"And what about repercussions here at Charité?"

Rudolf paused for a moment. Slowly yet passionately he said, "The monarch *must* be overturned. There are far too many people suffering and their suffering bores the king."

Walking past them, a doctor Rudolf recognized from the eye clinic slowed his stride.

Rudolf's said in a slightly louder tone, "Can you imagine the standards of public health being raised to such quality that it puts us out of work?"

The doctor turned and flashed a smile of agreement but continued walking away.

"You are a dreamer, Rudolf. But fortunately for you, many share your dreams." Reinhardt stopped and held out his hand. Rudolf put his hand in that of his friend's and they shook. "I'm proud of you," Reinhardt said.

A warm August breeze gently ruffled the curtains, carrying with it the complaining sounds of psychiatric patients who worked the grounds as part of their therapy, per Director Ideler. Looking down, Rudolf recognized some of his former patients and mused on his hope that this address would remain his for some time to come.

Standing by the open window in his sunlit room, Rudolf's attention oscillated between patients ambling on the common area below and the letter in his hand. Back and forth, back and forth. Ignored for now, on the cloth covered table in front of the couch, lay a draft copy of Schmidt's medical reform based on Rudolf's views. The joyful letter took precedence.

"It is official," Rudolf thought as he again read the words written by Minister of Culture Eck: *"...on the recommendation of Geh. Rath Schmidt, please report to the Kriegsrath Bercht, Chief Accountant, for disbursement of 150 thaler which represents your salary as prosector during your upcoming travel to study medical advancements of Prague and Vienna. Your trip to those cities will, no doubt, benefit Charité through your continued contribution to our quickly expanding reputation in the field of Pathologic Anatomy.*

"Further, I thank you for forwarding to my attention your published article of fibrin's chemical properties as it clots the blood. The article again demonstrates your brilliant research techniques as well as groundbreaking discoveries and I thank you for your attention to this matter. In recognition of your diligence and zeal, Kriegsrath Bercht has been notified to provide

you, in addition to the travel salary, with a special remuneration of 150 thaler.

"*Lastly, you are hereby bestowed the title of Interim Prosector of Charité Hospital. Should you require additional funding for equipment or research material, please submit in writing your request with a detailed explanation for its justification.*

"*It is through doctors such as yourself that Charité has acquired the status it has achieved and by its continued commitment to the advancement of medicine, Charité will remain competitive throughout Germany.*"

"This from Eck," Rudolf pondered, "who approved my speech yet refused to publish it." Then he decided, "I am most indebted to Schmidt who no doubt exerted influence in my direction." With gratitude too profound to contain, he at once determined to thank the man in person. He picked up Schmidt's memo from the table in addition to Eck's letter, grabbed his walking stick and headed to the home of the Gen. Rath Schmidt.

Rudolf saw little of the scenery. His gloved hand tap, tapped the cane with each quick step. Anyone watching him might have wondered at the diminutive man's brisk gait. It was, after all, a warm day made for strolling.

Dressed day casual, as always a model of high fashion, Virchow wore his single breasted brown coat buttoned from the waist to under the collar with tight sleeves and narrow cuffs. The coat flared from the waist and ended just at his knees with two deep diagonal pockets on the hem of its front skirts. Under it he wore a white frilled shirt banded with a bow, fitted trousers with stirrups and sharply pointed ankle boots. Under his narrow brimmed top hat he whistled a happy Christmas tune.

The streets of Berlin bustled as usual with the rich and poor, young and old. An old woman's full skirt covered the stool on which she sat on the cobblestone sidewalk vending crockery. Despite the warmth, she was wrapped in a checker-patterned shawl, her hands bobbing at needlework as she watched for those well dressed to lure to her wares. Diagonal to her and closer to the edge of the street a younger woman also hawked her basketry, sweating under her white bonnet. At the street's edge, a little girl in a lavender gown with lace collar teased two dogs with a piece of cookie, the dogs hitched to a milk cart. Horse-drawn carriages waited patiently outside stores for either their owners or for shoppers in need of rentals. Couples strolled casually through the street.

Schmidt's home faced the street, fronted only by sidewalk and three layers of zigzagging steps. Rudolf took the first four two at a time, turned right at the first landing, bounced up the next ten one at a time, turned left at the second landing and double stepped the last four, a pattern he had concocted from previous visits. Schmidt answered Rudy's knock and, after Rudolf greeted Fräulein Schmidt adding a polite hello to their eldest daughter, the two men entered the older doctor's private study.

Schmidt's study had two entrances on two walls, each opening comprised of two doors. One small carpet under the desk made it look like an island among a sea of books and papers. Six bookshelves did not contain all of his immense collection – some books were stacked on tabletops while more were strewn across the desk. Some books on the desk were earmarked by another book straddled atop them. Organized chaos. A mirror image of Rudolf's own study. Religious, political pictures and busts covered walls and a fireplace mantel added to the room's clustered feeling. As happened on his walk, though, no thought of Rudolf's was on his surroundings.

After closing the door, Schmidt turned to the abnormally quiet Rudolf who merely stood holding the papers in his hand. Rudolf's beaming expression was Schmidt's delight. Schmidt clapped his hands then rubbed them together. As Rudolf wondered what to thank the man for first, Schmidt clasped the silent young doctor in his arms.

"I've come to thank...."

Schmidt grabbed Rudolf by the shoulders and looking him in the face, interrupted, "Let's have a drink."

Smiling stupidly, Rudolf nodded. Schmidt strode from the room and returned with a silver tray bearing two tall, stemmed glasses and a bottle of schnapps. "To the newest director at Charité. Prosit – here's to you!" he toasted, their crystal glasses chimed.

Rudolf laughed aloud at hearing it for the first time. "Yes, sir!" he said.

"*And,*" Schmidt continued, "your obligations to the military are ended. The military can no longer claim you. You are now a civilian physician."

Slugging down his drink freed Rudolf's tongue and his words tumbled like autumn leaves in a wind. "As the interim director, it stands that what you say is true – that I will soon be named director. Nothing in the memo stated that my military obligations will end, though. That is of the finest news to me. How dear your support is to me, sir! And almost everything I wanted to see in print about medical reforms, you drafted in your memo to the minister." He read from the memo he'd already memorized: 'Things cannot be allowed to continue as they are at Charité as we are already being outstripped by the Viennese...' he looked up at Schmidt, his raven eyes shined. "You know, of course, I have been appointed Interim Director of the Morgue thanks to your praise of me, which I do not deserve..."

"NONSENSE!" Schmidt hailed. "You work long and hard, Rudolf, your enthusiasm is contagious, and your radical beliefs are *exactly* what Charité has needed. We have been complacent and lazy. You are shaking us by the shoulders," he grabbed Rudolf's shoulders and shook him with verve, "and waking us up! -- Let's toast again!"

Rudolf grinned while his head bobbed about like a marionette.

The door cracked open and Frau Schmidt peeped into the room.

"It's all right, it's all right," Schmidt said waving one hand at her in dismissal, filling his and Rudolf's glasses with the other.

"To the New Charité," Schmidt toasted.

"Ja!" Rudolf cheered.

After they downed the drink, Schmidt asked, "And what is your next step, young Virchow?"

"Next year, Reinhardt and I plan to publish a medical journal and recently I was elected a member of the local association for scientific medicine."

Schmidt looked puzzled. "What association is that?"

Virchow looked sheepish. "With all due respect, sir, it is comprised mainly of younger physicians."

Schmidt's bushy white eyebrows went up for a moment. "I see," he said.

"You would be most welcome to..." Rudolf stammered self-consciously.

Schmidt raised his hand. "That is quite all right, Virchow. The future is in good hands."

"Thank you, sir," Rudolf said while hoping his relief did not show. Not that Schmidt wouldn't be welcome but his presence might inhibit some tongues.

"And what of your trip to Prague and Vienna? Any word when you leave?"

"In just a couple weeks, at the beginning of September, after I'm finished teaching my current course."

"Vienna in September..." Schmidt murmured. "When you return, no doubt you will have strong words to pass on to the Charité medical staff about advancements, especially Vienna's. The wake-up call was sounded with this," Schmidt tapped the medical reform publication, "and you will describe to them in detail exactly how far behind we are."

Rudolf nodded solemnly.

"And you have sufficient funding for your trip?" Schmidt said with a wink and slyness that so characterized the man.

"For which I must also give you thanks." Mindful of his years of making do and doing without, Rudolf beamed at the thought of the generously financed and prestigious trip on which he was soon to embark. Then he added, "And for my article on the chemical properties of fibrin, the Minister has authorized bonus pay."

Schmidt pursed his lips and blew out. "Your parents will be proud of your achievements."

Rudolf's face clouded briefly then cleared. "I was so excited I raced over to see you without writing to them first. That is just as well, I will write to them after I get the distribution of the funds and send some money home," he said thinking aloud. Although feeling a pleasant slight burning in his stomach and a sense of warmth spreading through his body, a troubling thought occurred to him. He asked, "Schmidt, do you mind if we sit down?"

"Not at all," he responded. Schmidt walked to the spare chair in the room and removed the books from the seat. "Sit," he ordered.

After settling into the overstuffed chair, Rudolf's tone quieted. "I have a problem I would like to discuss with you."

From his seat, Schmidt said, "What is it?"

"A couple months ago I learned that Geh. Rath Müller, for whom I have only the deepest respect and regard..."

Schmidt nodded in acknowledgement.

"...opposes my viewpoint concerning ownership of pathologic-anatomical specimens."

"Bodies," Schmidt clarified.

"Yes, sir. Should Müller win approval from the Minister on behalf of his anatomy classes, the Chemistry/Microscopic lab would forever be completely dependent on the benefactor of Müller for specimens." He paused ever so slightly. "Müller's instruction of future physicians is critical but should specimen shortages continue, his students can do as my class had to do – share. Given no choice as to specimen type or number, my research would be under the strictest control of Müller and in the worst of cases, no specimens forthcoming at all."

"And for your stance, you are providing written defense?"

"It is in its final edit."

"Good. I can make no promises but I will see to it that it receives a thorough reading by the Minister. Müller's popularity makes him a powerful man at the hospital," he said explaining what Rudolf already knew. "He attracts many students who would not otherwise have chosen the University of Berlin. To put it crassly, a source of income."

"I know that, sir. It was his teachings more than any other's that inspired me to do research."

"Before you turn in the final copy to the Minister, then, please put it on my desk for review." The matter settled, Schmidt lifted his nose and sniffed, his belly grumbled. "Would you care to stay for supper?" he asked Rudolf.

"No sir, I have previous plans," Rudolf lied so as not to impose, stood up.

"One last thing before you leave," Schmidt said, saving some good news for last. "Although it won't happen overnight, but probably sooner than you think – I want you to apply an extra dose of your energy towards becoming a licensed teacher, a Privatdocent. Doctor's orders," he said sternly.

Rudolf darted from Schmidt's home before his heart burst from joy.

Without reservation Schmidt admired and served to further Rudolf's medical career. Although on this day he admired the changes Virchow would endow at Charité, it would not be long before the younger doctor's political bent soon found no support in Schmidt. Worse, the influential Schmidt would soon be instrumental in an event that would crash Rudolf's livelihood around him.

Charité

Friday, September 29, 1848

Dear Father,

My sole excuse for a long silence is that time slips from my hands, I know not how. Events press and force their way in great haste – hope and anxiety are on a seesaw, and neither politics nor medicine leaves me a moment of peace. Just now, it is somewhat quieter, but it is like the sultriness before the thunder. All around the horizon are thunder and lightning, thick threatening clouds are everywhere and nowhere a roof to protect us! The barometer has sunk low, very low! –

Mother had asked me to send 50 thaler to Dehnel. In addition, I am also sending another 25 thaler for your needs or spending them in whatever manner you deem fit. As for my coming, I do not think I will have time next month. The day before yesterday I started a new course that I would like to finish by the end of October so as to start a second one for the students at the beginning of the new term. I hope that on Christmas, if everything goes well, I shall definitely be able to make the trip. I much regret that I could not come in August to help you gather in the harvest, but at that time I was rather unwell, as was almost everybody in Berlin, but that is all over now; the cholera itself has almost completely subsided and I am now back on my feet. I am glad that you have been spared and I hope you remain so. Take proper care of yourself and be especially cautious with diarrhea. It should not be neglected now: go to bed at the right time, drink some peppermint tea, and do not leave your room too early in the morning.

Politics is now again going very badly, and I am very depressed. What is to become of Germany, I still do not understand. A reign of terror is everywhere in the making, and a state of siege more frightful than ever before. The long-feared reaction is now here. Everywhere military despotism and subjugated people, everywhere immorality of the rulers and demoralization of the people. My own involvement in these things is now very modest. Our District association, the Friedrich Wilhelmstadt, is definitely democratic and, therefore, cannot enjoy the support of the reactionaries. Your brother, the Major, meant this. If he calls the members wretched riffraff, he may be right from his point of view. True, many of them are proletarians, but the spirit of our time has made them human beings with a voice. You need not worry about this, persons such as Waldeck and Wentzler. Our posters and speeches received high recognition from enlightened men. We know no class distinctions, however, for in politics everybody is equal. If our people are to become a political entity they must also have a political education which cannot occur overnight. Apart from this association, I am a deputy in the district's central association; there I am vice president and I don't think I need to be ashamed of it.

You can best see my position toward the democratic party from the fact that on the recommendation of representatives Waldeck and Schramm I have recently been elected deputy to the constituent assembly in the district of Ziegenruck in Thuringia. I had 18 votes out of 25. Since I am not yet thirty years old, as required by electoral law, I, of course, had to decline. If I were old enough, I would at this moment be sitting in the National Assembly and would belong to the extreme left, although I do not always approve of the means that they propose to use for realizing their ideas.

I have already written to you that I, with Dr. Leubuscher, have founded a weekly paper, "Medical Reform." This periodical and the meetings of the General Assembly of Physicians along with their various commissions have taken much of my time. We are in entire opposition to the government, and Privy Councilor Schmidt has written for the Ministry of Medicine his own brochure, indulging in the most scathing criticism of me, my "materialism." I have heard the Prussian Secretary of Cultural Affairs also takes affront at our Medical Reform. Our cause is, however, so good that even such attacks do it no harm; of the course the struggle is not without danger but I think we can weather it. The Archiv continues peacefully on its course; two issues have appeared so that of the second volume, the one for the current year, only one issue is lacking.

You see how active I am. There is always a new struggle at hand, and I must admit that I would be exhausted were it not for the solace that I draw from being at rest with my principles and the fact that precisely such a period of struggle brings like-minded people closer. My relationships with my friends have become very much warmer, and I have made many an acquaintance who would otherwise never have come my way. Among such I count especially two of the noblest and most lovable persons from Konigsberg, Dr. Goldstucker, a Sanskritist, and Prof. Rosenkranz, who is presently reporting councilor in the Ministry of State and who has more than once been offered the Ministry of Culture. I hope that these friendships are going to last a long time.

Please give my kind regards to Mother, and ask her to be calm. I plan to write soon to her also; at the moment I am much too agitated to be able to write a decent letter. More next time. For now, farewell, and may a friendly heaven watch over you as long as possible.

Your ever loving son,
Rudolf

Late September, after his return from Prague and Vienna, Rudolf knocked on Benno's bedroom door at Charité and then let himself in.

Benno was standing in front of his open closet and just hanging up his jacket. He looked up in surprise, then smiled at Rudolf.

"Come on in, I just got here. Welcome back," Benno said he said walking toward Rudolf. "How was Vienna?

Rudolf strode over to him and thrust a large stack of papers toward Benno.

"And what is this?" Benno said, pretending to buckle his knees under the weight of the stack. "It must be something important to have inspired you *this* much."

"It's the young reforming the old, the new shredding old beliefs, replacing fantasy with facts..." Virchow rattled.

"All right, I understand. I suppose you want me to read this?"

Rudolf sat on the couch and offered Benno the seat next to him, as though Benno were the visitor.

"Now?" Benno asked.

Again Rudolf patted the seat next to him.

"Now," Benno said. "But then afterwards, you must tell me about Vienna."

"It's a deal," Rudolf agreed hoping that Vienna would be far from Benno's mind in a few minutes.

Benno's face as he read reflected his range of emotions – agreement, puzzlement, enthusiasm, scorn, and finally an expression of understanding.

He handed the papers back to Rudolf. "Do you not realize what you are saying? The backlash from this? I'm not telling you not to publish it and I'll support you no matter what because I believe you are correct, but you are twenty-six years old and Rokitansky is, what? Forty?"

"He's forty-two and, yes, I am twenty-six, but I am a correct twenty-six year old and he is incorrect forty-two year old. He

117

teaches and publishes incorrect information in his "Handbook of Pathologic Anatomy" and it must stop. Because he is such a popular and expert pathologist, he influences European doctors *and* doctors overseas. My paper is based on fact, not dogma. My attack is not against Rokitansky. I attack errors."

"Once again, you rattle the cages. They sent you to Silesia to report on an outbreak and they got a recommendation for 'full and unlimited democracy.' They send you to study the advances of pathology in Vienna and they get..." he pointed to the sheaf of papers in Rudolf's hands, "this." Benno shook his head. "And once again, I will stand up for you. When will it be published?"

"As soon as it is approved," Rudolf said wistfully. "Hopefully before the end of the year."

Nearly Christmas time, back in Charité, Rudolf and his jealous colleague Donner squared off at the far back end of the lecture hall. Donner would have preferred a small audience as he held Rudolf's just published criticism of Rokitansky's Volume 1, Handbook of Pathologic Anatomy in his hand but Rudolf was hard to catch up with at all.

"Let me see if I understand your educated views properly," Donner said.

"If my views were educated, they would be the same as yours..." Virchow retorted, "...incorrect. My views are based on research."

"Your research, correct?"

Almost a foot of height difference between them, Virchow looked up at Donner fixing his nearly black eyes in a steady gaze and said nothing.

"Rokitansky," Donner continued, "the greatest pathologist of our time who has performed thousands of autopsies and trained hundreds of doctors, states that specific fibrins in the blood humour determine the course of inflammations or cancers, and your public counterargument is...what?"

"I have no 'counterargument' against nonsense," Virchow said flatly. "I have published the result of my microscopic studies of fibrin."He crossed his arms and assumed a teaching voice he used with first year students. "Fibrin itself does *not* determine the course of a disease or cause a cancerous tumor. It has no properties that can do such a thing. Fibrin is a property of blood, Doctor Donner, which you would have learned had you read my recent publications which covered in detail my findings of fibrin."

Redness crept up from Donner's neck to his cheeks and forehead. "I have enough to read of the *learned* of medicine," he sniped.

Virchow ignored the remark. "Rokitansky has made remarkable discoveries without the use of the microscope and his eyes are well trained about the appearances of diseases from a *macro*scopic level." His temper softened somewhat despite the adversarial position of Donner. "It's like trying to study the stars without a telescope. Although stars can be observed without one, the telescope enables one to see much more clearly than what can be seen with the eye alone." He looked intently at Donner, hoping to break through his colleague's stubbornness that would, Virchow

119

knew, hold Donner back from medical progress. "Microscopes *must* be used in investigations and the prevailing dogma that diseases are based on 'constitutional disturbances' must end. Microscopes reveal what is indistinguishable with the eye, that diseases are not based on a humoural imbalance. If you are to keep up with the progression of medicine, Donner, you would do well to open your mind before... "

"Don't lecture me, little Doctor Virchow," Donner spit. "What you have published is a shattering difference in medicine and it will not be easy for doctors to understand or agree with. This reaches far beyond Rokitansky's reputation – your views contradict accepted medical theories of two thousand years."

"Not 'theories' – dogma," Virchow corrected. "Dogmas based on speculation, fallacies and imagination."

"The older doctors are going to tear you apart," Donner warned.

"Wrong again. It is my younger colleagues who seem most disturbed. The older ones are congratulating me on my findings."

"I am not disturbed," Donner said defensively. "Your views are rubbish! Time has, and will continue, to prove you wrong then you will be shown for the foolish work you do. You should never have been allowed to attend the University."

Virchow stared with pity at the Donner, and then turned and walked out the door of the lecture hall.

Leslie Dunn

BREAKS SHACKLES OF FOUR HUMOURS

In Rokitansky's dissection shed, his body dropped heavily into a chair as he finished reading. His Bohemian student assistant, Ignaz Semmelweis, listened as the pathologist read aloud Virchow's published criticism.

"Isn't this the 'Virchow' who visited from Berlin to study the vast progress of Vienna?" Semmelweis said incredulously. "The young, short one?"

"I remember him," Rokitansky said wearily. He rubbed his eyes. "He asked many questions and I remember there being as many I could not answer as the ones I could. But," he wagged his finger at Semmelweis, "he is also the Virchow that published the paper recently on the triad of thrombosis." Then he wondered aloud, "How can he be so sure of his findings? How can he sound this confident? Surely the young man wouldn't have gone so far as to publish his findings if they were not based on fact?" His voice rose in anger. "Doesn't he realize with what experience I base my writings, that I have studied medicine and disease of the body for nearly twenty more years than him?"

"You must write a response immediately, sir," Semmelweis said vehemently.

Rokitansky looked at the assistant, thought for a moment and then said, "No, I first must challenge his findings here in my lab." He glanced at the microscope on the shelf. "I started using that thing three years ago but perhaps I haven't used it enough," he said, then abruptly changed moods. "My handbook is referenced by hundreds of doctors! I'm on the third volume."

"And the things with which Virchow takes issue are in Volume 1," Semmelweis said.

"I know, I know," Rokitansky said irritably. He walked over to the shelf and snatched Volume 1. "Hundreds of hours went into this," he shook the book at Semmelweis, "all of it researched, catalogued..."

"And it is a mainstay of pathology," Semmelweis defended his mentor. He snatched the volume from Rokitansky and opened it randomly. "Here," he stabbed his finger, "the first pathological account of spondylolisthesis..." he opened to another section, "here, classification of patent ductus arteriosis as a congenital lesion..." he slammed the thick book shut. "How could Virchow, an *anatomist*, possibly find fault with such a work?"

Within time, Rokitansky calmed down. After thoroughly researching Virchow's views, much to the great man's credit, he eventually acknowledged the shattering significance of Virchow's findings, and their value to medicine. Illnesses and diseases originated from a single locus, or location, within the body and when no answer could be found, 'sick blood' or foul smelling air

Leslie Dunn

was not an answer. Rokitansky recalled all available copies of the first volume of his Handbook and entirely rewrote it eliminating all references to "crases and stases." Volume 1 was republished in 1855 void of the theory of humeral pathology. It is said that he never again looked at the first edition of his textbook.

Virchow's published views cast a spidery network of cracks onto medicine's two thousand year old spectacles. Although this epoch event pitted student against teacher, doctor against doctor and many against Virchow, it heralded a beginning of a new dawn in medicine. A medical revolution. The humoural theory had many associated treatments, such as bloodletting and emetics to induce vomiting – all of which were mainstays of the physician's prescribed treatments and medicines, all eventually replaced with theoretical medicine based on clinical research. Within a few years, Rokitansky and Virchow enjoyed a warm professional relationship as colleagues in their shared profession of pathologic anatomy.

At Charité, Virchow calmly waited out the uproar knowing it would pass neither applauding nor defending himself. In a letter to his father, he wrote that he hoped in the future, "people will be more cautious." Before the end of his life, Virchow would see the end of the treatment of bloodletting, but it would take a little longer than his lifetime, however, for elimination and replacement of the humoural theory.

Rudolf Virchow

About this time, the use of ether as an anesthesia during surgery had begun by an American dentist in Boston, Massachusetts. Although its usage was accepted in England, Germany as well as France viewed ether as Yankee nonsense.

Geheimrath Jungken, a chief surgeon at Charité, opposed the use of anesthesia in a lengthy letter he drafted to the hospital's administration.

Virchow, however, convinced of ether's humanitarian usage, demonstrated its effects on animals. Utilizing persuasion and persistence he learned from experience of his father, Virchow won Jungken over. With Jungken's permission Virchow administered Charité's first use of anesthesia on a surgical patient in February of 1847. His assistant was not another medical person but a servant, Herr Camille; the surgery witnessed by a large audience of other surgeons and medical students. Unfortunately the patient was an alcoholic with a magnificent tolerance to numbing agents. Still conscious after thirty minutes of inhaling the ether vapors, the man's leg was quickly amputated by Jungken.

To the delight of the surgeon, the attending audience and Virchow, the patient who enjoyed the newer form of unfeeling assured the doctor that the operation was painless.

PLOTTING AGAINST VIRCHOW

"Medicine Reform..." Donner muttered to Geheimrath Medizinalrat Joseph Hermann Schmidt, "...written by Virchow, no less."

Donner's appointment with Schmidt, limited to ten minutes, cut short Donner's usual effusive greeting to a simple, "How are you, sir?" Donner took the chair offered to him then launched into his subject. His favorite subject. "It's been four months since the barricades, Geh. Schmidt. Is Virchow content to speak at the worker's meetings, keeping those stupid men in a constant state of agitation? No. As vice president of the general physician committee seducing colleagues to his cause? No. As an author of 'Archiv' -- forum for every trivial thought and belief of his and Leubuscher's? No! Every week we are subjected to this paper - this radical, left wing propaganda, 'Medicine Reform'. Listen to this, Councilor Schmidt..." He paused and took a deep breath, reading from the single paged weekly: "Virchow pities 'all those who hope to endure the storms of world history by timidly taking refuge in personal or professional circumstances.'" Donner's voice rose and fell, mocking the tone of a fervent country minister which was his mimicry of Virchow's tone. "He *warns* us against those '*who attempt to judge the strivings of others who dare to sail their ship...*' his ship, I presume, and *he* is the captain," Donner sneered, then continued reading, "'...*in the storm of world history from the paltry viewpoint of their clique and their person.*'"

"'Paltry viewpoint of their clique and their person?'" Schmidt said indignantly, coming erect in his overstuffed desk chair. He had not yet read this most current issue.

During his years at Charité, Rudolf benefited from the teachings of Müller but, for two years, also from the politically powerful influence of Geheimrath Medizinalrat Schmidt. Schmidt prodded Rudolf to travel to centers of pathologic anatomy in Prussia and Vienna and voted on Rudolf's behalf for extra salary. Ironically two years prior, in 1846, Schmidt first published Rudolf's original draft of medical reforms and even praised Rudolf's reform proposals in a memorandum.

Minister of Culture Eichhorn asked Schmidt for his opinions and those opinions became Eichhorn's final decisions. Schmidt, for whom Rudolf remained grateful, affected military protocol to such an extent that it ended Rudolf's commitment to the military and allowed him to become a civilian doctor as well as other decisions of varying sizes that aided Virchow's career. But Donner had lately seen a more guarded look in Schmidt's eyes when Rudolf was around, a new tone in Schmidt's voice when Rudolf was the topic of conversation as happened more and more often.

"To whom do you think he refers – 'their clique and their person'?" the Director prodded Donner.

"I think it's obvious, sir. He mocks those of us who represent the firmly grounded, the substantial of society..." he took hold of his lapels, "...the well bred. Of course he would like the world to change, or perhaps that of his family's tiny little corner."

A slight ominous lift of Schmidt's wooly white eyebrow softened Donner's tone. "Of course, none of us can discredit the man for his achievements," he mumbled soothingly, as though suddenly mindful of Schmidt's personal influence on Virchow's achievements.

Schmidt stroked his length of his beard, his eyes firmly on Donner. "I've read Virchow's weeklies." He opened the large bottom drawer and pulled a large folder marked, 'Virchow' and waved it at Donner. One by one, he called out the names of weekly Medical Reforms: "Status of the Medical System; Medical Legislation; Medical Edict; Medical Appointments..." tossing each one to his desk. "Listen to what Virchow has to say in nearly every issue: '*As important as it may be that older physicians adhere to the new policy of socialized medicine...*' Schmidt paused. "Where does he get these terms that he fabricates? '*Socialized medicine*' – that has no meaning to me," he said in disgust. '*...the greater importance lies in the hands of the future of medicine, medical students, with whom lie the critical responsibility which modern society has given them. Their untarnished viewpoints molded by the needs of the people...*' "Needs of the people? I can't go on," Schmidt said. He removed his reading glasses and rubbed eyes, then continued, "Virchow holds in contempt," he paused as he scanned one of the documents, "'*colleagues who remain naïve enough to believe they can stay aloof from major social changes* *underway*' and mocks anyone who does not believe medicine plays a vastly important role to social and political developments. It seems Virchow adheres to the belief," his voice lowered, his tone altered to that of a conspirator, "that one's health is directly related to how much one owns. Seems he takes 'materialism' one step further than medicine – huh? What should we do then? Take our belongings to the center of town for the poor? Will that improve their health? Nonsense!"

He returned the papers to the folder and picked up another set of pages. From his seat Donner recognized the Charité imprint on the letterhead. "Do you know what this is?" Schmidt asked.

"No, sir."

"This," he grabbed the thick sheaf of papers, "is a copy of Virchow's soon-to-be-published 'recommendations' after his trip to Upper Silesia." His face reddened and his voice was stern and loud.

Donner had heard whispered references to Virchow's recommendations.

Schmidt said, "The medical administration fully expected in clear medical language methodology of transmission of typhus, medical guidelines for the Prussian government to prevent further spread of the disease – perhaps the usual humanitarian response to the villager's loss of lives...that sort of thing. Nothing like what Virchow produced," and slapped the papers on the table.

Donner waited.

Picking the papers back up, Schmidt turned to the last three pages and he said, "Here are the learned Virchow's *objective* recommendations..." then with words that sounded like a hammer hitting a nail, he read, "'*Political reform of Germany and local self-government of each state*,' then Virchow goes into great detail," Schmidt wagged a couple preceding pages of the report at Donner to show the length of Virchow's text on the subject, then continued reading, "'*Education sponsored by the government instead of the church...*'"

"Demeaning the authority of the Catholic church? The heathen," Donner muttered.

Schmidt cleared his throat, looked at Donner over the top of his glasses and again wagged pages, "...and he goes into detail." He turned to the next page. "Economic reforms...detail" he wagged the papers, "agricultural reforms...details," He turned to the last page. "Road building...details," then taking a deep breath and letting it out with a heavy sigh, Schmidt said finally, "*Requirements that teachers and physicians speak the language of the local people...*'"

"...details," Donner said.

Again Schmidt tossed the lengthy report to his desk.

"I'm surprised, sir, that he didn't mention fashion reforms," Donner said.

Schmidt answered in one breath, "Virchow's heart is in the right place, Donner, and he certainly acquired mastery over a number of subjects during his education. However, medicine is his profession and the only subject with which he needed to concern himself in this report – *not* politics."

Intimidated, Donner answered softly, "I agree, sir."

Schmidt's tone changed slightly, "Please do not misunderstand me, doctor...I have as great a heart for the poor as anyone else, but as physician I am primarily concerned with my patients health, *not* their pocketbooks. The Upper Silesians are well known to be slovenly, lazy slugs whose main goal for living is to outnumber their bottles consumed by quantities of fornication." He removed the white linen handkerchief from his pocket and dabbed his forehead. "I apologize for speaking so bluntly, Donner."

"That is quite all right, sir."

"Virchow's main point through his report is this for these people: '*Free and unlimited democracy'*."

For a moment, the younger doctor felt keen sympathy for the older one. Schmidt, one of Virchow's steadfast supporters, appeared distressed by the need to harness Virchow to protect Charité.

"May I speak my mind, sir?"

"You may."

"One cannot help but admire a man who has come so far from his roots. As much as he attempts to appear in high fashion, what exists inside the fine clothes is the son of a farmer. A very intelligent son, I'll give him that," he added quickly. Donner again saw Schmidt begin to react but this time Schmidt did not interrupt. "Perhaps the Upper Silesians reminded him of his village and that accounts for his strong reaction." He jutted his chin toward Virchow's report. "Had he been reared in a family similar to many of us here at Charité he might not have felt a kinship with that sorry lot, nor attacked the Catholic Church whose stewardship has benefited so many."

Schmidt said thoughtfully, "We need a counteragent to Virchow's influence among the doctors of your age group, Donner. Someone persuasive and a quick thinker like Virchow...would you know of anyone?"

"I have already taken more than ten minutes of your time, sir. Can I think about it and get back to you tomorrow?"

"Of course. Think about it as long as you need." Schmidt suddenly became animated again liked a horse kicked in its side. "Medicine is medicine is medicine," Schmidt slapped the back of one hand against the palm of the other, his voice boomed. "A treatment plan of *full and unlimited democracy*.' Utter nonsense! Politics has nothing to do with healing, and physicians do not need to concern themselves with democracy or 'Socialized Medicine'! The man has too much time on his hands, sits around, and thinks of such nonsense. Perhaps I should find him extra duties at this institution to which he owes his education. And his livelihood," he said ominously.

"It is my opinion," Donner said, "that Virchow too freely grants himself the new privilege of freedom of the press. Just a few months ago, a censor would have shut down their publication or recommended that Virchow, Reinhardt and Leubuscher's hospital privileges be revoked. Men have been exiled from Germany for less."

Schmidt said. "We'll talk tomorrow."

"Yes, sir," Donner replied then got to his feet and left.

Rudolf Virchow

CHRISTMAS AT HOME, 1848

Schivelbein

"Come on, Rudolf, buy your old mother a new pair of shoes."

"Mother, you are a worse child than I ever was," he teased. "You have asked for something at every booth except the tool maker."

Every Christmas, the Virchow's gathered with the other Schievelbeiner's, as did every village throughout Germany, at the Christmas market, Christkindlmarkt. In Schivelbein, over one hundred twenty booths represented craftsmen with wares of every description – from tablecloths to shoes to handmade musical clocks. Fir branches lit by candles decorated the booths.

Great festivity marked the opening of the market in late November and it stayed open continuously until Christmas Eve. In the center of each Christkindlmarkt, visitors pause to honor a crib surrounded by wooden nativity figures.

"Ummm, mother, smell the Stollen (fruit bread)," Rudolf grinned, snowflakes covering his top hat, his belly rumbling. He stomped his pointy black patent-leather boots. "Are you warm enough?"

"Don't worry about me. I have enough insulation," Johanna laughed. She perpetually dressed in black with hand-stitched collars surrounding her full neck. She kept her long dark hair flattened straight back, rolled into a bun. Her bonnet lined with ruffles and tied with ribbons gave her a merry look in contrast to her black dress.

Rudolf's visits highlighted her life; this one, in particular, brought her sublime joy. Neither her husband, nor Rudolf's letters, convinced her of Rudolf's safety in the months since the revolution. She would be unable to bear living should anything happen to her son. "We need to get you some of that Stollen and build you more insulation. You've lost too much baby fat. Give me a a pfennig," she said.

"I can hand it to the baker directly, dear mother," he teased. He turned to the baker, "Two Stollen, please?" and handed him two pfennig.

"Where is mine?" his father said, walking up to them.

"What is in the sack, Carl?" Johanna wheedled.

"Wife, you know I cannot tell you that," Carl said, too sternly for Rudolf's liking but he stayed out of their relationship. "Christmas Eve is in two days. Just like always, you can wait."

Rudolf pulled another pfennig from his pocket and got his father a fruit bread so warm and fresh steam arose from it. "Thank you," Carl said. "Aaahhhh," he sighed after biting into it. The three of them quickly finished the long narrow cakes sprinkled with sugar. "Are you two ready to go home?"

"Yes, father. Mother has shopped me numb," Rudolf said. Johanna smiled broadly.

"Let's go then," Carl said gruffly. He shared a deep attachment to his son, but his expressed itself more in a smothering manner. He found it harder to express his feelings than Johanna and for that he was a little jealous. Neither of them had enough time with Rudolf.

Rudolf's Christmas visit provided for him, especially this year, a sense of stability and respite from the chaos in Berlin.

Although his parents scrapped on a regular basis, had even discussed divorce, they stayed together. At no point in his meteoric career and intense political involvements did he ever put them behind him or distance himself from them. They were his anchor.

They walked toward his parent's carriage. Rudolf pulled the stepping stool from the carriage and placed it on the ground. He held out one gloved hand toward his mother. Grasping it, she gathered her skirt with the other. Her short legs had quite a stretch to board the carriage, even with a stepping stool; the buggy rocked and squeaked under her weight as she sat down, her back to the driver seat. She pulled a woolen blanket from a basket under the seat and curled up in it. Carl climbed to the driver's seat, settled his tailcoat and wrapped a woolen blanket around himself. After Rudolf boarded and wrapped in a blanket, Carl picked up the reins and snapped the horses to action. Traffic had muddied the path and even in the dark the dark, wet dirt contrasted keenly with the sparkly white, deep snow banks.

"Well, Rudolf..." his father said talking over his shoulder and Rudolf knew from the tone what was coming, again. "Have you met anyone... interesting?" The carriage bounced along its course.

"A couple of fellows from Konisberg, Dr. Goldstucker and..."

His father cut him off, "You know what I mean – not doctors. A girl. Any female friends?"

Johanna watched her son's face.

Rudolf thought of Rose, Mayer's daughter, then dismissed the thought.

His mother saw the fleeting changes in his expression. "If you had a wife, Rudolf," his mother said, "you would be content to stay at home, instead of attending all those meetings. She would keep you out of trouble."

"That may be true, mother," Rudolf conceded, "but my life is too..." he hesitated, not wanting to say the word that would confirm their fears, and decided on, "...hectic to accommodate a wife."

Before he left for vacation, Reinhardt told him disheartening gossip he'd heard about Rudolf. A few opponents had gained in strength against the majority – their goal: revocation of Virchow's privileges at Charité. Rudolf resolved to put it aside until after his holiday and to not frighten his parents with gossip.

"You can afford a wife now, couldn't you?" Carl asked. "I could understand when you were a medical student and earning less than a railroad worker. If you can afford Dehnel to watch over us because of enemies you may have and send us money from each paycheck, we know you can afford a wife and children."

"Besides," Johanna added, "others in your organizations would understand if you withdrew your support because of family needs."

Rudolf's face hurt from the cold air and he wrapped a scarf around his nose and cheeks. "It's obvious that the two of you have discussed this and think it time for me to have a wife for a variety of reasons, especially, it sounds as a convenient way to remove myself from politics."

"Huh?" his father said. "I can't hear you up here."

Rudolf dropped the muffler for a moment and repeated himself, then replaced the muffler.

"We only want what's best for you," Johanna said. Rudolf

Rudolf believed her with his whole heart. "I doubt there is a woman who would have me, Mother."

She gasped and put her hand to her heart. "Any woman would be lucky to have you, Rudolf," she said, her eyes wide.

He moved from his seat facing her to sit by her side. She raised the blanket and he wrapped it around himself, feeling its warmth. He leaned back for a moment and relaxed. He knew exchanging seats made it more difficult for his father to hear but it was too cold to stay facing the wind.

"Mother, most women are bored with politics, and sociopolitics as well as medicine consume my life. There are very, very few women involved in the committees and organizations. I don't even have the opportunity to meet women." He longed to tell her the truth – that within a couple months, he may no longer be employed at Charité, that on a regular basis he and the other 48'ers were threatened, ridiculed and scorned. He might soon be impoverished. Should things settle down, by all means, he wanted to have a wife to share his life. He dreamed of the children, too, that they would share.

"Father," Rudolf called out. "Would you like for me to take the reins?"

"No, we're near home. You can drive next time."

As they entered the lane in front of their home, Rudolf turned around to watch the approach. The home of his birth appeared so rustic compared to the grandeur of the buildings of Berlin. Nine windows fronted the two storied brick building with its high peaked roof. The door slightly off center to the right allowed for only the two windows to the left of it to be encased in shutters; the right two were bare, to his mother's embarrassment as shutters equaled a degree of status. The bottom floor windows were six paned, the second floor, four panes and the top floor attic windows, three. His mother's handmade lace white curtains veiled the windows of the first and second floors, the only sense of beauty to the face of the building. His father lined the front of the home with rocks to keep animals from going underneath. No plants decorated the front of the building except a tree to the right of the structure. As plain and unappealing as it appeared to others, though, at the moment there was no place he'd rather be.

Early on the morning of Christmas Eve Johanna rose early and began cleaning the home, stopping only to prepare breakfast and lunch. The Christmas tree lay on the table and placed upright during the evening, adorned with candles and homemade decorations. While the home filled with scents of cleaning soaps and baking goodies, his mother bustled around humming happy tunes. Rudolf and his father spent the day in conversation -- arguing politics, Rudolf's medical anecdotes and gossip of the neighbors. Tomorrow they, like all the other villagers, would spend part of the day visiting others and receiving guests. Then, finally, Christmas Eve arrived.

Candles on the tree were lit and together they sang, "O, Tannebaum" and "Stille Nacht" (Silent Night). Carl read aloud, as always, the story of the birth of Christ (Christkind), followed by exchanging of gifts. His father was genuinely pleased with the snuff box Rudolf gave him, and his mother with the porcelain vase made in Berlin. They gave him slippers, a new pipe and a knitted washcloth. The surprise Carl bought Johanna at the Christkindlmarkt, he'd even wrapped it in brown paper and string, was a matching plate and bowl hand painted with a forest scene in her favorite shade of blue. The joy on his mother's face as she ran her fingers over and over the hand-painted pottery and the pleasure in his father's face at his wife's contentment soothed Rudolf's soul and for a moment all was right with the world.

Leslie Dunn

POLITICAL ACTIONS ENDANGER VIRCHOW'S CAREER

Berlin

Friday, April 6, 1849

My Dear Father,

I believe you may have gathered from a news item in the *Kreuzzeitung (newspaper)* that your warnings came too late. I am sorry that you had to get this information first from this newspaper that repeatedly vents its spleen on me. I had continued to delay writing to you, although I have known the actual state of affairs for eight days, because negotiations were still going on and I was not able to foresee their outcome. Now things are gradually settling down and, thus, I can present the case with greater composure.

You must have learnt from the newspapers that a month ago the Ministry of War dismissed two Charité surgeons because they acted in favor of the opposition party during the elections. At that time, I had been asked by the Ministry of Culture how I, holding the position that I do, could permit myself the liberty of distributing provocative pamphlets. My answer was that my *official position has nothing to do with my political activity, and that I had not misused the one in order to carry out the other.*

Exactly a week ago, March 31, 1849, I was informed by the administration of Charité that the Minister of Spiritual and Medical Affairs, etc. had dismissed me, that my official duties would be terminated on the 15th of this month, my housing on May 1. The immediate occasion for my dismissal were the elections, the next my ceaseless and organized opposition to the government. In reply to this, I wrote a letter to the minister pointing out the inadmissibility of his action. Several influential people took the matter in hand likewise, and while I saw to it that not too much noise was made in the newspapers, there arose among the physicians, students and others a great agitation, which gradually assumed such proportions that it has finally dawned on the gentlemen in the Ministry that they have to be more reasonable. Today steps were first taken by me; tomorrow I shall probably have a "confidential" talk with one of the gentlemen and, thus, gradually reach an agreement. Of course, it is difficult to make out how far they will go now in compromise. It is easily possible that I will lose board and lodging and be allowed only to retain the post itself. This, I shall have to put up with. As a precaution, I have, therefore, already rented a dwelling diagonally opposite Charité, and if the occasion arises I will be moving into it on May 1. For the moment, I have to reckon with much loss, but then it is for the moment, mind you. Let there be a change in the governmental system and you will find that the tide has turned. You still need not worry about me. My courses are going so well that they completely cover this loss;

140

and even if everything were taken from me I would still be able to survive.

In all this, the thought of your well-being worried me most; but there was still nothing to be done, and in the end there remains the prospect of an outside position. In Bavaria, where I am considering a post, a definitely reactionary ministry is in control; it wanted to make Phillipps, dismissed last year from Charité because of his ultra-Catholic views, professor at Würzburg and, therefore, came in conflict with the University. This conflict exists in my case in an inverted fashion. Phillipps high Catholic views offend the Bavarian ministry and University. So far, my views have been met warmly there.

The medical faculty at Würzburg has unanimously requested the Bavarian Ministry to offer me the professorship of pathologic anatomy. This will bring 1200 fl as salary and about 800 fl as honorarium. The Ministry has not yet made any decision, probably because the situation in Bavaria is as chaotic as here. Thus, to some extent my fate will depend on the formation of a new ministry in Munich. If it is liberal, there can scarcely be any doubt as to my appointment. And if so, I can then again state my conditions here.

In any case, be comforted and don't let this spoil for you the Easter holidays, which promises to be very fine. Write me soon that you have not lost your peace of mind on this account, and that Mother too, whom I hope is again quite well, has calmed down. If she is all right, she must now take some thought for me. In the event that I have to give up my quarters and move out, I will have to acquire bed linen, towels, etc. Since I have a sofa bed,

I need only sheets and blanket-covers as well as pillowcases. In a few days, I believe the affair will be decided and more detailed information can follow; in any case, I need nothing before May 1.

The political situation in general has again improved from the moment. The reports from Italy and Hungary today sound very favorable; war has broken out in Schleswig. The King and his dynasties seem bent upon ruining themselves. They are losing all moral prestige; power and organization alone will sustain them for a while. Indeed the King has said more than once: Against democrats only soldiers can help!

I will write to Mother as soon as I have definite information, that is to say, in a few days. Many regards to our good friends, my heartiest good wishes to you.

Your Rudolf

"Minister von Ladenberg has refused my request for a chance to defend myself," Rudolf said to Leubuscher, co-author of Medical Reform whose privileges also had been revoked.

"Ahhh, but what a tumult when word got out about the Ladenberg's decision to revoke your privileges at Charité, Virchow. There is not much need for you to defend yourself – your colleagues and students did it for you. The Minister stopped all appointments so he could get some of his work done and still they waited for him to come out of his office. All the work at Charité was affected, short of patient care. Unfortunately for me, my popularity is not as great as yours at Charité and I am being shown the way out the door. I believed we were in this as a team..."

They sat together on Rudolf's burgundy brocade sofa bed with rolled wooden arms and pillowed low back. Rudolf lowered the velvet curtains, the room darkened as the evening grew late.

Three pictures, one each of his parents and the middle one of the three of them, were centered less than a foot above the couch. Above the family pictures hung a large gold framed picnic scene done in the current romantic style. The twelve foot high ceiling was framed with beige crown molding and a chandelier suspended by six chains hooked to a single long rod looked like an upside down elegant umbrella in the middle of the room. In front of the sofa, on a round table covered with burgundy cloth edged in lace and tassels, sat two glasses of beer and a pitcher.

"We are in this together, no doubt, Leubuscher. I am pushing your name to the forefront with mine with every letter I write and with everyone to whom I speak."

"Doesn't seem to be helping, Virchow. My letter requesting a chance to defend myself was returned to me and the Minister had himself written the word, 'NO' across the top of it."

Rudolf nodded with understanding and sympathy. They sat in brooding silence, sipping beer. "The Archiv has not been at all affected by all of this," Rudolf said. "That is the only good news at this point. Do you have any idea where you will go, what you will do?"

"I plan to stay in Berlin, no matter what the outcome. There is nothing for me in my hometown of Breslau and no place else I want to be."

Rudolf smiled at his friend's tenacity and passion for the city Virchow, too, had come to love.

Rudolf Virchow

"What about you, Virchow? Are you considering Giessen University's offer of a professorship? Would you be willing to move to Frankfurt and be a university doctor?"

"Würzburg's offer seems more likely. It is an inexpensive city in which to live and the hospital there is one of the largest in Germany. Giessen's offer, I'm afraid, might contain contingencies that I refrain from political activity. A year ago, they removed Professor Carl Vogt who is now a leader of the left wing in Frankfurt."

"Wouldn't Würzburg also expect you to refrain yourself from politics? Would they not expect you to disengage yourself from it altogether?"

"A lot depends on the ministry. Würzburg first sent queries about me to Charité in January and since my current activities are the same as they were three months ago and three months prior to that, I'm sure they are well informed about me yet they still pursue me. That is encouraging."

"What does your uncle Major Virchow say to all of this?"

"Except for initially criticizing my speaking ability, uncharacteristically, nothing. I think his strong opinions about the lawyer, Waldeck, caused him to withdraw support from our district. Waldeck continues to gain in popularity; still Uncle sees him as "riffraff." Uncle Hesse, my mother's brother, though, frequently sends me warm greetings and invitations to his home. I'm going there this weekend just to get away for a little while. It's always such a pleasure to visit my uncle and aunt and my cousins."

"Rudolf, I just had a troubling thought. What if you lose your place at Charité and suddenly Würzburg withdraws their interest?"

Leubuscher didn't know that two weeks ago, deciding to take him into his confidence Rudolf shared that same concern with his father. "Several months may pass that find me without a position, but even in this jam of trouble there would be a way out. Such are the discomforts of life. Archiv is successful and that is a source of income. The number of students attending my classes increases with each term, another source of income, and private practice might be another. At least we don't have wives to support."

"Unfortunately," Leubuscher said and then added, "no, it's better this way. Despite all the current problems, Anna clings to Reinhardt. She, though, is the female exception. Are you still planning to attend meetings?"

Rudolf nodded emphatically. "Meetings at Mayer's home continue. The Mayer's have become nearly as dear to me as my family. Especially Rose. Röschen."

Leubuscher's eyebrows lifted in surprise. "She is 'Röschen' then? Virchow, she is just a girl."

"She is 18. She's petite and appears younger than her age."

"She's also very quiet. I suspect *too* quiet for you," Leubuscher said teasingly.

"For two years now, Rose has been learning." Rudolf chest expanded against his vest. "From me."

"You sound proud."

"I am. She doesn't talk much, but when she speaks it is with intelligence and strong, sound beliefs. After all, she is a Mayer."

145

He smiled, the smile reaching his tired eyes. "I realized only recently how fond I am of her and it seems she has been fond of me for some time. I've been too preoccupied to notice."

"Then the Archiv is not the only good piece of news through this mess."

Smiling, Leubuscher raised his glass and Rudolf clanged it with his own.

"Have you considered marriage?"

"Yes, but that is an impossible thought at this time. My future is so uncertain."

"Would she be willing to relocate to Würzburg?"

"My friend, I have not and will not make my intentions known to her and her family until I know what is going to happen next. I'd prefer to stay here at Charité. I know it will trouble you to hear this, but the Minister is willing to compromise on my behalf to quiet the tumult of those in my support. Even now, the students and other doctors plan a more vigorous protest."

"I wish you no ill will, Virchow. I only wish it were on my account, too."

Rudolf saw the pain in his friend's eyes and felt a profound sadness.

"Do you know what type of compromise?" Leubuscher said.

"I'm willing to concede my residence here at Charité...," he waved his arm indicating the room, "...giving up my free room and board. That is as far as I am willing to go to spare the Minister a charge of weakness. In anticipation of his decision I have rented a room nearby. If you remember when I was elected Chairman of the Volkspartei (People's Party), Mr. Lehnert, Director for Medical

Affairs, was excluded from the elections and, therefore, he did not vote. When I wrote to the Minister I told him that it was my influence that swayed the decision that Mr. Lehnert be excluded and from this arose the charge of 'misuse of my official position.' That was only because the Charité had been, quite improperly, turned into an election department. If this hadn't been the case, those same activities of mine that are now taken as official could only have been regarded as private. And if I had not been living at Charité, I would not have come into conflict. No fault was found with me to support my suspension so I could not justifiably be removed from my scientific position. I asked him to limit my removal to the lodgings."

Berlin

Friday, April 13, 1849

Dear Father,

My request to the Minister was considered. Today I was called to the Director for Medical Affairs, Privy Councilor Lehnert, who told me that I would continue as a prosector, in other words, an anatomist, but lose board and lodging, provided I state that in the future I will refrain from exercising political influence on the Charité and its officials. I accepted this and will, therefore, continue to perform my duties undisturbed, at least for the moment.

On May first, I leave the Charité and move into the house diagonally opposite, Charitéstrasse, No 1. I must now again ask Mother to send me bed linen and towels; should she not be able to do so, let me know without delay, in order that I can equip myself here.

As for the Minister, he has asked Lehnert to pass on the complaint that I had not gone to him personally, and to advise me that I had better do so after the event. I shall probably meet this demand, too, so that I can tell him what an unjust and ignoble act he has performed. He now seems to be capable of anything, for today Lehnert was willing enough to grant me 150 thaler for experiments on animals. But I must be very cautious at this point, so as not to be suspected of weakness, for I have already made concessions enough. Moreover, I do not know how long such a Ministry will be able to sustain itself. Everybody it has to bear defeats in the House, and yet it continues!

I shall write soon again.

Your Rudolf

WÜRZBURG WELCOMES VIRCHOW, WITH CONDITIONS

Seated together for dinner, the Mayer's enjoyed their finest time of the day. Their two eldest daughters were married and one of their sons studying medicine at the city of Halle leaving four children surrounding them at the dinner table. Frau Mayer again noted with sadness, though, the changes in her husband's demeanor since the beginning of the repercussions after last March, especially after July's storming of the Armory. Nothing lessened his commitment or altered his opinions – his enthusiasm, though, that tireless zeal that attracted others waned month after passing month.

And now the news about Rudolf seemed to have affected Röschen more than it did her father -- not a surprise to her mother. Frau Mayer's amusement these days was founded only in that it had taken Virchow this long to notice her beautiful, tiny daughter and the love Rose had confided in her mother that she felt for him.

At first Rose stood quietly through all the months of biweekly meeting then as she began to speak more often, Frau Mayer noted Virchow's opinions becoming her daughter's as though Rose was

Virchow's student. Sometimes it was harder to determine what Rose and Rudolf enjoyed more – when they united with an opinion against the rest of the room or the few times they debated against one another. Both she and Rose understood, even admired, Virchow's reluctance to speak for her hand, mother and daughter certain that his love grew more and more evident in his face when he looked at Rose.

Glancing at his daughter over bowls laden with potatoes and asparagus, and the roast veal on a platter, Dr. Mayer said, "Lisette, have you washed your hands?"

"Nein, Papa."

"You may be excused."

"But what difference...."

"You may return after your hands are clean," he said firmly.

Her chair squeaked against the wooden floor. She muttered, "I'm not a doctor," as she popped from her seat and raced out of the room.

"With no added sounds, and a soft return to your chair -- thank you Fräulein," he added.

Barbara and Max giggled.

His father cleared his throat. "And, you, Max? Have you washed your hands? And Barbara?"

They held up their hands up, palms facing their father. "Ja," they said in unison.

"I hoped this issue had been settled with this family. Its demon enough that constant reminders must be drilled into other physician's at the hospital," Dr. Mayer said loud enough for his daughter to hear in the kitchen. "The next time, there may be no dinner for the offending party."

Silently the petulant Lisette returned to the table and slipped into her seat.

"Let me see," the doctor said.

"Papa," Lisette protested, hiding her hands under the table.

"To your room, now!" he boomed.

Tiring of the commotion, Max said, "Mmmm, mama, roast veal and asparagus. My favorites, it smells soooo wonderful."

His mother laughed at her teenage son. "what meal isn't your favorite?"

The family laughed softly as Lisette stormed to her room, her mother troubled by another empty seat at the table yet supporting her husband's decision.

"Rose, you haven't been eating well lately," her mother said.

"There is a meeting here tomorrow night," her father said hoping to encourage her appetite. He noticed that on meetings days Rose dressed prettier, seemed more animated and lately voiced more of her opinions. He decided that his quiet daughter's political interests finally sparked to life.

"I suppose the usual crowd will be here?" she asked casually.

"Ja," said her mother smiling at her. "Including Rudolf."

Rose smiled at her mother.

"Ah, yes, Virchow..." Dr. Mayer stated thoughtfully, his mouth pursed.

Frau Mayer heard concern in her husband's voice. "What about him?" she said looking at her husband.

"There is word that the Bavarian Ministry has asked the Senate of the University of Würzburg to begin negotiations with him on a position there."

Rose's mouth fell slightly open and she sat still, her eyes on her father.

Frau Mayer looked at her daughter whose face grew pale, then back at her husband. "The University of Würzburg? So far away! What does he say?"

"I laughed at what he told me. The first thing he did was request a new hearing with the Minister of Culture at Charité for a counterproposal, with specific requests of Charité." He shook his head, amused. "I wish I could say he was my son. Suspended from Charité, then reinstated. Offered a position at a rival facility and uses it as a negotiating tool at Charité."

"What did he ask of Charité?" Frau Mayer asked.

"Three things that I remember: an appointment to the prosectorship without conditions, an assistant professorship, and a raise to 800 thaler a year."

Each Mayer had been drawn vicariously into Virchow's drama of this past year. They now paused and gauged each other's reactions, unsure of just how to react.

"Wasn't it just a month ago that he was fired?" Max said.

"Without conditions?" Barbara repeated.

"Ja..." Frau Mayer answered Max, "...and then reinstated," she reminded him.

"Of course without conditions!" Rose fired indignantly at her sister. "How else can he continue to improve things? Unless they agree to his appointment without conditions, he will be silenced.

He must be able to speak his mind and publish without censors chopping at his words."

Surprised and chastened by her sister's vehemence, Barbara slouched in her chair.

"And what was the Minister's reaction?" asked Frau Mayer, her voice a mixture of interest and deep concern.

"Virchow says it was his impression that the man was ashamed. I believe his exact words were 'The Minister vacillated between shame and fear,'" answered her husband.

"'Shame and fear?" Rose echoed. "I don't understand."

Her father explained. "Shame that the Bavarian government was more liberal than ours, and fear that should the Minister favor Virchow, the Minister would be attacked by his own party." He saw the puzzled faces around the table. "In other words, on one hand it shamed the Minister that Bavaria has become more progressive than our government and he fears that any show of support for Virchow, whom he truly cares for and admires, will create problems for him, the Minister."

"Poor Rudolf," Barbara said softly. Sympathy for one of their heroes coursed around the table.

Rose stared at her plate and swallowed hard.

That evening, Rudolf, Reinhardt, Anna and Leubuscher walked slowly through solemn Berlin streets to Mayer's house for their regular Thursday night meeting. The Army's infiltrating presence in Berlin mollified the town. Rudolf and Leubuscher lead, Reinhardt and Anna behind them. Anna's gloved hand rested on Reinhardt's bent arm; the four of them talked softly.

Rudolf Virchow

Reinhardt so often saw Anna in her nurse's uniform that when he saw her in normal clothes, he couldn't stop from staring. At first, the attention caused her discomfort but gradually she accepted it as a compliment and now she enjoyed it. Her bonnet cupped from below one side of her chin, over the forehead down to the other side of her chin, tied with thick pink ribbon under her chin, its edges making her profile barely visible. Ringlets of hair framed her face under the bonnet, the rest of her long blond hair gathered at the crown braided and pinned down. All three men wore evening clothes of single-breasted black tailcoats. Silk scarves wrapped around the high collars of their crisp white shirts. Each wore black silk pumps with pointed toes and carried walking sticks in their gloved hands.

"We are blessed this evening to have a wind carrying the cesspool smells away from us for a change," Reinhardt stated to the group, and they mumbled in agreement. Berlin had no proper sewerage disposal. The number of cesspools and nauseating odor increased in direct proportion with the growth of the population.

"Reinhardt," Leubuscher said over his shoulder, "your diagnosis was accurate about Frau Boettcher, may she rest in peace. Uncontrolled hemorrhage of a ruptured artery that fed a uterine tumor." Leubuscher was a pathological anatomist like Rudolf, Reinhardt in obstetrics. "What do you think is the cause of the higher morbidity rate of your obstetrical patients in the past couple of months?"

Reinhardt answered, "I don't think there is a higher morbidity rate but rather a higher pregnancy rate. Since December, early January, I have noted an increase in the number of pregnancies and you two unfortunately see the tragic results of complications related to those pregnancies."

"The revolution was in March," Rudolf said, then counting on each finger, "April, May, June, July....December -- the ninth month post Revolution. I have read that in the past, as is currently happening throughout Europe, populations experience a rapid increase after a time of war."

They walked quietly, each deep in thought until the familiar site of the ivy-covered trellis appeared.

"After you, madam," the men parted allowing Anna to pass through first. Her gown softly brushed the cobblestones and a leaf attached itself to her hem. Reinhardt quickly bent down and pulled it free.

"She's got you wrapped up," Rudolf whispered teasing Reinhardt as Dr. Mayer opened the door.

"You're just jealous," Reinhardt whispered teasing back. "You'd like to wrap up a little Rose..."

Rudolf pierced him with a look. "Don't you dare say a word, Reinhardt."

"I won't, I won't. Now calm down," he said softly.

"What?" Dr. Mayer said. "Calm down? What are you two debating? Sounds like my kind of discussion," he laughed. "Come in, come in, the others got here just a few minutes ago. We can hardly wait to hear about the three of you...excuse me, Anna, we want to hear about you, too, but you don't get in high trouble like these three. Rose, move aside and let them come in – Max, MOVE!" He sounded exasperated.

As usual, the crowded home felt cozy and busy, but not under tension. Until they began to talk.

Reissner and Wentzler filled the others in on talk of the streets, a blend of gossip and fact, differentiating between the two for those in the room.

Over the past few months, Reissner's strength of character and sense of responsibility won over each man in the room. Waldeck, too, matured in his role as Virchow predicted as Vice President of the Prussian National Assembly. Waldeck learned to not let circumstances form his character but rather his character formed his party. His politics remained unswerved but his presentation greatly calmed down, and, therefore, a great asset to the cause.

As experience showed them, position alone did not spare Rudolf's friend and co-author of the Archiv, Leubuscher, and the group could only guess what consequences attorney Waldeck faced. Rudolf's popularity protected him. The group's love for one another united them into a brotherhood, but like their soldier counterparts each knew that should it happen, danger must be faced alone.

"And what of you three?" Mayer said as moderator after Reissner and Wentzler had spoken. "Any news, doctors?"

From her chair, Rose stiffened slightly.

"The schism at Charité is ever deepening," Reinhardt answered his greatest colleague and teacher. "No doubt, you have felt it too, Prof. Mayer."

"I have. But most of it seems centered around Rudolf. Other matters..." he eyed Leubuscher as he searched for the words, "...are unfortunately settled."

All in the room noted Mayer's tone. Unspoken yet keen sympathy swept through the room toward Leubuscher.

Mayer continued, "And just when we think things are calmed down, Dr. Virchow again stirs the pot."

Most of the room laughed. Leubuscher's eyes stayed downcast and Rose watched Rudolf's face as the proletariats looked with curiosity at Rudolf.

"What have you done now, Virchow?" Wentzler quizzed.

"I've received an opportunity in Würzburg that I am considering," he said pulling a letter from his coat pocket, he fixed his eyes on Rose, "because of this."

"'Dear Dr. Virchow,'" he read aloud, "'I, the Minister of Culture at Charité, acknowledge the just appreciation of your scientific accomplishments as well as that of your teaching, and regret all the more my inability to offer you any advantages which could lead you to decline such an honorable call as that as heeded by Würzburg.' Inhaling deeply he refolded the letter and crammed it back in his pocket. His shoulders sagged.

He looked again at Rose, noticing the glimmer of pooling tears in her eyes yet distracted by the softness of her neck and shoulders above her pale yellow dress and her eyelashes casting shadows on her cheeks. He looked away to the others in the room. "The Minister goes on to explain that neither the University treasury nor Charité has money, that the number of assistant professors at the University has exceeded the normal allotment." Rudolf paused

157

briefly, "and that he is not in a position to make me definite and binding promises. In other words, he offers nothing in response to my request for negotiations."

Reissner said, "In other words – take it, or leave."

Rudolf's shoulder's sagged again. He looked at Reissner. The man could always be counted on for making things clear. He nodded. "Yes, Reissner. That is what I'm being told."

Rose clutched her handkerchief to her eyes and with a gasp ran from the room, her mother trailing behind. Rudolf started to rise from his seat, then sat back down. For the first time, he felt his emotions responding to the disappointing attempt at negotiations. If you let go, he told himself, you won't be able to stop. Deep breath. Control yourself.

Rudolf said, "I immediately wrote to Würzburg that I am definitely ready to enter into negotiations with them."

Only Reinhardt and Leubuscher knew the answer to the next question – "When would you be leaving then?" said Mayer looking as though he suddenly felt a hole in his life.

"October."

Berlin

Tuesday, May 29, 1849

Dear Father,

At last the official notification from the Senate of Würzburg University has arrived. It states that my "excellent achievements in the field of pathologic histology" have attracted attention, that for this reason a request for my appointment at the University was sent to the Ministry of Culture, and that permission has been granted. Therefore, I am now being asked to give a definite answer as to whether I wish to take over the public, regular University professorship of pathologic anatomy along with the direction of hospital post-mortem examinations, in which case an annual salary of 1200 fl is offered, with an obligation to deliver a course of lectures on pathologic histology once a year. This course of lectures up to now carried an honorarium of 10 fl.; it was up to me whether I desired to tap further sources of honoraria by giving private courses.

I replied to this letter at once, without ado, stating that I was prepared to start at Würzburg in the next winter semester. Now only the appointment by the King of Bavaria is necessary, and I believe that under the circumstances it is sure to follow.

For my part I have done everything to keep the affair in order; I am as cautious as possible. I would certainly not be so frivolous as to put my future and your own at stake. In the present circumstances, it is useless, or at least almost so, to involve oneself with general causes other than where it seems reasonable, given the disadvantages for the individual arising thereby. Where it is useful, in medical reform, I continue my opposition without concern, as you perhaps know from that newspaper that again vents its spleen on me, the Kreuzzeitung. The statement recently cited in it is, by the way, a total distortion.

How the general course of politics will take form may perhaps become clearer in a few days' time for the French chamber opened yesterday. Once again there is talk of the constitution of the Reich and of election legislation in the Staatsanzeiger, which comes out tonight.

159

We hear nothing about our political prisoners. All that has been spread abroad so far about lawyer Waldeck consists of lies or guesses. In any case, there is as yet no serious aggravation and it will perhaps be necessary to withdraw the charges. Should anyone be called to appear before a jury or a court martial, God help him! The structure of both is such that an acquittal is hardly to be expected. These are our constitutional achievements.

I hope that my letter with the daguerreotype portrait and the other contents has arrived. I am always very desirous of reports from you; now I wish in particular to hear of the arrival of this mailing.

Your much loving son,

Rudolf

Months passed with no word from Würzburg in response to Virchow's agreement to terms of employment. As was his nature, Rudolf calmly rode them out. He taught classes during the summer and, just in case, he scheduled classes for the fall. He accepted the finality of the publication, Medical Reform, last date of publication, June 29, 1849. Not one to go down quietly, Virchow wrote the following in its last issue:

"The Medical Reform is closing down solely on account of the political situation in our nation and the ensuing impossibility of a reasonable reorganization of public health, of medical education and of medical conditions in general. The medical reform we had in mind was a reform of science and society. We placed too great faith in the power of reason as against brute force, in the power of culture as against that of the cannon."

It was a cool August day, three months since Rudolf sent his letter to Würzburg. As he walked through the exiting corridor in Charité, he noticed the man leaning sideways against the wall in the hallway, but family members of patients frequently did that. They, too, sprung to his side when Rudolf walked by, as this man had done, halting Rudolf from exiting Charité. Nothing in the reporter's attire triggered Rudolf's guard.

"Dr. Virchow, can I get a statement for the press?" the reporter asked with professional coolness.

"What newspaper are you with?" Rudolf said, annoyed.

"Edward Gunter, of the Spenersche Zeitung. I need just a minute of your time, sir." Without hesitation, Edward proceeded, "We would like to be the first to report your explanation about Würzburg." He watched with keen attention for Rudolf's reaction.

"Explanation? About what?" Rudolf asked. The hairs on the back of his neck rose. Had something happened to the Bavarian politics in the last couple of months - an uprising affecting his his new post? Had someone influential swayed them against him? Is that why he had not received any word?

Virchow's power and role in Berlin, as well as the Spenersche's steadfast support of Virchow's political activities, controlled the reporter's glee at being the first to report Virchow's explanation about Würzburg, *and* Virchow's initial reaction to the news. Edward spoke slowly, cautiously aware he was talking with a powerful and influential man. "Um...about why Würzburg rescinded its job offer to you."

Rudolf tossed on a cloak of indifference. "Oh, yes, the information is so new I haven't had time to investigate it. I just got word myself," he said truthfully. "After I investigate it, though, I will write to you for my official stand on the situation...your name was Edward, correct?"

"Yes, sir." If Virchow was covering his feelings he was damned good, a professional in fact.

"As you have been told, Edward, the matter will be more thoroughly researched and I will get back to you. Good day." Rudolf tapped his walking cane for emphasis, then turned and strode down the hall away from the exit.

Edward walked out of the hospital, certain of the fresh misery in Virchow's eyes.

Rudolf did not turn around to check the reporter's distance until he reached the left hallway that led to his office. The man was gone. Virchow then turned in the direction of the maternity ward to seek out the only man who might possibly know the truth – friend turned foe, Schmidt.

Rudolf found him leaning over a patient's swollen abdomen, his eyes closed as he listened intently through the stethoscope on the woman's abdomen. Donner and Reinhardt, enemy and his best friend, attending other patients on the ward stared at Rudolf.

Schmidt's eyes opened and then widened when he recognized Rudolf. Rudolf's ability to remain calm under pressure was part of his Weltanschauung, or world view. This uncharacteristic look of consternation on Rudolf's face cut through Schmidt's hostility and he responded with concern. "Do you need to speak with me?"

Rudolf nodded.

"Now?" Schmidt gestured with his head in the direction of his patient.

"As soon as you can, sir."

Schmidt turned to his assisting nurse. "Can you please ask Dr. Reinhardt to come here? Tell him Frau Rasa's presentation is most likely breech and she needs close monitoring."

"Yes, sir."

Turning to his patient, "Frau Rasa, there is something that I must attend to. I'm leaving you for the moment in Dr. Reinhardt's care but I will return soon."

"Thank you, doctor."

They walked to Schmidt's office, and Schmidt closed the door behind them. "I hear things are not going well for you," Schmidt began bluntly. For appearances sake, he did not want much personal time with Virchow.

"I have not heard anything recently, until just a few minutes ago."

"And you have come to me to find out what is being said."

"Yes, sir."

Schmidt looked gravely at Rudolf. Despite everything, he still admired the young doctor. "There is not much for me to tell you except a new ministry is in control in Bavaria. Since Munich is a Bavarian town, Munich must concede to the new Ministry. Because of that influence, operations have turned against you in Munich. How far they have turned, I cannot say. Your position at Würzburg is in serious jeopardy."

"I don't know what to do," Rudolf said. "All my plans were made, the move seemed imminent. I accepted their offer months ago..."

"I know, I know. I'm sorry, Rudolf."

"What do you suggest I do?" he asked.

"How long has it been since you've written to them?"

"Nothing since May."

"Then I suggest that as your next step. If you need help drafting the letter, please let me know. But you are quite a writer..." he smirked half-teasing and got a sad little smile in response.

A week later, Rudolf looked up from his desk as Reinhardt entered Rudolf's office.

"I've heard from Würzburg," Rudolf said drumming his fingers on the desk.

"I'm glad you finally wrote to them and even gladder that they answered you quickly," Reinhardt said. "I have the feeling, though, you did not get the answer you wanted. Have you answered them yet?"

"Of course. I just got back from posting my letter."

"Let me hear their letter."

Rudolf pulled the letter from Würzburg out of the folded sheet used as an envelope. Enclosed with it, also, was a clipped article from the Bavarian newspaper, the Augsburger Postzeitung – an article written by the Ultra Catholic party.

First, Rudolf read the article publicly informing the Bavarian Minister that the minister would be guilty of high treason if he forwarded to the King Würzburg's nomination of Virchow as staff physician.

Then Rudolf summarized the letter for his friend. "The Minister worked himself into a state of rage over the newspaper article and wrote to the Würzburg Senate that the Minister would appoint me only if I change my views *and* provide guarantees that I will not make Würzburg 'a playground' for my radical tendencies."

Rudolf looked at Reinhardt, his serious look melted with an impish thought.

Reinhardt noted the look. "You and your radical tendencies," he said. "How dare you try to improve people's lives."

Rudolf opened his mouth to retort then held up his index finger as if to say, I'll get you later, then completed the summary of the letter. "The Senate decisively rejected the first demand, that I change my views, as unreasonable. The second, however, that I not continue political activities at Würzburg, has been put to me."

"And how did you respond?"

"I wrote, "*I have no intention of acquiring a playground in Würzburg for radical tendencies.*"

Shaking his head side to side, his eyebrows lifted, Reinhardt said, "Then you don't know what is going to happen to you next, do you, my friend?"

Rudolf Virchow

ROSE AND RUDOLF MARRY, MOVE TO WÜRZBURG

Rudolf and Rose silently strode together on the sidewalk by the river. Their linked breath vapors formed a streaming chain on the freezing November day in 1849 thinking about all the events since the barricades twenty months ago that brought them here. Snow laden massive Linden trees lined the water's edge. They stopped at well trodden steps that led down to an open embankment of the river.

Standing at the top of the steps, they stared at the icy river for a moment. Rudolf tugged his Röschen by the waist and turned her to face him. He felt awed by the love in her eyes and sure of the love in his heart.

Rose uncharacteristically spoke first. "Ever since you told Father in August you'd received official word from Würzburg that your employment was accepted, the pain got stronger and stronger until I could not help from showing it. You've taught me everything I know, dear Rudolf, and my admiration for you is endless. I could not bear not seeing you anymore, you not being anywhere in my life."

Rudolf took her tiny gloved hand and raised it to his lips.

She took a shallow raspy breath and whispered, "I will never forget the first time you did that."

"Did what – kiss your hand? When?"

She playfully tweaked his nose. "It doesn't matter. Even if told you, you wouldn't remember," she said sagely for an eighteen year old. She stopped and gazed at him. "Why did you wait so long to tell me how you feel? You came to the house to say *goodbye*." She sounded wounded.

He looked tenderly at the wispy dark curls encircling her face under her bonnet, her pert nose, tiny chin, her sky blue eyes that grabbed him.

"Things have been so uncertain, my Röschen. I face this great move to Würzburg knowing I may never be able to return to Berlin. Yes, I came to say goodbye. But when the time came, I couldn't bear to say it. To you."

Silent, she stared at him. Waiting.

"I will have to supplement my income giving private lessons, hope that my travel allowance will be sufficient until I am settled...your family is here! I almost hoped Würzburg would say 'no' so I could be with you!"

She broke her silence. "My family is where *you* are," she stated resolutely. "You may be ten years older than me, Rudolf, and I still have a lot to learn but there can be no one else for me, I will marry you."

Rudolf grinned, smiled and then giggled. He threw back his head and broke into laughter from the bottom of his soul. "You little sprite. Knowing there will be time before we are comfortable..."

She shook her head solemnly yes.

"Knowing you will have to follow me there..."

She nodded a sad little yes.

"Knowing that you will have to leave your family.

She looked at the ground and nodded.

"Knowing I love you more than I ever dreamed possible."

Her face came alive. Her blue eyes sparkled as she yipped with joy and they embraced through bulky coats.

"We must begin our engagement immediately," Rudolf declared.

"Yes!" she said.

Months of walled off emotions surged between them as the held back words gushed out. Shy looks gave way to bolder stares, hugs deepening to tender embraces, tentative kisses to stirring passions. The revealing, the uncertainty, the thrill, the sadness, the joy – the joy!

"I'll tell your father and mother we are engaged when I take you home," his face beamed.

"Yes! Mother and Father will be so excited to have you as part of the family..."

Rudolf's grin got one shade softer.

"What did I say? What is it?" she asked, her soul and spirit intimately connected to his.

"You will..." he said slowly, "become a part of...*my* family."

"And?"

He did not want to tell her of his financial commitment to his parents, not that she wouldn't understand, but worried that to his father word of a new daughter-in-law would be interpreted only as a decrease in the amount of available cash that Rudolf sent home. He chose to respond to Rose along a less direct, but just as honest, path.

He said, "I have written nothing about you in my letters."

She stomped her foot in the snow.

"Nothing?! Not even a mention of my name?" she bridled.

He pulled her rigid body to him. "I will fix that right away..." he said contritely, then, with all the tenderness he felt inside, he whispered, "...future mother of my children."

She sighed deeply, and he felt her body relax. Wrapped in a blanket of love, they held each other in silence for a few moments above the riverbank, no longer just dreaming of how it would feel to be in each other's arms.

"Let me take you home. We have a lot of plans to discuss."

While they walked, though, they shared the harsh awareness that within the hour, months of separation would begin. They talked of the wasted months with regret then of their bliss that they finally opened up to each other, if even at the last moment. Their engagement had begun – baptized with tears and confirmed with kisses. Plans would have to wait.

Rudolf kept to his word and wrote to his father about their engagement. Only after dealing with his move to Würzburg, though, did he answer his father's concerns about Rose's dowry as well as her family's status, both of which his father overestimated.

Würzburg

Friday, November 30, 1849

My dear Father,

Rudolf Virchow

Now at last I find myself in a well confirmed and recognized position as professor in the prosperous Main University. Today I reported for duty in the Julius Hospital, and on next Monday I will begin my lectures. This is the end of a long train of events packed into the last days, about which I still owe you some details. You will find it natural if I first speak of my engagement.

Privy Councillor Mayer is not, as you said, a high official but an ordinary practicing physician who bears the title of Privy Sanitary Councilor without office. You need therefore have no fear of him, and you can rest assured that as a man without office he is in any case more honorable and charming. I have already written to you about his family, but you have no doubt forgotten this in part, and I want therefore to give the family background.

Mayer has a brother, who is court gardener in Monbijou (Berlin) and a sister, who is married to the court gardener, Fintelmann, in Charlottenburg. His wife's maiden name is Martins. The well known jurist and defense attorney Martins, former Oberlandsgerichtsrath and at present a member of the Upper House (opposition) and Oberbergrath Martins in Halle, are Mayer's uncles. Two of her brothers are artificers (Pistor and Martins). One of her sisters is married to Geh. Cabinetsrath Illaire, another to his brother, secretary of the royal household in the office of the court marshal, and a third to Professor Dage (painter and member of the Academy of Art).

The Mayers have seven children, five of whom are or were girls. The eldest daughter is married to the physician Dr. Ruge in Berlin, the second is married to Geh. Finanzrath Seydel; Röschen is the third, and there are two younger ones. Of the sons, the oldest is at the moment studying medicine at Halle, in the first semester; the second is still in high school.

If you ask after the outside possessions of the Mayer family, I have no answer. I have never asked whether Rose was going to be provided with a dowry, rather I have hesitated to offer her my hand until I believed that I myself was in a position to support a wife. I do not think that Mayer has or will assemble a great fortune, although he may be quite well off. With the number of children (seven), no very large share remains for them individually. It will always have to be more or less my care to keep house with Rose, and I rejoice in this.

I have known Mayer since the beginning of 1846. He is and was even then the most sought after obstetrician and gynecologist in Berlin, and was Chairman of the Society for Obstetrics when I first made his acquaintance; we soon became confidants and then friends. I came to know his family much later, in the course of the next year, the summer of 1847. Röschen was then still almost a child and concerned me not at all, but her mother soon grew to like me, and a confidential relationship took form between us, particularly since March 1848, which in its development had given her a motherly attitude toward me even before there was any talk of Röschen. Not a week passed when I did not visit the Mayers one, two or even three times; I generally arrived late and did not leave before midnight. We had long conversations, philosophized, and talked politics. Aristocratic members of the family have long since complained that I was

171

lowering the tone of the Mayers, and my eventual engagement has aroused great alarm within these circles.

Now, as for Rose, it took a long time before we came close to each other, and as late as the beginning of this year it would have caused me little regret to part from her. Rose is very quiet when she feels no need to speak, and so in my talks in her home, she was more a listener than a participant. But in this listening she paid such careful attention to me, and in a sense was educated by me, that I can think of no one who better understands me. And as for me, I have grown fond of her, I don't know how and when; but one fine day I noted that she had unexpectedly grown into my heart and spread herself into its every corner. This came at a very sad time, when I had received the ministerial decree of my dismissal.

At that time I considered it a point of honor to conceal my feelings for Röschen because of the uncertainty of my immediate future. So I remained cold, even after my appointment had come, and yet I could not leave Berlin. When I finally saw that Röschen was day by day less and less able to hide her troubled feelings, when I saw that she was suffering, and clearly on my account, I could no longer restrain myself. On Monday I went there to say goodbye, and by noon we were in each other's arms.

So much for today. I am enclosing 50 thaler in the form of treasury bills. I am sure you will need some money. Give my kindest regards to Mother.

Your

Rudolf

"Finally I get to meet the great Dr. Virchow," Kölliker joked, pumping Rudolf's hand up and down. They stood just inside the baroque pavilion of the building they would be sharing at Julius Hospital in Würzburg. They'd not seen each other since Kölliker's visit with Rudolf at the Mayer's. "I am proud to say I am both coworker and friend to Germany's first chair of Pathological Anatomy. Berlin's comet has come to Würzburg. Again, Dr. Virchow, you are making history."

Pulling his hand free, Rudolf embraced his friend. "It was a long journey to get here," Virchow said, thinking of his eventful past that culminated in the move. "But this next year brings with it *many* new things – new position, new city, new wife..."

"What?! New wife – do I know who it is?" Kölliker asked.

"You know her," Rudolf said with a smile. "Rose, my Röschen – Mayer's middle daughter."

Kölliker pursed his lips and whistled. "That beautiful little slip of a girl is traveling all the way to Würzburg to marry you?"

"No, no, of course not," Rudolf said. "We became engaged just before I left and her father asked us for six months of probation. The soonest we can marry is next summer and we'll marry in Berlin."

Kölliker's eyebrows raised. "In Berlin? You are not permitted to return there by the King's order."

Rudolf put his finger to his lips. "Shhh. It is where we must marry. We will find a way."

"I'm sure you will find things around here to occupy your time and your mind for the next six months," Kölliker said mischievously.

"Ahhh, my friend, unless you mean related to work only. No politics," Rudolf stated flatly.

"No politics? What happened? Come on, let's go sit in my office...better yet, let's go sit in your new office and we will close the door."

They walked slowly down the hallway, the floor's shiny wood reflecting the morning sun. Virchow's portion of the building, the Pathology Department, was to the left; Kölliker's Anatomy and Physiology department down the hall to the right.

Würzburg, a much smaller town than Berlin, would take some getting used to, Virchow knew. He thoroughly enjoyed the travel from Berlin but a little dismayed that the town was even smaller than he remembered.

The pavilion where he would work was an elongated building with two symmetrical dome-crowned wings at each end of Julius Hospital, named in honor of Julius Echter von Mespelbrunn, Prince Bishop and Priest of Würzburg, 1545 to 1617.

Other than a desk, two chairs and a filing cabinet, Rudolf's office was as barren as his heart. He detested the distance between him and Rose. He and Kölliker sat in the chairs.

Kölliker asked again, "What did you mean – 'no politics'?"

"Before leaving Berlin, I had to give my word – signature even – on the King's demand that I would not engage in politics of any sort. You are watched as closely as I."

Kölliker nodded in agreement. They stared glumly at one another for a moment.

Rudolf continued, "Nothing will be gained to continue resisting the government. Not only has everything been undone since the barricades, the situation is even worse than before, and I decided months ago to acquire the role of observer rather than participant." Staring at a knot in the floorboard, his whole being projected sadness and weariness. "Military presence is seen everywhere in Berlin. It's just a matter of time before the people strike again." He shook his head and looked up at Kölliker with pain in his eyes. "The proletariat is the result of the introduction of machinery. Shall the triumph of human genius lead to nothing more than to make the human race miserable?" he asked in true despair.

Kölliker predicted, "Hopefully soon, but certainly within our lifetime, Virchow, you will see the German nation unite. All our efforts and the prices it has cost us *will* matter." He paused for a moment. "What of Waldeck, what is happening there?"

"Do you know he was taken as a political prisoner?"

Kölliker closed his eyes for a moment, his face reflecting profound sadness, and nodded yes.

"He was of great influence in drafting the constitution last December, then five months later accused of being part of a conspiracy." Rudolf paused and shuddered at the enormity of Waldeck's ominous turn of events.

"Do you believe it?" Kölliker asked quietly. "That he is part of a conspiracy?"

"I would sooner believe the sky rained pigs. No. I believe the charges are false and designed to silence a very influential man. Shortly before I left Berlin I heard from a reliable source that Waldeck may soon be released." He shuddered again. "I did all that I could..." he said helplessly.

Kölliker jumped up. "You did more than most! Why do you berate yourself? He stood on the battleground as an attorney and as an attorney, he will defend himself. With what would you have defended yourself – a microscope?"

Despite his misery, Rudolf smiled, glad for the first time that he'd come to Würzburg. Then his smile ran away to some dark place inside of him. "I may never be able to return to Berlin. The damned newspaper, Kreuzzeitung, kept mentioning my name while I was waiting for the final answer concerning my employment here. They would have *loved* it if Würzburg had turned me down. I'm sure the newspaper accurately and timely broadcasted my leaving Berlin and urged the right parties to never allow me to practice medicine there again."

There was a light rapping on the door. The two men quizzed each other with their eyes wondering if the other expected someone. Even in the safety of the hospital, months of harassment led to suspicion at the arrival of an unexpected guest. Both shrugged their shoulders and shook their heads no.

Virchow opened the door and behind him heard Kölliker sigh and say, "Scherer, come in, come in."

"I've come to meet the famous Virchow. I heard he just arrived..." Scherer glanced at Rudolf, his head snapped as he did a double take, then he simply stared.

At age twenty-eight, Rudolf's youthful plump cheeks, serene gaze and small stature took many off guard.

"Rudolf Virchow, I'd like for you to meet Johann Joseph Scherer, Professor of Organic Biochemistry and partner in crime."

Not much taller than Rudolf, Scherer had an intellectual and scholarly appearance; the quiet type, Rudolf thought. As deep as Kölliker's hair was parted to the left was as deeply Scherer parted his hair to the right such that standing next to each other their foreheads formed both halves of a heart. Scherer's hair length was to the middle of his ears as men do when self conscious about the things, the brown a shade deeper than Rudolf's.

Scherer took a couple steps into the room and reached for Rudolf's hand. "We need to persuade you to grow a beard and wear spectacles, young man," he chided as the two shook hands.

Rudolf liked something about Scherer immediately and his spirit lifted a small notch.

"How old are you anyway?" Scherer couldn't help himself. He'd heard Virchow was young, but *this* young?

"I turned twenty-eight a couple months ago, October 13. And you, old man?" he teased back.

"Born in '14. Makes me your elder at thirty-five," he bantered.

"And I'm in the middle at thirty-two," Kölliker added.

"Now that the important things are settled, Virchow," Scherer said, "how was your trip?"

"Cold, long, and I loved it."

"Ahhh, a man who loves to travel. But I think you are here to roost for a while?"

Rudolf smiled sardonically. Of course word was out about his circumstances. "My traveling boots are in the closet, the hotel's closet, for now. I hope to soon find other, uhhh, less expensive living arrangements, soon," he said. Rubbing his hands together enthusiastically he said, "And I especially can't wait to get to work with all the new equipment and resources...and the arrival of my new bride next summer."

"New bride? Your intended's name is..."

"Rose Mayer."

"Mayer..." Scherer said. "Might she be related to Dr. Carl Mayer of Charité?"

"You've heard of our Mayer?" Rudolf said not at all surprised.

"Dr. Rotterau, our obstetrician/gynecologist here at Julius Hospital, speaks highly of your future father-in-law. He is well known in his specialty."

It pleased Rudolf to hear this. It was known to Rudolf that Dr. Rotterau traveled to Berlin to study under Mayer after which Rotterau and Virchow corresponded. Virchow's, as well as Kölliker's employment at Würzburg was the fruit of combined efforts of Rotterau and Julius Hospital's rector, Franz Rinecker.

"I hear from Kölliker...well, from many sources, that you, too, despise romantic medicine in favor of scientific medicine. I read and learn a great deal from every issue of *Archiv*. I have some things I hope you will consider for publication...as well as joining forces with Kölliker and I for a publication associated with a Medical Society here at Würzburg. Interested?"

Rudolf warmed toward the man even more. "We are going to become good friends, Doctor Scherer."

Three days after Virchow 'reported for duty,' on December 2, 1849, Kölliker, Scherer and Virchow along with twenty-one other faculty members began the Physical-Medical Society in Würzburg. Proceedings of the meetings were published and the first volume lists these three as the editors. The stated purpose of the society was to advance medicine, natural science and research through meetings held every fourteen days. At meetings discussions would be held of current research across Europe, research methods and provide demonstrations.

Within months of aborting his publication, *Medicine Reform*, and successful continuation of the *Archiv* with Benno, Virchow together with Kölliker and Scherer would continue publications of the Medical Society for the next ten years.

Würzburg

Saturday, December 15, 1849

My dear Father,

I hope my first letter reached you some time ago, and I also hope that your silence does not mean that special circumstances have arisen to prevent you from writing. Nonetheless, it saddens me not to have heard from you for such a long time. I have been here only fourteen days but it seems as if months had passed; everybody is friendly and attentive but I still cannot get rid of the feeling of being a foreigner. So every piece of news from my old home is like the arrival of an old acquaintance. Röschen was also somewhat lax in writing and has therefore received a scolding letter from me. Mother Mayer has written to me, and only your letter is missing. This time I sincerely hope that our letters have crossed.

On Thursday, the Rector "bound me by oath," that is I had to swear three oaths: an oath of allegiance to the constitution, one to duty, and one against secret societies. So I am now well settled in every respect and hold the post of secretary at the meetings of the faculty, where I am the youngest voting member. In addition, the members of the University who teach medicine and the natural sciences recently founded a Society for Physical Medicine, in which I was elected first secretary and member of the commission for editing the reports that are to be published. My lectures began last week before a very large audience. How many of them have actually registered for the course, I do not know. Things here move very slowly and money comes in late.

The day before yesterday I left the hotel and moved into small but cheerful and moderately warm quarters at cabinetmaker Reppenbacher's house on Grabenberg. My furniture and books have been unpacked, in short all is in order. I told you that I did not take all my furniture with me; only the better pieces are here. Whatever I lack will be supplied temporarily on a hire basis by the owner of the house, who has a furniture shop.

As to my financial status, which probably will interest you most, it is correct that four Prussian thaler are equal to seven gulden, as you can easily see for yourself on the two thaler coin. I do not know yet whether the other calculation, that one gulden here is to be considered equal to one thaler, is correct but it seems to me exaggerated. It is only true that our lectures are paid according to this standard. Where in Berlin I received ten gold thaler, here I take ten gulden, so that there is a very substantial difference. My travel allowance has been spent, for out of the 160 florins left after paying for stamp fees and taxes, transport alone cost me over 80. As I see now here, it could have cost less, because while I had to pay two and a half thaler per hundredweight, here

I could have gotten it for one and two third. My salary for the first half of the month has been used up by the hotel bill, so that I would hardly have been able to survive had I continued to live in this way.

However, I hope that with suitable arrangements things will improve. Of course, I will again give private lessons in order to increase my income, and for my scientific needs I must devote myself to writing. In this way, and with a degree of austerity, I shall be able to manage a household without having to accept anything from my future father-in-law, and I shall also be in a position to help you on occasion in your difficult position. I think that we must speak to each other openly in this matter. You must be in a position to tell me roughly what your prospects are in the coming years and how much of a deficit you reckon on in your budget. In turn, I can make arrangements for this, and I hope that you will not pain me by making fewer demands on me than I made on you earlier, under most unfavorable conditions in your household with the poor crops.

And now, having settled these matters, let me express my heartiest and fondest greetings on your approaching birthday. This past year was perhaps one of the most eventful and significant. We have all passed through changes of fortune, and now, at its end, we can nevertheless look back with feelings of satisfaction. Probably no other year was more decisive for my entire future, and thereby for a part of yours as well. Never before could I express my wishes, as long as I was involved in fulfilling them, with greater hope for their fulfillment than now. Never before have I more strongly cherished the conviction that it would be possible for me to contribute to your happiness than now, when I myself am thinking of building a house.

Stay well, dear Father; I hope we shall succeed together in remaining mentally alert and physically fit. And my chief wish is: may I succeed, on each coming anniversary, in making you ever happier.

> *Your grateful and much loving son,*
> *Rudolf*

For eight months, the gears of Rudolf's daytime clock blurred in hectic movement but sharp fanged teeth gnashed his nights into one intolerable hour after another pining for Rose. Already called 'bride' and 'groom' by German customs, Rudolf looked at the engagement ring on the ring finger of his left hand. After the wedding, the same ring would be placed on his right hand. He marveled that such a thin band of gold could so intimately connect him to another human being and wondered if ever he and Rose looked at their rings at exactly the same moment. Most of Rose's belongings had been transported to their new home in Würzburg and the thought of the traditional doll nestled in its cradle that he had not yet seen amused Rudolf.

Finally August arrived and Rudolf returned to Berlin for his Hochzeit (marriage).

Carl and Johanna Virchow also traveled to Berlin and stayed in a local hotel. Carl accepted Rudolf's offer to pay for the bill. Carl joined Rudolf and Rudolf's friends at their favorite drinking hole, Seeger's Tavern, two nights before the wedding for the traditional Junggesellenabschied (bachelor's party). His friends considered kidnapping the soon-to-be bride, as was done in small villages and suggested by Johanna, but they knew their conservative and anxious Rudolf would get impatient searching for his bride throughout pubs. And not a little drunk.

As required by law, their marriage license hung 'at a public place' for a week – outside the door of Mayer's office inside Charité. Despite its inconspicuous hanging, news of the banished instigator's return to Berlin for the occasion of his wedding somehow leaked to the newspaper and eventually the Prussian police.

On the morning after his bachelor party, Rudolf and Rose married during a civil ceremony at the Registry's office on August 24, 1850, with a church wedding planned for two days later. On the eve before their church wedding, the party, Polterbend (rumbling night), was held at the Mayer's. Friends and family, as well as the engaged couple, tossed cheap chinaware deliberately breaking it all. Rudolf and Rose worked together to clean up, fulfilling the custom to demonstrate the couple's willingness and ability to work together.

Finally the day arrived. Rudolf wore his tailored black single breasted low cut silk tailcoat with its long collar and double breasted revers. Under it he wore a single breasted low cut silk waistcoat with a white shirt, stand up collar to his chin and black cloth trousers. Around the collar of his shirt was a white silk stock tied into a large bow. He drove an elegant black carriage with black horses to Rose's home to carry her to the church.

Immediately ushered into the family room, the family cooed over his appearance until Rose appeared in the doorway. Rudolf stared in silence at his bride-to-be, his tears blurring her into an angel all in white. She stared back at him with radiant blue eyes.

From her tiny waist, ruffles flowed up the sides of the gown to her shoulders, the ruffle getting ever wider as it approached her shoulders. Encircling her shoulders, another layer of ruffles underneath supported the top layer. Under both was a small puff of silk and it appeared to him as though she had wings. Tight fitting lace sleeves buttoned down her arms and ended in a trumpet-like flare of lace around her wrists. A ribbon was tied around her waist. Five garlands of gathered silk played up from the hem to the level of her knees, each garland topped with a dainty spray of pink flowers. On her head was a wedding crown of tinsel, flowers, pearls and ribbons and in her gloved hand she carried a draw string purse. She extended the purse to Rudolf with a teasing look dancing in her eyes.

For once Rudolf was speechless.

"Aren't you going to ask me what is in the purse?" she asked, well aware of the effect she was having on him, loving his rare inarticulate moment.

"You are beautiful, my Röschen. *My* Röschen," he repeated, "soon to be my wife." Then, smiling, he managed, "Salt and bread for good luck?"

Smiling at him, she happily nodded. "Yes!"

Still smiling, he gave his waistcoat pocket two pats.

"Grain?" she guessed.

"Yes. Double good luck." He extended his elbow to her and she glided across the room slipping her hand through his arm. Blissfully unaware of another plan taking shape, they walked down the sidewalk toward the carriage as the rest of the Mayers followed close behind in another carriage.

Arriving at the church on the glorious August day, they innocently laughed at the thick log straddling the sawhorse in the church yard. Immediately after their wedding, in their wedding clothes it was the custom for them to again work together and saw the traditional log. Their hands would never touch the bow saw resting against the log.

They waited together in a separate office in the church, then, after their guests had been seated, Rudolf and Rose walked to the front of the church and what was supposed to be a one and a half hour ceremony began.

As the priest began to speak the church the doors burst open. In stomped four policemen who lined themselves shoulder to shoulder, brazenly staring down the aisle at Rudolf as the crowd gasped.

"What are they doing here? They've come for you, haven't they? Why now? No, no..." Rose whimpered. She clutched his sleeve.

Rudolf put his arms around her and pulled her tightly against him.

Seeing the terrified couple enraged their fathers who both sprang into action. Carl Mayer and Carl Virchow charged from their seats and strode down the aisle. Male guests arose throughout the church with clenched fists and faces like a storm cloud gathering. Women gasped and clutched handkerchiefs to their mouths, children huddled close to their mothers.

185

Agonizing over what to do, Rudolf stood with Rose in his arms, watching their fathers approach the police. The minister stepped close to the embracing couple and put his arms around them both.

"Halt!" the police ordered the two advancing fathers.

"THIS IS NOT THE TIME!" Carl Virchow shouted at them.

"Go away!" yelled Dr. Mayer. "HE WILL LEAVE BERLIN AS SOON AS HE'S MARRIED!"

The police did not budge. "NOW," they ordered. "He is to leave *NOW.*"

Rose cried against Rudolf's jacket. "We must finish our wedding," she sobbed.

The minister administered the briefest version of wedding vows and walked the bride and groom to the front door of the church.

The Captain's voice boomed throughout the silenced church. "RUDOLF VIRCHOW – YOU ARE TO LEAVE BERLIN IMMEDIATELY!"

Rudolf tilted his head slightly upward, then with a slight tuck of his chin toward Rose who stood to his left, he said, "Captain, you have the honor of being the first to whom I introduce the new Mrs. Virchow."

The officer opened his mouth and stared, then closed his mouth.

Rudolf's father chuckled, marveling at his son's precociousness. As the comicodrama overcame him he began to laugh out loud. By his side, laughter, too, began deep in Dr. Mayer's chest. The sounds bubbled up, the guffaws grew louder, then clutching his belly, they rocked with laughter. The rows of people close to the scene glanced from one to another unsure if the whole scene was a prank or not – who ever heard of police barging into a wedding? – and then finally deciding it was a grand joke they joined in the merriment.

Regaining their dignity and composure, the police lunged toward Rudolf, who was caught off guard. As the crowd gasped, an officer on each side of him grabbed him by the arms. Instantly the crowd bristled – this was *no* prank. The new groom was yanked out the church door so brusquely that Rudolf's head snapped backwards. With an officer on either side of him, he barely kept his balance as his feet skittered down the four concrete steps. Both fathers rushed after Rudolf.

Standing alone just inside the doors, Rose buried her face in her gloved hands and wept. Her mother and her new mother-in-law raced to her. The three women clutched each other and stood like a rock in a creek as the guests flowed around them to look out the doors.

Rudolf violently worked free his arms of the officers clutch. The sympathetic crowd poured down the stairs and surged between the officers and Rudolf. Rudolf turned toward the door and opened his arms toward Rose. The crowd quickly split a path and without a word, Rose flew down the steps to her new husband. Rudolf and Rose grasped hands and while the crowd maintained a protective barrier against the police, the newlyweds raced to the carriage.

The officers yelled ineffectual threats as the crowd stood firm. Rose gathered up her wedding dress while Rudolf helped her from behind and they dashed into the decorated carriage. Carl flung himself up to the driver's seat. The horses snorted sensing the tension around them and restlessly shifted their weight from one leg to the other. Carl snapped the whip. The horses reared up pawing the air with their front legs. As their feet hit the earth, they charged. Inside the carriage, Rudolf and Rose leaned their heads back against the cushioned seat and Carl hunched against the force. Pebbles and dust flung out from behind them.

Rudolf held his weeping new bride as she buried her face in his neck. He kissed her forehead, whispering words of comfort on their ruined wedding day. "One day, Röschen, we will tell our children about this day."

She wept louder. "We didn't do the log..."

"Not to worry, my love. We know we will work together for the rest of our lives."

"We must leave Berlin immediately," she cried.

"Yes," he said in a low, wretched voice, "we must leave immediately." He pulled her chin up. Tears clumped her black eyelashes and he thought, *her eyes look like stars*. The mixture of emotions he saw in her eyes – anguish, fear, a tinge of stubbornness – tore at his heart. He aimed a kiss at her mouth but a sudden jolt put his lips on a salty, wet eye. He silently cursed the police for destroying their dream and a twinge of regret for his past that had brought this upon them. He pulled her head back to his shoulder. They rode in silence and sullenly watched out the window, the scenery passing by as quickly as their broken day.

Carl drove them to the Mayer's home. While Rose stayed in the carriage, Rudolf and Carl grabbed Rose's packed trunks and tossed them in the carriage on top of Rudolf's. Coming up the street was a police carriage.

Rose leaned out the carriage door, looked at her father beseechingly and in a pleading voice cried, "Mother!"

"She'll understand you had no time to say good-bye," her father promised, and climbed back up to the driver's seat. Glancing behind them at the approaching police carriage, he snapped the whip then tight lipped, his brows pulled into a deep V, pulled out and headed for the train station at a less jarring clip. He knew by now that the police did not intend to harm Rudolf; ousting him not only from Berlin but the entire Prussia area was their main intent.

As they drove away, Rose craned her neck keeping her teary eyes on the house, on the dogs who stared questioningly from the front yard but kept their distance from the commotion. Rudolf watched her keep an eye on the trellis of ivy and knew she wondered when she would see any of it again. He never expected that their departure would happen under such dismal circumstances. Rudolf sat quiet by her side, guessing what she was going through. Taking a deep calming breath, she assured him that she reminded herself she was now the wife of the man she adored and soon they would be on their way to their honeymoon. They both relaxed a little and held each other in silence.

"Those hateful, hateful men," she sputtered. "Do you think we will *ever* be able to come back?" she asked wistfully.

"I hope so, Röschen," Rudolf said, "I hope so."

Rudolf Virchow

Würzburg
Wednesday, October 2, 1850

Dear Father,

You must by now be impatient to hear from us. Here we are again now, like an old married couple with many adventures, after rich experiences, shaken and bruised. Our journey, though not enjoyable throughout and even not without danger, was nevertheless so pleasant on the whole that now in retrospect it appears to us as a perfectly happy whole. The petty sorrows are gradually forgotten, and more and more our memory of the whole presents itself as a chain of sunny and happy days.

You know how we came as far as Kreuznach. From there we left on Tuesday, September 3, made short rest-stops only in Baden-Baden and Frieburg in Breisgau, and reached Basel on Thursday evening. From there we went to Interlaken via Bern and Thus, stayed there a few days, and made excursions to Giessbach and up the Abendberg, where there is a well known institution for cretins. On Tuesday, we then went to Lauterbrunnen to view the famous Stabbach. There – until then we had used steamers, post- or private coaches, Rose was seated on a horse and we briskly climbed 6000 feet in the sky to the Wengernalp, which lies just across from the huge snow-covered horns of the Jungfrau, the Monch and the Eiger, so that one could see this colossus from top to bottom.

Just as we arrived above we were greeted by a noisy rumbling and powdering, from slope to slope, into the valley below. After having enjoyed some chamois ragout and trimmings, we descended 300 feet on the other side. This takes only four hours, but for an hour at a time in places it is so steep that one's knees start buckling. It was just there that Rose could have suffered a serious mishap. I was standing on a high rock and examining the path which we were supposed to take. It continued along the slope of the mountain and was so full of rubble that the horse slipped at every moment and moved very unsurely. It seemed so risky to me that I had Röschen dismount. About two minutes later the horse slipped and went head over heels down the slope.

Then we arrived in Grindelwald, a village situated in a wide valley, but still 3000 feet above sea level. The grain was everywhere green and the cherry trees were laden with fresh fruit, big baskets of which were set on the restaurant tables for dessert. It was here that we saw our first real glacier and stood for a while in a green ice cave, enveloped on all sides by ice, so that light could penetrate into the cave through its layers.

The next day we climbed the Faulhorn, approximately 8000 feet, the highest inhabited spot in Europe. Our travels eventually took us to Gotthard. All this, from Interlaken to Gotthard, took eight days. Rose was on horseback most of the way, although she also covered large stretches in between on foot.

At Lake Lucerne, a steamer at the Tellplatte took us to Lucerne, where we found our first letter from the Mayers. On Tuesday evening we went on foot up the 3000 foot high Rigi, where we made camp until the following Sunday. Undoubtedly the most marvelous spot I have ever seen! One can survey almost the whole of German-speaking Switzerland, the Alps, mountains, plains, lakes, rivers and countless villages and towns. From Rigi we descended, again on foot, and traveled by train to Zurich, where we again spent two days. A week ago yesterday we hurried from Zurisch over Winterthur to Lake Constance, crossed to Friedrichshafen by steamer, and then returned here via Ulm, Stuttgart and Heilbronn. And it was marvelous!

The roughest part of moving in is now over. Our kitchen is in operation, all chests have been unpacked, the cabinets have been partly arranged, and part of our calls made, acquaintances found for Röschen – and it seems that things will go very well.

Röschen is really happy; she likes our place, she is satisfied with the people, and she is getting used to the local customs. It is very good that the vacation enables me to be by her side and help her in many ways, and once she has done things herself all will be easier. Since her brother will be coming soon now, I hope she will not be too homesick.

There you have a preliminary report. More will follow soon. Write soon, too, how things are with you, how it was in Berlin, and whatever else that is good.

Your loyal son,

Rudolf

VIRCHOW AS PROFESSOR

Soon after the new year in 1851, Rose told Rudolf that in August they would be new parents. Although it thrilled both of Rose's parents and his mother, his father received the news less than joyfully. Still, if it was a boy they agreed to name the baby after Rudolf's father, Carl.

After the honeymoon and settling in, Rudolf began teaching classes of pathologic anatomy to pathology students as well as medical students. Weeks slipped by. Rudolf continued his lifelong practice of five hours of sleep a night enabling him with time to become engrossed in multiple tasks at one time. His studies of disease processes affecting individuals naturally led to studies of disease processes affecting groups of individuals. The horror of the Upper Silesians remained a part of him.

Virchow began pioneer work in the field of physical, not cultural, anthropology with studies on the skulls of cretins (those born with severe hypothyroidism that resulted in stunted growth and mental retardation). These studies led to other studies, beliefs and involvements for Virchow.

Rudolf Virchow

It was a cold March Monday morning in Würzburg in the year 1851 and Virchow was performing a meticulous post-mortem (after death) procedure for the benefit of his students, a hands-on autopsy, as opposed to teaching in the lecture hall. Autopsies performed on colder days better suited the student's noses.

"Can you state the disease, the underlying pathology, that indirectly caused this patient's death?" Virchow inquired of the young medical student. They stood side by side looking down at the laid open elderly male body on the autopsy table. Virchow guided the student through the autopsy process while other students watched.

"The heart is extremely enlarged with contraction of the left ventricle..."

"That would make heart failure the *primary* cause of death," Virchow interrupted.

The student took a deep breath. "It appears the patient had two types of cancers, sir, of which one was the cause of death."

"Go on," Virchow prompted.

Making his decision, the autopsying student clipped free a piece of an abnormal section of rib and held it up for viewing. "Cancer of the bones."

Virchow pushed his glasses up higher on his nose, and sighed deeply. "Cancer of the bones," he mumbled. He grunted, then exhorted at the young medical student, "Think microscopically!"

The student replied, "But sir, I can *see* the tumor," then realized from the reaction of the others that it was a foolish choice of defense.

Detecting the student's southern Germany accent, Virchow said, "Where are you from and what is your name?"

"Hans Lewenhart, from Munich."

"And since there are only two Pathologic Anatomy classes in all of the German states, you find yourself in *my* classroom."

The student squirmed. He didn't like the turn of the conversation. "Yes, sir."

"Are you familiar with the microscope?"

"Yes, sir."

"And do you recall from the classroom the pictures I drew of the microscopic difference between cancer cells?"

"I recall them, of course, Prof. Virchow, but I could not depict one type from another by memory."

"Of course not, nor would I expect that you could. The pictures are merely representations of what can be seen through the barrel of a microscope."

"I'm trying to understand the significance, Prof. Virchow, but if a condition is clearly visible, why would we need to view pieces of it under a microscope?"

Again, Virchow pushed up his glasses and fixed his dark, piercing eyes on Hans who unflinchingly stared back. The fixed stare told Virchow that the young medical student truly was trying to understand, and not argue against, Virchow's insistence on the use of a microscope.

The master indicated to the student to replace the rib piece back inside the opened chest cavity. Virchow pulled a sheet from underneath the gurney on which the tattered body lie and gently covered the body.

Rudolf Virchow

He cleared his throat, then in his somewhat monotonous, droning voice, repeated the analogy that five years earlier in 1846 he had told his Berlin colleague and foe, Donner: "Imagine for a moment you are students of astronomy. It is a cloudless night and we have gathered in a field where we have a perfect view of the heavens. There are more stars in the sky than there are jewels in the king's treasure room." He looked around the room for signs of boredom. Loathing of boredom would in time become part of his reputation, scaring students to attention. "I point out the Milky Way, Orion's belt, other galaxies, a star just south of the Northern star...and next I set up a telescope. Directing it toward one of the stars and bringing it into focus we see that what we mistakenly believed to be a star is, in fact, the planet Venus." He grew silent for a moment and looked around him.

"We cannot imagine an astronomer making a study of the sky by eye alone. Gentlemen, the microscope is to medicine what the telescope is to astronomers through which we not only confirm or correct diagnosis, but even more remarkable is its use for discoveries about disease processes. And to answer your question, Hans, what is seen with the eye must not be trusted as fact and must be regarded as a working theory. Just as the telescope revealed the heavenly body not to be a star at all but a planet, the piece of bone that you held, although yes, it demonstrates cancer, but a cancer that did not originate in the patient's bones. Hence, the bone cancer is a symptom of the patient's underlying indirect cause of death. The difference will be of great interest to accurate statistics as well as to his progeny. Do you understand?"

With no conviction noted by Virchow, Hans nodded yes.

"We must maintain records of the incidence rate of our findings. Analysis of those records would indicate the incident rate diseases of specific areas of a population. In that way, we help more than one patient. We help a community."

Hans' again nodded, this time with a more solid understanding.

"It is imperative to inform the next generation of the diseases of their parents. They may make choices to help prevent the occurrence of the disease, if prevention is possible. A slide will be prepared of the 'bone cancer' and the subject of our next class. Class dismissed!" Virchow announced with a wave of his hand.

Hans was correct about the bone tumor but incorrectly answered the question Virchow asked – "the indirect *cause* of death. Despite the popularity of microscopes they were used improperly, and because of that viewed as a passing fad. Virchow was determined to not let that happen. Through a microscope Hans would have clearly seen the primary prostate cancer cells that metastasized, or traveled, to the bones.

Mid-April, Kölliker walked into Virchow's lecture hall and knocked on the open door. Although it was more than half hour before class time, he knew Virchow would be there.

The room was multi-tiered, like any large university classroom. Students sat on benches. In front of the benches, the students scooted their knees under a lengthy continuous ledge just wide enough for taking notes or resting their arms when they hunched forward to hear the soft-spoken Virchow. In front of the first row was a table in the shape of a half moon.

Virchow was busy laying what appeared to be tiny railroad tracks on the lengthy ledges. He looked up at his friend, smiled and waved him inside.

"What have you got going on now?" Kölliker asked. "I feel like I've walked into the wrong classroom. Are you doing an experiment?"

"No. I'm setting up a railroad. I am Chief Engineer Virchow of the Microscope Express," Rudolf chuckled. He pulled on a string attached to a model train and pulled it along the track. Attached to the train was a box car that Rudolf sawed to half its height so that it appeared as a gondola on wheels. Inside the boxcar was a microscope and on the front of the boxcar was a piece of paper on which Rudolf had written two words: *Think Microscopically!*

Kölliker said, "Let me guess. The hospital will not buy you a number of microscopes so you are setting up a track to send one around the room?"

"They would buy anything I requested, but to ensure that the students see precisely what I *want* them to see, I set up a track around the entire classroom to send around the microscope that I prepare."

Kölliker laughed. "No wonder I hear so many of them talking about your classroom antics. You've been here less than a year and already the number of students are increasing."

"Good." Switching the subject, Rudolf said, "You look even more miserable at this early hour than you do later in the day – why are you here instead of in bed where you usually spend most of the morning?"

"I'm here at this ungodly hour is to ask your help. I know this is the only quiet time of your day."

"Help with what?"

"There are multiple skulls I use in my classroom but not all of them look normal to me and you deal with abnormalities a great deal more than I. Do you think you can look over them to decide which ones are normal from those that are not?"

"Love to. Are they all of any particular race?"

"Mixed races."

Over the course of the next few months, Rudolf sorted out twenty-nine abnormal skulls which piqued a new interest for him: the development of the skull and how it relates to deformities. Through careful analysis and measurement he derived the classification still valid today: macrocephaly (enlarged skull); microcephaly (small); pathological dolichocephaly (enlongated) and its subgroups; pathological brachycephaly (short) and its subgroups. Also he eventually formulated his opinion, based on microsopic research and documented measurements, regarding deformity with regards to premature closing of the sutures of the skull.

During the year 1851 when Rudolf and Roses' first child entered the world, thirty-year old Virchow did most of the work for his book, *Researches on the Development of the Cranial Bases*. This book would become one of the most important contributions in the field of anthropology.

Although when he and Rose vacationed in Pomerania and she would soon bear Carl's first grandchild, Rudolf's father's attitude toward his daughter-in-law often brought her to tears and angered

Rudolf. The two men's dispositions were too opposite – the father was mastered by his senses and the son mastered by his intellect. His father accused Rudolf of beliefs that Rudolf previously denied, or read something in the intent of Rudolf's words that clear-minded Rudolf had not written. Or worse, provoked Rudolf about politics knowing his son must stay away from that simmering bed of coals.

As hard as Rudolf tried to placate his father, his reserved character shined through his words frustrating his father all the more, as did Rudolf's adamant desire to disengage from politics. Although Rudolf continued to send money home to his parents, because of the anguish his father caused his beloved wife and the aggravation his father caused him, his letters became less frequent, less informative about daily living and more about attempts to settle issues.

Würzburg
Monday, April 7, 1851

Dear Father,

You were certainly right in not responding to my letter in the first surge of feelings. And it was the same with me, too, for I almost repented that I had written to you under the influence of my first impression, and that I had put aside a plan to send you another, more appeasing letter. I thank you therefore from the bottom of my heart that you waited, and that what finally emerged from the conflict of your feelings was only love that forgives and reconciles. May the grumbling and resentment which has again and again welled up in you now yield place to a gentler, milder mood. You will than always find in both of us, in Röschen as well in me, affectionate cooperation and cordial understanding.

This conflict has finally shown what would otherwise have developed more gradually, namely that time, distance and different surrounding circumstances have resulted in many differences in our views and feelings. Your judgment of persons and things does not coincide with mine. You have accustomed yourself to making fixed pronouncements that are opposed to my convictions with ever increasing certainty, whereas my feelings have taught me to find certain allusions, which appear quite ordinary to you, coarse and painful.

Under similar circumstances, such a state of diverse views and feelings is bound to develop anywhere, and under such utterly different external circumstances one cannot hope for complete agreement. In such a case we are left with no other choice but to acquiesce, acknowledge the disagreement – and tolerate it. It is the great question of tolerance. If there is real love, it is not difficult to exercise tolerance, for tolerance is the daughter of love – it is the truly Christian trait, which, of course, Christians of today do not practice. When we know that we are sure of each other's love, and that each of us is at pains to find out what is true and act accordingly, what else do we need to reach satisfactory mutual understanding?

I cannot deny that I would be happier if we could go beyond tolerance to a complete union of feelings and convictions. But this would perhaps hardly be possible even with a lasting association, with continuous understanding on all questions; how much less with this separation? For instance, you touch constantly on politics. First come, as Auntie Voss (author's note: a reference to Vossische Zeitung – a Berlin newspaper) and the Party of Order require, communism and socialism in gruesome clothing. It is nothing to you that I wrote once to you earlier that I held communism as madness, and that I rejected the systems of the French socialists because they would bring back absolutism. But you forget that the Manteuffel ministry is mobilizing the army and the militia to suppress the Prussian people, is behaving in quite the same way as the communists and socialists; one part of the people works to feed the other, or the one gobbles up the other. If they let the system take its present course, it will lead directly to the French systems. We, who want social reform and are socialists in the free sense, want to avoid such a state of affairs. But you, the taxpayers, you want to see nothing. So you reproach me saying that I went wrong in holding that Europe would become either Russian or republican. This is too comical: don't you already feel the knout? Do you believe that Count Brandenburg died of mere affectation after he had been in Warsaw? Don't you know that it is always a Russian note or a Russian emissary who carries the orders of the Czar to Vienna and Berlin as to how to behave?

You seem to have concluded from my silence that I have begun to consider my earlier views wrong. And yet you admonish me to remain quiet, as if you did not really have much faith in peace! Now I accept the admonitions when my wife, too, is always a new admonition. I do not keep away from politics because I reject with horror my earlier politics but simply

202

because I want to abstain, because I do not want to play an
active part in politics.

    Farewell dear Father, and remain kind to
           Your much loving son,
           Rudolf

Rudolf remained out of the political arena in Würzburg not only because he had given his word, but of equal importance on behalf of his friends who argued for his employment at Würzburg. Both he and Kölliker were constantly under surveillance and both shrugged off all but the most vitriolic of the attacks by right wing politicians. The energy Virchow could no longer use for politics he channeled into other areas in his life: research that laid the foundation for his epoch cellular discovery, teaching and influencing the future leaders of medicine, membership in scientific groups, publishing five articles in Archiv and thirteen in the Physical-Medical Society, and his growing family. Carl Virchow was born August 1, 1851 and Hans on September 10, 1852.

Meanwhile, an event occurred that would eventually affect Virchow's life as well as alter the course of German history. In September of 1851, Otto Bismarck received official confirmation of his appointment as Prussian representative to the German Confederation's Diet.

ENTER OTTO BISMARCK

Otto von Bismarck was born on April 1, 1815 at Schönhausen in the Old Mark of Brandenburg in a typical Junker estate within the Prussian boundaries. Junkers are the descendents of a Slavic group conquered and enslaved 700 years ago by German knights. To Junkers, in particular Bismarck, true Germans were Protestants and especially *not* Roman Catholics. While tiny Virchow and the brawny Bismarck viewed Catholics with disdain, each for different reasons, it would be the only thing on which they would agree.

Bismarck was the youngest son of an intellectually sophisticated mother and easy going, less than brilliant father. To Bismarck's disappointment he derived his character mostly from his mother. Nonetheless, by his appearance he spent his life emulating his hefty, earthy hero – his father.

It was his mother's desire that her children have the finest education, so the family moved to Berlin and, unlike other Junker sons who attended the cadet corps, Bismarck went to the finest grammar school of his day. Through his mother's connections with the court, Bismarck rubbed elbows with members of royalty which rewarded him later in his career.

While attending the liberal University of Göttingen in Hanover, ironically Bismarck joined the student union, the Burschenschaften, the same group whose flag of black, red and gold was adopted during the Berlin revolution of 1848. Although comfortable in his role as a radical with the Burschenschaften, he soon turned against the group. He decided to no longer affiliate himself with its middle class members and joined the more elite student corps, the first public demonstration of his lifelong character trait of personal relationships steering the course of his political beliefs and immunity to his own inconsistency. Bismarck was a man of his word but his word, priorities and plans changed according to his feelings. One thing that never changed, though, was Bismarck's belief in the superiority of Prussia. At the age of twenty years he entered the Prussian civil service.

During the next ten years, he separated from the Prussian civil service, worked eight years as a landowner on his parent's Pomeranian estate (his mother died when he was twenty-four; his father when he was thirty), then re-entered the Prussian civil service. For one month. By the time he was thirty, life was dreary and void of meaning.

Soon, though, Bismarck found a rock on which he could stand. Through the love of a woman, Johanna – his future wife who was raised in and adhered to strong religious beliefs – Bismarck truly became a man of religious faith.

They planned to marry believing that they would settle in the country and they might have had it not been for two occurrences – in May 1847, the retirement of a regular diet member whose replacement was Bismarck, and the illness of Herr von Brauchitsch, a regular diet member. King Frederick William IV requested the diets to unite in Berlin for the King's effort to raise a loan for a railway to the eastern provinces of Prussia. Compelled by the King's request, newly-appointed diet member Bismarck traveled to Berlin to stand in for the sick Herr Brauchitsch.

In Berlin, Bismarck soon found himself protesting against the very liberals he had once embraced. And he found he liked to protest. Against the liberalists, Bismarck argued in favor of cooperating with Austria despite the fact that this argument conflicted with his deep-seated beliefs. Although the King's effort at a loan failed and the diet members dismissed back to their homes, Bismarck's sharp wit and clever tongue landed favorably on the King. Bismarck branded a name for himself – a reactionary, one always ready for a duel.

Life suddenly became interesting.

Bismarck returned home and married Johanna.

In his responses to the so-called German question raised during the revolution and barricade fighting less than a year later, Bismarck developed ideas and arguments which foreshadowed his later policies and actions. He never left anyone in doubt that he was a Prussian patriot, *not* a German nationalist. He rejected the Frankfurt Assembly, of which he was a member as a representative for Prussia, plan for unification because it would absorb Prussia into Germany. "Prussian we are and Prussian we wish to remain," he said in June 1848. Throughout the German states, Prussia was viewed as a natural leader of a new nation due to its efficient government and superior military power.

Bismarck also despised the King's compromises with the liberals after the barricade fighting. The National Assembly, of which Virchow was a member, met at Frankfurt with the purpose to create a united German state, to include Prussia as well as the other seat of power in the German states – Austria. However, the prime minister of Austria refused the offer to join German nationalism. His refusal triggered events that eventually unraveled the Frankfurt Assembly.

Soon after the end of the failed effort at unification, Bismarck sold his share of the family Junker farm and rented a home in Berlin.

After the revolution and its sequelae were squashed, eventually there was restoration of the German confederation and Prussia needed a delegate to the federal diet at Frankfurt. Having spoken publicly of his short-lived belief in cooperation with Austria, with only six month's experience Bismarck became the only man ever to be appointed to a high diplomatic post without previous service. At age thirty-six, six years after he felt his life was useless, in 1852 while Virchow remained a political pariah in Würzburg, Bismarck took front stage in German politics as the Prussian representative in the Frankfurt Assembly.

For the next thirty-nine years, he would wield tremendous power over the people of Germany, especially with the monarchy. Within time, Bismarck would verbally duel with another powerful figure in German history, a doctor with wit and a tongue as sharp as his own.

Leslie Dunn

SPESSART, ZÜRICH, BATTLE WITH BENNETT

On February 21, 1852, Virchow, accompanied by Administrative Councilors Alexander Schmidt and Robert Koch, was officially charged to study the reports of a health crisis in the isolated city of Spessart located northwest of Würzburg. Although not a distant city, they did not reach the mountainous region with ease. Ironically, Bishop Julius, founder of the hospital in Würzburg, was a descendant of the noblemen who in the 1700's settled in the borders of Spessart.

Virchow's report on his study determined the population suffered from typhoid, not typhus, induced by near starvation. Again he rebuked Catholic domination of the populace for its higher regard for member's souls than their physical well being, similar to what he found in Upper Silesians he studied four years prior. But unlike the Silesians, health returned to the Spessartians with prompt improvement in diet from soup kitchens proving him correct that malnourishment predisposed a population to diseases. As he previously recommended for the Silesians, for which he was so thoroughly scorned and ridiculed by administration as well as his peers, he once again recommended as his treatment of choice

209

for the permanent health of a nation: "Education, wealth and freedom."

Virchow's examination far exceeded a physical examination of his patients. Beginning with the very bed on which his patient lay, he noted its condition and how many other occupants slept with the ill person, room temperature, location of heat source for the home and the source's proximity to his patient, size of the room, the room's proximity to the kitchen, on what foods the family subsisted, location of food storage, number of rooms in the home, its geographical location in each village as well as surrounding animals, plants, streams - even rocks. As a doctor he was like a detective sifting through clues to find the root cause of his patient's illness, and as an anthropologist he compiled charts, calculations and regional statistics of each finding.

Sensitized by his recent interest in skulls having studied them in Abendberg during his honeymoon and in 1851 in Franconia, he noted with particular interest the incident rate of cretins in Spessart. In his report, he described a twenty-seven year old weighing no more than thirty-one pounds and found two brothers whose living conditions disgusted even their filthy neighbors. The brothers lived an animalistic life – their bodies, meager clothing as well as the hay on which they slept was covered with their urine and feces. Of bread and new clothing given to them, the former ravenously devoured and the latter destroyed so that in the end, their state remained unimproved. When they stole, they were beaten. Of these unfortunate men, impossible to study them as he did the others in the town, Virchow noted only their condition.

Leslie Dunn

After six years of friendship and coauthoring the *Archiv*, Benno Reinhardt, age thirty-three, died on March 11, 1852 from pulmonary tuberculosis of which he had showed signs as early as 1846. In a eulogy written for his dear friend, Virchow noted that perhaps the scientific method of medicine might have flourished without their work, but believed that they had made a difference in the direction of pathology.

The new path that Virchow and Benno helped blaze with powerful words based *on irrefutable* and *reproducible* facts would eventually penetrate and wipe out thousands of years of romantic, vitalistic theories of medicine. Did miasma's (poisonous air currents) cause diseases? Was cretinism the work of the devil? Was pus a substance that melted tissues, or the result of melted tissue? Were the Silesians struck down because God wanted to wipe them out for their slovenly and sexually promiscuous living? No. Materialistic medicine, the study of what can be seen and touched as opposed to ethereal humours, vapors and miasmas was the antidote of which Virchow, as well as other physicians courageously administered in liberal doses.

After Benno's death, Virchow continued the *Archiv* alone. The newly reorganized publication of the Physical-Medical Society also provided venue for his prolific publications. Virchow's meticulous research as well as his comprehensive approach (including French and English studies) toward his subject material garnered him a growing reputation as a renowned pathologist; each article carried more weight and like a pebble thrown out into water, the circle that carried his name reached ever further with each publication. Like Johannes Müller at Charité, Virchow provided the University of Würzburg with a growing source of income due to his discoveries, fame and classroom antics. Other sites began to woo Virchow. Especially Zürich. Beginning in 1852, that city began what eventually would become a relentless, shameless and zealous pursuit of Virchow's talents.

It was another Monday morning autopsy on a frozen December morning. On the table laid the remains of an unfortunate twenty-nine year old woman who had succumbed to a massive intestinal infection that perforated (ate a hole through) her intestinal lining until she bled to death.

As he deliberately covered up the lower half of the body, Virchow began to lecture that which he had repeatedly spoken and written for the past seven years: "Life is the expression of a sum or phenomena which follows physical and chemical laws. We...," he looked around the room, "...*deny the existence of a vital force, a healing force. There is no such thing as a 'vitality' giving rise to life. Life itself, as well as illness and disease, adhere to and are governed by cellular laws. Contrary to current beliefs, diseases are not based in the nerves only nor are illnesses caused by sickness of the blood.*"

At the murmuring in the room, Virchow paused for a moment. "Gentlemen, this is intended as review and not as new information. Who is still not clear about these fundamental messages?"

No one moved.

"You are the doctors of the future and, as such, you must learn knowledge based on the scientific method. You may spring ideas from a hypothesis, but you may not base your beliefs on a hypothesis. Beliefs are based on facts alone. Trust only what can be seen, tested and reproduced. If a patient's family insists that a patient's insanity is punishment for wicked behavior, that patient might be suffering a brain tumor or a ringing of the ears, tinnitus, that has driven them beyond sanity. Never accept as fact a diagnosis attributed to that which cannot be tested. Nerves and blood will be affected by pathological processes but these are not to be assumed as the bed of the disease process."

Pointing to the body, one by one Virchow asked the nine pathology students surrounding the autopsy table the same question: "Returning to our lesson involving this unfortunate young woman, based on what we see what organ was most affected by the infection?"

Incorrect answers of "the heart," "the lungs" indicated to him that the students were guessing. Doing his best to tamper his frustration, he reminded himself that these pathology students attended fewer than ten autopsy demonstrations. Still, was it that difficult to notice the enlargement of the spleen? An organ normally no larger than a man's fist filled the patient's left side. *"There would be no, 'Think microscopically,' mentioned here,* he thought ruefully. *These students need to learn to think pathologically."*

"This is not a question about systems. This is a question about specific organ response to the deceased's bout of infection and a question that, should any of you pause for a moment and think, can be answered from textbook learning with little more than a glance at the body."

213

The students squirmed uneasily.

One of them squeaked, "The spleen appears a little large. Splenomegaly?"

"Ah, ha!" Virchow chortled. "Yes! The spleen is, indeed, enlarged due to its response of the body fighting the infection. Who can tell me of other reasons for splenomegaly?"

And so it went with each lesson, each class. Virchow gained a reputation as a demanding teacher, one who insisted that students learn not only medical terminology ("pia mater" – delicate membranes surrounding the spinal cord and brain) but also the native language from which the word was derived (Latin) as well as the meaning of the root words ("tender mother"). Students described colors in full and exact detail during the course of a physical examination on a live patient such that when one pressed on a red mark on the patient's skin, did it blanch and completely whiten out, or did it retain its redness? Did it blanch out but retain redness only in the center? Or turn pink? Scalpels must be held just so, as well as any other piece of equipment.

Despite Virchow's deservedly earned title as a difficult instructor, students from as far away as America pressed Würzburg University for acceptance as much for an opportunity to learn from Virchow as for an opportunity to be near the now internationally famous doctor. If a student had trouble understanding a lesson, and if Virchow perceived the trouble as anything *but* boredom or lack of intelligence, with a gentle arm around the student's shoulder, Klein (Little) Dr. Virchow presented an invitation to spend time after class for a session of one-on-one teaching. However, if the lack of understanding arose from inattention or less than extreme intelligence, these students became targets against which Virchow would sling verbal knives. It was not to the great doctor's credit that some students who lacked Virchow's genius endured his public humiliation.

Virchow finished the autopsy and, as usual, students cleaned equipment and returned things where they belonged. Yet, during class Virchow sensed an undercurrent of something among them. They seemed easily distracted, less focused than usual. A few times he looked up and saw expressions in their eyes which he could not put into words.

As they gathered up their books, Virchow called to one of his most promising students. "Hans, would you stay behind for a moment to give me a hand?"

Hans glanced at Virchow. "Yes, sir." His friends looked at him but he waved them away. "Save me a seat in the cafeteria," he said.

As the students shuffled out Hans placed his books back down and walked to the front of the room. A thin young man, not much taller than Virchow, he approached the doctor with near reverence.

Virchow busied himself cleaning up until the last student exited the room. Hans stood quiet. "You were quieter than usual today," Virchow said.

Hans looked down at the floor, stared at the tips of his shoes and shifted his weight from one foot to the other. Virchow noted the young man's discomfort.

"Is it your grades?' he prodded.

"There is an article in today's paper, sir...about you."

Rudolf Virchow

Virchow pushed his glasses up his nose and felt a tingle in his neck. "I haven't read today's paper yet. Do you have it with you?"

Hans nodded. He walked to his books and pulled out the newspaper, folding it in half so that the bottom of the front page was clearly visible. With head tucked, he handed it to Virchow who stood with an outreached hand. Hans thrust his hands into his pockets.

Scanning the headline, Virchow read the article with a half smile and then a shaking of his head. Next to him, Hans' body twitched so that during his reading Virchow was tempted to ask the young man if he had an urgent body need.

After Virchow read it, Hans blurted, "Is it true, Professor Virchow, that you are leaving Würzburg to take over a clinic in Zürich?"

Virchow removed his glasses and tucked them into his pocket. "Unless there is another Professor Virchow of whom the paper writes, I have no intentions of leaving Würzburg."

"Then how..." Hans stammered.

"Zürich has written to me and offered me the post," Virchow admitted. "However, I see even before they have received my letter informing them of my decision, they informed the world of their opinion." He smiled mischievously. "They are working from a hypothesis."

He and Rose discussed the possibility of moving to Zürich. Although she missed Berlin, she insisted once again that her home was with Rudolf and that whatever he decided to do was all right with her. As the years passed, though, Rose's yearning to go home to Berlin deepened until she lived a life of near mourning. Eventually her physical condition reflected it, too.

Zürich's offer was appealing, no doubt. As director of a clinic, Virchow could set policy, practice medicine, continue to teach...but what of his research? Every week brought him closer to answers he sought and laid more and more groundwork for the major publications he wanted to write. He immensely enjoyed the camaraderie of his colleagues as well as the Physical-Medical society and its publication he helped edit. Also, he stood firm to his sense of responsibility to the friends who had helped him secure his position at Würzburg. What if Virchow chose personal gain – a higher status, more salary – yet left behind years of work? Although one day the results might gain him fame, for now he decided he must stay in the trenches.

"No, Hans, I am not going to Zürich."

Hans relaxed at last and grinning as though Virchow had just told him he was excused from exams from now on, Hans reached for his teacher's hand and pumped his arm up and down, up and down, up and down.

"Thank you, thank you, Herr Virchow!"

"You're welcome," Virchow laughed, his voice shaking with his whole body being moved as it was by Hans.

Despite their professor's stern teaching practice   and that he was often the bullseye of the local newspaper political attacks, it upset them to think he was leaving.

Letting go of Virchow's hand, Hans hugged his teacher who hugged him back. "I've got to tell the others!" he announced. Hans raced from the room.

Virchow gathered up his papers and ambled from the room, his face aglow.

During Virchow's afternoon class, one of the students asked him if he might stay later, meet in Virchow's office, to review some subtle findings the student noted while examining a patient in clinic. Of course Virchow would stay. Rose had long ago grown accustomed to Virchow's erratic hours, like those her father maintained during her whole life.

The December German evenings bring darkness early in the day and by 4:30, daylight was fading. The student brought good questions and the two of them spoke for nearly two hours until both were satisfied of the student's understanding. After the student left, Virchow considered the day, after all, a blessed day and looked forward to seeing Rose and their sons.

Now well after dark, Virchow put on his thick woolen tweed overcoat with its shawl-like hood and flare sleeves, next his tan leather gloves and narrow brimmed top hat. He heard a curious tapping on his office window.

Pushing aside the thick drapes, Virchow breathed the cold air that had been insulated by the drapes. Seeing flickering lights outside, he scratched a small hole in the ice on the window. Cupping his hands around the hole he peered through the glass.

Hans, his cheeks reddened from the cold, stood jubilantly waving one hand, in his other he waved a torch set afire. Beside him stood other students Virchow recognized, their breath vapors streaming out, snowflakes gently drifting down spotlighted by the torches they all held high.

Virchow felt chills up and down his arms and legs. His throat tightened and his eyes got misty. He pulled the drapes together and walked briskly to the entrance of the building. As he stepped out the door, there was a deafening outburst from the students.

"HURRAH, HURRAH" they yelled as they thrust their torches in his direction, the fires making golden streaming ribbons of light in the darkness. Then holding their torches high, they began to slowly parade past him, all eyes glowing, smiling. Virchow openly wept.

Looking down the column, he saw that nearly every medical student, about two hundred, gathered in the procession, a cherished honor reserved for revered professors. Slowly he raised his cane until it pointed toward the sky. Standing erect before them, his arm held high, tears coursed down his face. He could not speak for the lump in this throat.

A voice yelled out, "PROFESSOR VIRCHOW, WE HONOR YOU!"

"YES! YES!" the crowd chanted. From the beginning of the column to its end, the students began to sing the Latin song of tribute to their esteemed teacher: "Gaudamus igitur" (Let Us Be Happy):

"Let us rejoice therefore,

While we are young.

After a pleasant youth

After a troublesome old age

The earth will have us.

Where are they who were in the world before us?

You may cross over to heaven; you may go to hell if you wish to see them.

Long live the academy!

Long live the teachers!

Long live each male student!

Long live each female student!

May they always flourish!"

A blessed day, indeed! Virchow thought.

The next morning, Rudolf posted the following letter to his father.

Würzburg

Thursday, December 2, 1852

Dear Father,

You may have read the latest news about us in the newspapers, I mean my appointment to take over the clinic in Zürich. It is the same position that Schönlein held before he was invited to Berlin, and in which Pfeufer and Hasse were later engaged. Despite the very favorable conditions I have declined, since I feel the necessity of bringing the work that I have been pursuing for so long a time to a definite conclusion, which would be impossible for years to come in a new position. Here an increase in salary, a position as examiner, and a small infirmary have been requested for me, but I would have decided to stay on here even without this, as much as I would like, for many reasons, to be in Zürich.

Leslie Dunn

*I believe that eventually there comes a time when one must
limit one's activities to goals that offer a sure prospect for
success.*

> *Your much loving son,*
>
> *Rudolf*

In 1853, an issue that had been simmering for seven years
boiled over. Rudolf wrote an article, *Report on Studies in the
Doctrine of Tumors* published in the medical journal edited by him,
Kölliker and Scherer. In this article, Virchow reviewed a paper
written by Scotland's John Hughes Bennett. Virchow's abrasive
criticism of Bennett's beliefs (*"With singular obstinacy Bennett
always comes back to the cell theory of Ascherson* [a physician
researcher in Berlin]") provoked Bennett and a battle ensued over
each one's claim for the new medical term, leukemia, with the
definition of word itself a close secondary battle.

In an article published next in Virchow Archiv, Virchow stated
that two years ago he had distinguished two forms of "leukemia" –
splenic and lymphatic – and devoted much of the article to
descriptions and elements of these two forms. In the article, he
noted Bennett's desire to have the disease called 'leucocythemia'
rather than leukemia, and like a cat batting a skein of wool
Virchow noted that Bennett's 'leucocythemia,' although
unacceptable, is preferable to Bennett's original, "suppuration of
the blood," that Bennett believed the white cells were those of pus
and *not* of blood. Trivializing the matter further, Virchow appended

his article with a mention of Bennett's claim to having first published a description of the disease.

With over one hundred fifty years passed since then, no mention regarding the outcome of this clash exists available to this author except phrases out of context from articles published years after the event. By virtue of the fact that the disease is known as leukemia and not leucocythemia, the evidence speaks for itself regarding the outcome.

In the November 1853 issue of Edinburgh's Monthly Journal of Medical Science, an 'anonymous' writer wrote a seething criticism of Virchow's *Report on Studies in the Doctrine of Tumors,* using two words against Virchow from Virchow's own article – 'singular obstinacy.' Who was it to whom Virchow had directed those very words? Bennett. To flush out the culprit, Virchow published a rebuttal in Virchow Archiv stating Virchow's belief that the anonymous writer was no one other than Bennett, whose anger must be directed toward Virchow undoubtedly because Bennett believed he, not Virchow, first recognized leukemia, or rather leucocythemia.

Colleagues on both sides of the battlefield joined in, and in a very public manner.

The debate continued into the next year and in June 1854, another 'anonymous writer' declared in the Edinburgh Monthly Journal of Medical Science that, indeed, Bennett discovered 'leucocythemia.' But the faceless, nameless writer, *admitted* Virchow first made the statement that the corpuscles were not pus but rather colorless cells of the blood.

Soon after the publication of the admission as to Virchow's originality regarding the accuracy of the source of the disease he named 'leukemia,' Virchow published notice in the Archiv that the admission settled the question once and for all, endorsed by his colleague, Kölliker.

'Once and for all' lasted until only a couple months, until October of 1854. In the Edinburgh Monthly Journal of Medical Science, Bennett at last revealed himself. He publicly and irrefutably declared himself as the first to describe leukemia and, therefore, its discoverer. *"I must be excused,"* Bennett wrote, *"from entering into literary warfare against revolutionary combatants whose chief weapons are detraction and attacks on character...But since Professor Kölliker has descended into the arena as a champion for his colleague, I have no longer any objection to enter the lists with such an opponent – trusting that one so distinguished in the field of science, like the chivalrous knight of old, will conduct himself not only sans peur* (without fear), *but also sans reproche* (without reproach)." From this, even though he slung a barb in Virchow's direction, it seems Bennett's concern was that of professional retaliation by Kölliker.

Unlike Virchow's conflict with Rokitansky, no historical mention can be found that Bennett and Virchow ever attained professional camaraderie. Virchow's distinguished status especially at such a young age led to professional jealousy, his outspokenness intimidated some or led to bitter conflict or, conversely, his youthfulness and forthright nature charmed others into allied teamwork. The same is recorded as fact regarding

Bennett. Both instances, though, conflict and teamwork, spurred others who also blazed trails advancing medicine.

Leslie Dunn

OMNIS CELLULA A CELLULA –
CELLS ARISE FROM CELLS

During the years at Würzburg, Rudolf cultivated groundbreaking research and international fame. During those same years Otto Bismarck's political career flourished in Frankfurt as well as Berlin.

By 1852, four years after the failed revolution, the thirty-nine separate German states remained just so, with seats of conflicting power in Prussia and Austria. Concerned about giving up rights and power to the other, like bickering sisters, Prussia and Austria settled into alliances with foreign countries – a fact that Bismarck eventually utilized to his Prussian advantage.

Austria had recently triumphed over Hungary and Italy and the triumph infused her with haughty superiority. Her delegate to the Frankfurt Assembly, which Prussian Bismarck attended, did not feel the need to consult with other delegates, a regrettable attitude among any assembly. The Austrian delegates smug attitude especially provoked Bismarck who took it personally. Discarding his earlier public statements co ncerning his stance to unify with about unification with Austria, Bismarck once again changed his politics and sided against Austria.

Post-revolution, a newly created German customs union, the *Zollverein,* included nearly all the states except Austria. Due to a gradual weakening of her power since the Hungarian and Italian victories, Austria asked to be included in the *Zollverein*. From appearances, Bismarck acquiesced. In reality, he influenced the vote against Austria's inclusion for which Austria suffered economically.

By 1852, international politics forced German republics into an alliance. A conservative union was formed, The Three Northern Courts – Russia, Prussia and Austria – against France. The alliance was short lived. In 1853, conflict started first with Russia against France, followed by Russia against France *and* England. Russia's conflicts did not rally Prussian and Austrian support as expected by Russia. One year later, outbreak of the Crimean War exposed Bismarck's cunning and ruthless traits.

At the outbreak of the war, King Frederick William's advisors fought among themselves, each with differing opinions as to German's course of action. The King's unofficial advisor, Gerlach, urged the King to fight against France and England for Russia. Foreign Minister Otto Manteuffel counseled the King to unite Prussian forces only with Austria and another advisor offered a third option – to fight with France and England against Russia.

Bismarck presented the King with another option, once again revealing his personal brand of tactic: deception.

"Let us frighten Austria by threatening alliance with Russia, and frighten Russia by letting her think that we might join with

France and England." He outlined his mock battle plan. "If we mobilize 200,000 men in Silesia, this will threaten Russia. With that threat in place, we will demand of Austria the full seat of power in Prussia."

In order to sway the King's opinion, Bismarck persistently made repeated and lengthy trips between Frankfurt and Berlin. King William found Bismarck's tactic interesting but the King was not moved to action.

"A man like Napoleon could pull off this sort of stroke, but not me," the King told Bismarck.

Choosing to follow his Foreign Minister Manteuffel's advice, the King ordered what would remain for three years an alliance between German sisters, Prussia and Austria.

Despite Austria's sporadic efforts to engage Prussia to enter into battle on Russia's side, Prussia adamantly remained neutral. France and England appealed to Austria, persuading her to approach the Russians on their behalf and impose peace terms on Russia.

Austria's sole involvement was her undoing.

Regretting her decision, Austria pleaded with the rest of the German states for military support to disentangle herself from any involvement in the war. Bismarck successfully convinced the states to remain neutral.

By late 1855, pressured by France and England, Austria sent an ultimatum to their old allies, the Russians, warning that Austria would enter the fray against Russia if peace terms were not accepted. Exhausted by three years of battle, Russia conceded. A Congress in Paris was called and rather than heralded for her efforts to end the war, Austria defended herself on all sides – against Russia for not fighting on Russia's side, and against France and England for not fighting on *their* side. Quick to turn a situation to his advantage, Bismarck pointed out to the King that Prussia had, after all, followed the course he had originally advised. As an added coup, because of Prussia's neutrality and Austria's defensive posture, foreign relations in favor of Bismarck's Prussia strengthened. In April 1856 with the war over, Bismarck uselessly droned to his Prussian counterparts about Austria, "Germany is too small for us both."

Gaining no support, Bismarck turned instead to countries other than his own to sharpen his underhanded foreign relationship skills.

As the Crimean War spun into its third and final year in 1855, Würzburg sat untouched by the event as Rudolf's career continued its upward spiral. Even grander employment offers arrived on a regular basis from Zürich as well as offers from other universities. This, to a man who remained a pariah in Berlin, under surveillance and viciously attacked in newspapers.

Virchow cocooned himself with his classroom, his family, research and friends while vigilantly avoiding political activities. Skulls, fibrin, tubal pregnancy, cholesteotomas, tumor classification, cellulose, amyloid degeneration, leucine and tyrosine, rabies, anthrax, pus, albuminous fluids – Virchow's myriad research subjects were recorded in over two hundred published papers.

Students enrolled at Würzburg to attend his classes and some competed for the cherished and funded position as his assistant. Sensing the revolutionary changes about to occur in medicine, young doctors were eager to sign up. Virchow ensured that his assistant's received generous salaries and, unlike other professors who jealously insisted on receiving credit for their assistants work, he encouraged them to publish under their own names. Despite generous professional stewardship, he exerted unreasonable control over their personal lives. He offered his opinion as to whom they could or could not marry, whether or not they could teach and when they could leave his employ. After working hours, Virchow was a jovial, music loving, snuff-indulging individual. Working and learning at the master's side was either a very good place to be or an awful episode in their life to endure for the sake of their career.

A stillborn premature infant laid on the autopsy table, the baby's mother defending herself against a charge of infanticide. She gave birth to her illegitimate child alone in the woods and the infant died – highly suspicious circumstances to the authorities. Virchow's forensic report would either prove the young woman killed her newborn or clear her of the hideous crime punishable with death. Having studied, lectured and published reports on the 'revolutionary' changes that occur at the moment of a healthy birth, difficult legal cases frequently came Rudolf's way.

Even the most case-hardened assistant recoiled at the site of the pearl white tiny body that lay silent on the cold metal autopsy table. Having his own children further softened Rudolf but watching his scalpel poised over the tiny lifeless body, no one would guess the grief piercing his heart. Virchow's acts of kindness toward the experimental animals impressed his students and his assistant, Karl, knew that despite Virchow's cool demeanor, autopsying this infant was difficult.

Virchow bent under the table on which the body of the baby lay to turn the wheel which would lift the table higher. Doing so brought his face closer to the body and he smelled an odor emitting from the dead infant.

"Karl, I smell alcohol," Virchow said.

"Yes, sir. Yesterday when the body arrived, I immersed it in spirits, per protocol."

"Have you read the requests of the court?"

"No, sir."

Virchow picked up the chart, flipped it open and stabbed his finger at the paper. "Here," he said, shoving the chart toward Karl whose face flushed red.

The third year medical student read for a moment, then looked up puzzled. With a pang of regret, Rudolf recognized Karl had more learning to do. But under what circumstances to do it!

"The court asked specifically for chemical analyses," Virchow explained. "They asked that we check for traces of poison in the tissues..."

Karl nodded, appearing as though he still did not understand.

"...tissues that were chemically testable until you immersed the body in alcohol."

"Oohh," Karl intoned, followed by rapid sequence of his eyebrows going up and down in consternation and his eyebrows raising up as he looked at Virchow with fear. He then lowered his eyebrows and chin in shame as he understood that he botched the case and possibly condemned the young mother to a charge of murder. "What should we do?" Karl asked forlornly.

"The autopsy, of course," Virchow responded with a tinge of anger. He would have no choice but to inform the court of his student's blunder and pray that the error would not cost the young mother her life.

The autopsy began with a complete external examination. Karl recorded the infant's weight and height and noted no signs of trauma. If the baby was born alive and then beaten to death, fresh hemorrhages would be evident. There were none. This provided no answer to the question, though, of the woman's guilt or innocence. Lack of trauma indicated either that the child was born lifeless or murdered without violence, such as drowning or, as the court suspected, by poison.

The internal examination began with a V-shaped incision from both shoulders to the breastplate, or sternum, continuing with a single slice to the pubic bone such that the incision resembled the letter Y. Student and teacher worked closely together tugging back and clamping the skin exposing the rib cage and abdominal cavity. Next, the front of the rib cage was removed exposing the organs of neck and chest allowing for the removal of organs such as the heart, thyroid gland and lungs. Virchow carefully checked for signs of internal trauma. He would check for liquid in the lungs. Water would indicate drowning, amniotic fluid would prove the child had never taken even one breath; instead, alcohol seeped from the infant's lungs.

After removal of the chest cavity organs, next the abdominal organs – tiny liver, stomach, gallbladder, spleen, kidneys, ureters – were dissected, or cut free, from the body. The assistant obtained thin slices of each organ in preparation for microscopic studies. If it were not for the abnormal appearance of the infant's kidneys, attention would next have gone to autopsying the head and brain.

As Virchow sliced open the kidneys, he motioned for Karl to stop. Both of them noted the collapsed and enlarged appearance of the kidneys. This time a microscope would not be needed to resolve the cause of the infant's premature death. The kidneys were littered with cysts. Gently they placed the tiny organs into preserving solution in separate little bottles and completed the rest of the autopsy.

The mother forced to defend herself in the middle of her grief was innocent. Cystic kidney disease had throttled life from the child as it grew her womb.

Within time, Virchow's autopsy method – studying the *entire* body - became a standard in the industry and is the method used today.

Mindful that research suggestions given to him by his professors began his career, Virchow frequently assigned assistant's with tasks or specific studies. Just as Virchow shared his assistant's foibles, he also shared in their triumphs. Friedrich Grohé, another of Virchow's assistants, was assigned the duty of proving or disproving specific medical publications involving cholera patients. Two researchers published papers stating that when the crystalline amygdalin, found in the seeds of apricots, peaches and almonds, was introduced into the blood of a cholera victim, the blood emulsified, or broke down, the substance which then emitted a bitter smelling odor. While the claim was not disproved, Grohé did prove that the same thing happened when amygdalin was mixed in the blood of patients who had died from other diseases. In other words, amygdalin emulsification was no marker for cholera.

Some of the greatest minds in history found a new thread and through profound work and greatest diligence, wove a new pattern able to withstand the test of time. Virchow was one of these. As though working a loom with a beautiful but blemished tapestry, he took his place on the stool, shuttled and blended his own magnificent patterns into the piece. His work removed the flaws of others. While doing so, he cultivated the minds of those who would take his place on the stool, some of whom would even correct flaws in Virchow's work – their total work culminated in the sturdy fabric of today's medicine.

Not all of his assistants fortified a place in history with their discoveries alone. One of his assistants, Ernst Haeckel, renowned himself not only by his work but also by eventually pitting himself against his respected but feared mentor during the years of the dawning Darwinian beliefs.

Proficient in Latin, Greek, Hebrew, Arabic, English, French, Italian and Dutch, Rudolf kept abreast of discoveries in other countries. He then applied the discoveries of others to his work. If his research advanced due to the application of another's work, he wrote about it giving credit where credit was due; if it proved another's work to be in error, he wrote about it.

Rudolf Virchow

During the nineteenth century, monumental biological discoveries regarding life itself made print; specifically the locus of life or the point of life in the body. Throughout the centuries, religious beliefs blanketed, blinded and handcuffed medicine. Doctors fought and often lost the battle with well-meaning priests who tended to parishioner's spiritual as well as medical needs. Virchow made no secret that he despised the Catholic Church's influence in particular. It would be his stance throughout his life, one that would eventually be the one and only grounds for agreement with Otto Bismarck, a man who represented all that Virchow passionately despised. From this singular alliance between these two sworn enemies against the church, Virchow derived another word to describe the conflict, a word that remains to this day: *Kulturkampf*, meaning "culture struggle."

In 1838, German botanist Matthias Schleiden was the first to bring light to the rational or mechanical (not spiritual) question of life. He loosened the grip of the church on medicine when he discovered that all plants were composed of cells. Next Theodor Schwann further freed medicine one year later with his discovery that all animals were composed of cells. With the undeniable fact of the cellular composition of living creatures established, it would take another fifteen years before superstition and religious dogma felt the nudge of their removal from medicine.

A prolific writer, Virchow published an article in Archiv, Volume III in 1855 built upon the foundation previously set by Frenchman, Louis Pasteur. In his article, Virchow's most profound and famous axiom appeared for the first time. It destroyed the basis of humoural medicine, pioneered cancer research and treatment and permanently opened the door to disentangle medicine from the church: *Omnis cellula a cellula* – cells arise from cells. Simply stated, life arises from life.

For centuries the church was convinced that illness and diseases sprang from sinful behavior and used those beliefs to maintain control over the population. The church maintained that crop failures and resultant poor health of a village were evidence of sinful thoughts and behavior. The more widespread the disease, the harder the priests thumped their message of damnation which justified withholding life sustaining necessities. In proof, they said, those in good health and wealth obviously lived a good Christian life. Virchow proved for the first time that cells did not spontaneously generate from poisonous air to grow warts, muscle tissue did not sprout worms from unclean thoughts, and tumors did not grow from sins. Wart cells grew warts, pus was a byproduct of inflammation, worms in muscles grew from other worms, and tumors arose from other tumor cells. Whether it was healthy tissue or unhealthy tissue - where a cell exists a cell *must have preceded* that cell, and one generation of cells led to the next. Four simple words revolutionized medicine and became known as the Law of Biology or simply, Virchow's Law.

As the medical world reeled, Virchow's name was uttered in every continent. While he intently followed published reactions to his discovery, his hours spent with his family were quiet and loving. Rudolf and Rose had a baby girl, Adele, on October 1, 1855. Virchow was a devoted father to his three children and loving husband to their mother. At no time in his life did he seek riches, status or fame. These germinated from the rich soil of his intelligence fertilized by his passion and his enlightening discoveries.

Despite her husband's devotion, seaside vacations, climbing mountains with her husband and children and visits from her family, Rose's health and spirits in Würzburg grew weaker and weaker with each passing year. In 1856, as the faculty of Charité mourned the death of Professor H. Meckel von Hemsbach, his passing was an event that would change the lives of Virchow, Rose and their children.

Leslie Dunn

KING'S PERMISSION TO RETURN TO BERLIN

Throughout Rudolf's years in Würzburg, the professors in Berlin at Charité were aware of Rudolf's burgeoning fame, that his had become the final word in the field of pathologic anatomy. Although not permitted to visit Berlin by order of the King, Virchow's publications reached his colleagues desks at Charité and they sometimes referred cases to him. Johannes Müller boldly requested of Charité that Virchow replace the recently-deceased Professor Hemsbach. Indeed, it was Müller's intention that Virchow replace Müller teaching pathologic anatomy.

The King's belief in his counter-effect after the revolution and the silencing of its participants was so complete that neither the King nor Bismarck viewed Virchow as a threat. Royal permission was sought and given. Virchow could return to Berlin. As if to highlight the king's belief in Virchow's subjugation, the king asked no political conditions of Virchow. The king grossly underestimated the courage, energy and now powerfully influential and famous former revolutionary.

Before he left Würzburg, medical students again paraded and sang for Virchow. Under his tutelage, the number of students had grown from ninety-eight to almost four hundred. Nikolaus Friedreich, who abandoned clinical medicine to study pathology under Virchow, succeeded Rudolf.

Rudolf and Rose were going home.

One to capitalize on a situation, Virchow provisionally accepted the position at Charité. As part of his agreement to return, he requested that Charité construct a new Institute of Pathology. Charité complied. It speaks volumes of his character that Virchow asked for separate areas for mourners of his autopsy patients and lodging for his experimental animals. It speaks highly, too, of Charité that Charité complied. He also asked for a Department of Chemistry in connection with his Pathological Institute. Charité complied.

With all his conditions met by the famous and caring Charité, on October 6, 1856, Rudolf, Rose, Carl, Hans and Adele left Würzburg for Berlin. Shortly before their departure, his father received the following letter:

Würzburg

Friday, September 26, 1856

Dear Father:

We returned from Brückenau about ten days ago. The baths suited us very much, the children especially, whereas Röschen has still not lost her headache and weakness. On October 6, we intend to leave for Berlin. I have hired two big coaches for transporting the luggage, so that we can take along almost everything. This is really a bitter business, since freight and packing, which the coach-master handles entirely, costs 500 florins: But the railroad would not have cost much less, and in addition I would have had a host of troubles. In Berlin we will be living at first with the Mayers, since our future home (Leipziger Platz 13) has yet to be furnished. If I can spare the time, I also plan first to attend the centennial celebration of the Greifswald University. Setting up the new institute of pathology will take up so much of my time also that I will hardly be able to begin my lectures before the start of November.

There you have my plan of action for the immediate future. But you must write to us once again, so that we do not have to leave here in uncertainty as to your state of affairs.

You will also no doubt remember that the first birthday of your granddaughter is very close, and although you do not yet know her great charm by sight, her sex will beguile you into not forgetting your great and heartfelt gallantry toward her. I am really very sorry that you cannot see her now. She is the most cheerful and lively of our children, so sturdy and plump that it is a great delight. Her head is indeed still very bald, but then you see its beautiful form all the better, and I expect that unless some great changes take place she will one day be a very pretty girl. She already stands very well, sits down and gets up, has her own language and gestures, behaves very sensibly toward strangers, in short she is worth seeing. She has almost learned to walk here in her hometown or, better, the town of her birth.

And now a fond farewell, and let us hear some good news. Röschen and the children send you warm greetings. Give my best regards to Mother.

Rudolf Virchow

Your loyal son,
Rudolf

After settling in the children and his ecstatic wife, Virchow oversaw construction of his new institute and by the end of the year 1856, eight years after brandishing a pistol on behalf of the working poor, Virchow opened the doors of the brand new Pathological Institute that still stands today. Its initiator would remain director until his death forty-six years later.

In this climate of burgeoning medical discoveries, chains of events link up apparent disparate activities. As hammers, chisels and dynamite blasted away at the Rhine Valley for building railroads and later limestone extraction, an accidental excavation occurred that would soon have the attention of the world. As a leading anatomist in the world, one who had published a great deal on the subject of skulls, Virchow was the natural choice to study a skull discovered in the Feldhof Cave in Hundsklipp valley, also known as Neanderthal Valley. Due to his expertise, Virchow was the first to study the Neanderthal skull.

Virchow stated: "The skull has a deep suture between the low vault and the upper edge of the orbits. Such a suture is found only in apes, not in man. Thus, the skull must belong to an ape." This opinion provided the impetus that, his assistant, Haeckel, would one day use to grandstand against Virchow in defense of Darwin.

After his return to Charité, it wasn't long before Rudolf realized something unhealthy was transpiring with the syphilis patients. Venereal diseases spread rampantly among the overcrowded, poor population. The barbaric treatments based on the still popular humoural medicine ended the suffering of many in a most unfortunate manner. The third floor of Charité housed syphilis patients in a room known as the 'Salvation Parlor.' Hermetically sealed rooms, impossible to open from inside, were heated in the belief that profuse sweating flushed out the syphilis. To enhance the treatment, patients were given mercury which induced salivation.

Felix von Baerensprung, director of the syphilis ward, mercifully determined that mercury was harmful to the patients. He devised a diet, instead.

Reviewing his statistics on causes of death, Virchow noted over the months an increasing number of syphilis patients among the dead. He made an appointment to speak to Director von Baerensprung personally.

"Come in, come in," von Baerensprung said jovially to his famous colleague. The aristocrat, much like Virchow's old nemesis Donner, felt obliged to recognize Virchow only on Virchow's merits. "To what do I owe this honor?"

Virchow said bluntly, "An increasing number of your patients are dying."

Clearing his throat, von Baerensprung pulled charts together and stacked them in a neat pile on his desk. "That is not at all true, Herr Virchow, and I strongly protest your belief."

"It is not my belief, Herr Baerensprung." Rudolf opened the file he held in his hand, turned it facing the direction of Baerensprung and sat back in his chair and waited.

Without even a glance at the file, Baerensprung asked, "What is it?"

"It's the past two months of total cases I've autopsied with separate columns for each cause of death. If you will turn to the next page, you will see the number of syphilis cases over the past two years from my predecessor. In the last month alone, we are nearly half of the previous year's total."

"I don't need to look at your papers," von Baerensprung blurted. "Since I've ordered the withdrawal of mercury treatments and instituted a new diet..."

"A new diet?" Virchow asked with consternation.

"Ja. And it's working," he said defensively. "We see fewer and fewer patients returning with recurrent episodes of acute syphilis."

Virchow removed his glasses, closed his eyes for a moment and rubbed them. "Herr Baerensprung," he said as he felt his temper rise, "would you please do me the professional courtesy of describing your new diet?"

Baerensprung spread his thick fingers on the blotter covering his desk, stared at Virchow for a moment, then started to tap his fingers. "I've ordered a well balanced diet," he answered vaguely.

"That includes...?" prodded Rudolf.

"Meat, potatoes, vegetables and so on. I don't need to explain a well balanced diet to you, good doctor."

"Is there more?" Rudolf felt himself becoming exasperated. So far, nothing made sense.

"After a period of a well balanced diet, the patients are then fasted."

Rudolf's paused. "How long are they fasted and what do they receive during these periods of fasting?"

"During their period of fasting," Baerensprung said with a bit of pride, "they are given plenty of clear water and ample amounts of sarsaparilla tea." He clasped his hands together, his rings flashed. "I, too, keep logs, Dr. Virchow and since instituting my new diet plan, my records indicate a lower recurrence rate. The diet is a successful treatment," he finished.

"It is true," Virchow's voice lowered as he put his glasses back on and pushed them up his nose, "that recurrences are less common because instead of going to the clinic your starved patients are turning up at the autopsy table."

Virchow's arrow reached it mark.

Baerensprung's chin lowered. He growled, "I ask that you now leave, Dr. Virchow."

His pride sorely wounded by Virchow's remarks, Baerensprung decided on another course of action to help his patients. Perhaps from this encounter he also initiated research to prove his expertise in his field. Without obtaining consent from a female gonorrhea patient or even informing her of his deed, Baerensprung injected her with material from a first stage syphilis chancre. She inevitably showed signs of syphilis. Baerensprung again repeated his experiment on an eighteen year old woman, this time from a second stage chancre. When she, too, effected syphilis symptoms, Baerensprung took credit for proving that syphilis was infectious in both its first and second stages. He rationalized that due to the lifestyle of the two women, they were candidates for contracting syphilis anyway.

243

Rudolf Virchow

Baerensprung's experiments led to enduring, uncompromising disputes with Virchow. Virchow's heart remained steadfast to those without a voice. From this experience Virchow began advocating for patient Informed Consent, today a routine practice.

Nine months after Virchow's return to Berlin one of Charité's greatest teachers died - Johannes Müller, age fifty-six, reportedly by his own hand. Had he advocated for Virchow to replace him, that he could 'take his leave' knowing his position was in Rudolf's competent hands?

His death was an indescribable loss to Charité and to his students. Müller's enthusiastic teaching, insistence on the practice of scientific method and profound knowledge of the human body empowered Virchow to all he later aspired. Of Müller, Virchow wrote: "The worship of nature, which was his vocation, united his pupils just as in a religious community. Müller was the University of Berlin's greatest instructor."

Less than six months later Rudolf received a belated letter from his father about the death of Rudolf's beloved mother. Although one is not impressed with his anguish in the following letter to his father, through records of his relationship with his mother one can guess Virchow's struggle to control his anguish, remain calm and convey his concern for his bereaved parent.

Berlin
Tuesday, December 22, 1857

My dear Father,

244

My birthday greetings to you come this time in sad company. Every day there were hindrances that still held me up, and now what sad news! I found your letter this afternoon when I returned from the Charité. Since the burial is to take place tomorrow at 9 a.m., it will be impossible for me to arrive so early, and now, after the event, I can do nothing at all for Mother. How sad I am now for not having brought her here earlier! Perhaps she could still have been helped if she, as you say, had been moaning for quite some time. I do not yet fully understand how she died, and you would be doing me a special favor by letting me know what she actually complained of -- whether the abdomen, chest or head, whether she sffered from cough, cough, vomiting, giddiness or whatever. Of course, all this is of no use to her now, but it gives some comfort to know how her death came about. When we were with you, she had complaints only about her abdomen, which in themselves were really not threatening, and news of her death was certainly the last thing I expected.

Now more sincerely than ever I wish you good health and a long life; may everything go well with you and may you feel happier in your lonely home than has hitherto been the case. But may you also consider how quickly death approaches man and breaks off his long-spun plans! You have many difficulties before you. You will have to weigh them seriously, and decide whether you will and can overcome them at once, or whether you should restrict the circle of your affairs and economize on your means, as I and the deceased have long wished. May a peaceful and cheerful spirit be with you and give you clear judgment at the right time! Yes, I cannot help also adding the wish, which agrees with my depressed mood perhaps more than with clear anticipation, that you may be spared further heavy blows of misfortune; may a slow decline of the farm, which now you alone have to manage, may a gradual decay of the house, which you alone have to look after, or a disposal of your possessions to strangers, not be the next thing to take place!

I have no wish more urgent than that we understand each other, that we live together and in peace. I will be too glad to open my house to you, if you wish to live here! It will be very sad for you now over the holidays. How would it be if you closed your house and spent Christmas with us? Of course, it will be a quiet holiday, but the children ought not to be deprived of their joy and you also will find some pleasure thereby. Come any time you wish and you will be welcome. The distance is now short, the expense light and you can, if you so desire, soon return.

Or do you want me to come to you? I would prefer not to leave Röschen, who is very anxious and has been awaiting her delivery with gloomy thoughts. (She was pregnant with their fourth child, Ernst.) There is also no other wish that I would like to realize personally in Schivelbein than to see to the raising of a dignified tombstone for Mother. I would like that if the children should later visit Schivelbein they could easily find where their grandmother is buried and remember it because of its impressive outward appearance. I would most prefer a polished granite plate that would cover the whole of the grave and have her name engraved on it. Or do you have a different plan? It will also be necessary to maintain the tomb as long as possible to ensure that within living memory her grave is not turned up and destroyed.

If you want me to come to you to talk over such matters or perhaps for other purposes, I will gladly join you between Christmas and the New Year. Of course I cannot stay away long, but I put my time at your disposal.

And now I send you my warm greetings and may things go well with you. With us everything is fairly cheerful at the moment and with better weather the children will probably thrive. Greetings and kisses from everyone. Reply soon to

Your much loving son,

Rudolf

His mother's death saddened his Christmas of 1857, especially after the recent loss of his most beloved instructor Müller. Time off for the holidays allowed him time to grieve. When he returned to work in January 1858, it was with renewed vigor for the wheels he set spinning in 1856 with the publication of his work on cells. While others continued research based on centuries of mythical medicine and sought inanimate causes of human ailments, Virchow successfully cultivated organisms, sifted through possibilities against his platform and found cures, causes and effects that did not occur to others simply because they continued to follow ancient myths.

During the months of February, March and April 1858, Rudolf held a twenty lecture course devoted to cellular pathology and, based on the series, published his revolutionary book, *Die Celluarpathologie in ihrer Begrundiung auf physiologische und pathologische Gewebelehre* (Cellular Pathology Based on Physiological and Pathological Histology). In the first chapter, in addition to the new fact that all living things are made up of one or more cells, Virchow stated his two tenets for which he is now famous: All cells arise from cells and the cell is the base unit of all living organisms; and that all life is bound to cells. In other words, the cell is not only the vessel of life but the living part itself. His other chapters covered: normal tissues, diseased tissues, nutrition, vascular systems, pyemia, infection and metastasis, his views of dyscrasias, peripheral nervous system, brain and spinal cord and finally Life of the Elements: Their Activity and Irritability. Words published over the years in his frequent articles were brought together under one cover – thrombosis, embolism, leukemia, fatty metamorphosis, hyperplasia, neuroglia (nerve glue) – medical terms created and defined by Virchow.

In 1859, one of the benefits to mankind that Virchow's cellular discovery first led to was the lowly worm, specifically ones that infested human beings, dogs and other mammals: *Trichinella spiralis*.

In England 1833, John Hilton of Guy's Hospital in London described what is believed to be the most complete first description of worm-infested muscle. Two years later, the hard as bone, cyst-like bodies of the worms blunted the scalpel blade of James Paget. After microscopically viewing the worms, Paget's became the first published account of the 'minute whitish specks' which set off rounds of reported cases as well as extensive research.

Until Paget's discovery, the nematode parasite, *Trichinella spiralis,* was "...heretofore considered as peculiar to the human species," wrote an American doctor, Joseph Leidy, in 1846 after studying a slice of mealtime pork. Symptoms associated with Trichinella include fever, nausea, vomiting and diarrhea at the early stages. In later stages, the worm larva migrate throughout the body resulting in pneumonia, encephalitis, myocarditis (heart muscle inflammation), deafness, eye damage and kidney inflammation. It must be noted that at the time, meat infiltrated with the white cysts was considered normal.

That humans self-infested themselves by eating raw pork proved a groundbreaking discovery. How to stop that unfortunate process fell into Virchow's domain. Such that the deadly issue affected millions spurred Virchow to tackle it with top priority.

After feeding an experimental dog fresh muscle tissue riddled with white flecks of Trichinella spiralis, the dog died within days. Upon autopsy, Rudolf observed the worm in the tissues of the unfortunate canine's small intestine confirming Rudolf's belief that the worm traveled beyond the stomach and infiltrated itself into the body. At this point, he wasn't sure exactly how, only sure that it did. He next discovered that heating meat to 137° or greater killed the worms.

With this discovery, Rudolf literally set out to the streets of Berlin. His conviction that his role as a doctor obliged him to pass on important health information to the public could not wait. His book on the subject would not be published until four years later.

He informed people of the danger, particularly in light of the German fondness for Rawfleish – raw meat – as well as the simple solution to make the meat safe by proper heating. What Rudolf lacked in stature he more than compensated for with chutzpah. Not all the public appreciated his message.

Public notices were posted on poles and building around Berlin: *Rudolf Virchow, Director Pathological Anatomy and Physician of Charité to speak on the Importance of Not Eating Raw Meat, Sunday, 2 o'clock, Linden Street Park.*

Rose sat in the shade nearby while their children played on the swings and slides. It was a perfect summer day except for the stench of human waste that no Berliner could escape. Even the children commented on the disgusting odor. The summer heat cooked the brine of waste making it impossible not to notice. Berlin's population had grown considerably during their six years away. Even though the city regularly flushed the gutters, the foul, almost palpable stench of human waste filled the air.

This was the fourth Sunday Rudolf spoke to the citizens. Rose noted that each Sunday the crowd increased in size. One man in particular, though, attended each meeting and heckled Rudolf. Rose frowned when she spotted him positioned dead center in front of her husband. So far, Rudolf's verbal jousting with him provided stimulating tension but the man would not go away.

Rudolf found out through friends that the man, Herr Borgman, was a veterinarian and a member of the German Veterinarian's Society. Borgman took Rudolf's warning personal. It's admirable to confer to the people scientific advancements but quite another to point the finger at fine German swine as the source of a disease outbreak. From hog growers to markets to the professionals who specialized in animals, pigs represented income to a number of Berlin citizens. Virchow threatened their livelihood.

Rudolf rubbed his hands together, pleased to see that so many had come to hear his message. He squinted in the sunlight and glanced over at his children playing.

"Good day," he began. "My name is Dr. Rudolf Virchow and I'm a physician at Charité. I have some important news for all of you. After I'm done speaking, I will gladly answer any questions you may have."

"So you want all these people to stop eating pork?" The man interrupted Rudolf. He appeared startled when Rudolf smiled at him.

Rudolf had a surprise ready for him. "No, I'm not telling anyone to stop eating pork. I'm telling everyone to stop eating *raw* pork, Herr..."

"Borgman. Herr Borgman," the man said. "That's as good as saying to stop eating pork," the man argued. "What are we supposed to eat instead – potatoes?"

Someone near Schultz chuckled. Schultz turned in the chuckler's direction and nodding his head, chuckled, too.

Ignoring them, Rudolf bent down and picked up a small white package near his feet.

Rose smiled. Herr Borgman was about to get a good taste of Rudolf's medicine.

Holding the little package high, Rudolf announced to the crowd, "I hoped to see Herr Borgman today so I could give him a gift for his perfect attendance."

Rose recognized that sardonic smile. She covered her mouth with her hand and giggled. Nearby the children swung and climbed. A few in the crowd clapped for Rudolf's thoughtfulness.

Borgman did not smile but only stared at the doctor, the heckler momentarily silenced.

Lowering the package Rudolf continued, "Inside of this package is a piece of fresh, raw pork I brought *especially* for Herr Borgman."

"Ha!" the heckler found his tongue. "It's probably a piece of dog meat," he said. "Why would you bring me anything – you don't even know me."

Some in the crowd giggled. It was an unexpected drama in the middle of a Sunday lecture.

"You are correct, my friend, I do not know you but I do know that you are fond of pork, Herr Borgman, and so I brought you this large piece of *fresh* pork," Rudolf said. He slowly unwrapped one side of the package, turned the lump in his hand and unwrapped the other side. He folded down the pieces of paper so that the red chunk of meat was clearly visible to the crowd. He lifted his arm above his head displaying the piece of meat. Then he looked up at the meat he held aloft, looked with a puzzled expression at the crowd, then looked again at the meat. Slowly, deliberately, he lowered the pork, brought it near his face and inspected it. He glanced at the crowd who by now had forgotten Herr Borgman.

Drawing his face into a sour expression and making a sound in his throat as though gagging he extended his arm toward the direction of Herr Schultz. He smiled a wry, wicked smile. "Herr Borgman, I must apologize...."

Borgman gulped, his eyes opened wide. It looked as though Rose suspected that he regretted pitting himself against Dr. Virchow.

Rudolf continued, "I see flecks of white throughout this otherwise delicious appearing slice of pork and I apologize for the worms. But not to worry, good sir. For weeks you have been telling me that I am wrong - I invite you to join me on stage for a bite."

The amused crowd's chant, "Esse, esse, esse" (eat, eat, eat) grew louder and louder.

"I'll join you but only if you take the first bite, Dr. Virchow. It would be only fair."

"What? Partake of a gift I brought for you?"

The crowd continued its chant, "Esse, esse..."

The man growled, "Nein!"

The crowd cheered.

Rudolf saw his wife applaud.

With this and months of public lectures, demonstrations, articles and posters, the public learned what, is today common knowledge, how to properly prepare meat to kill potential and inspection of the meat is mandatory for public safety.

CLASH OF THE TITANS: VIRCHOW AND BISMARCK

It wasn't long before Rose had yet another reason to be proud of her husband. An old friend of Rudolf's, Dr. Salomon Neumann, suggested that Rudolf consider running for the city council. After a nine year hiatus from political activities, and now old enough to accept the election, thirty-eight year old Rudolf won. A year later, in 1860, in addition to being a city council member, he became the co-founder of the democratic German Progressive Party (Deutsche Fortschrittspartei), a robust member of the Council of Scientific Advisors to the Prussian Government and chosen into the Prussian Federal State Parliament. No longer militantly fighting against the government. He immersed himself in it.

A year after King Frederick William gave his blessings for Virchow's return to Berlin in 1856, the King's mental condition deteriorated into complete insanity. Some historians contend that the King suffered from an advanced case of cerebral arteriosclerosis (hardening of the arteries that lead to the brain). Either case - insanity or arteriosclerosis - rendered him incapable of making rational decisions. His brother, William, ruled as regent on Frederick's behalf from 1857 until Frederick's death in 1861.

King William, armed with a stronger military awareness than his dethroned brother, set about appointing a more liberal ministry that held no appeal for Bismarck and, in fact, dismayed him. The liberal ministry meant close cooperation with Austria – a most repellent course of action for Bismarck.

The new King found insufficient grounds to dismiss the reactionary Bismarck. Augusta, William's wife, detested Bismarck and for a while Bismarck feared that his career was ended. Instead, Bismarck was made Prussian minister to distant St. Petersburg and early in 1859, the Bismarck's left Frankfurt for their new post.

In St. Petersburg he was, in his own words, "Put on ice." Gone were the days of successful lobbying against Austria, rubbing elbows with the refined and elite in Frankfurt, endless cigar smoking and swimming in the Rhine. As no railroad yet existed from St. Petersburg, the five day trip to Berlin sufficiently stranded and frustrated Bismarck. His pay suffered, also, as the St. Petersburg diplomat received the lowest salary of all the diplomatic representatives. Subsequently, the family endured a dramatic reduction in their lifestyle and social status.

Bismarck soon found to his liking the Russian diplomats, though, and he learned their language. The Russian's arrogant nature appealed to him and he made such a good impression on them that Alexander II offered him a post in the Russian diplomatic service. However, Bismarck's loyalties remained with Prussia. With an eye on the neighboring country of Poland, Bismarck knew an alliance between Russia and Prussia would secure Poland to Prussia. The root of all his maneuvering remained his anti-Austria stand. It was, after all, no problem for him to create alliances with foreign countries; just not within his own.

Volatile politics in Europe challenged the early years of King William's regency. Despite he and his wife's misgivings concerning Bismarck, whom William secretly feared, the King summoned the man to return to Berlin. Anointed King in January 1861, William guardedly appreciated that conniving Bismarck would boldly oppose the deadlock of his Chamber. For three years the Chamber fought among themselves regarding the army, its role and budget. King William knew nothing of the military and preferred it that way. William offered Bismarck the position of Prime Minister.

Bismarck appeared in Berlin and offered his solution to end the Chamber's impasse – unconstitutional rule without a budget act. But he presented the king with an unacceptable demand in accepting the position as Prime Minister. A free hand in foreign policy. Bismarck desired an alliance with France and Russia and opposition to Austria. King William refused to consider an alliance with France and responded to Bismarck's demands by dismissing him back to St. Petersburg.

As European uprisings intensified, the King relented to a degree and moved Bismarck closer to him. He appointed Bismarck Prussian Minister to Paris. Misinterpreting the move, Bismarck aligned himself as deputizing a Russian-French alliance. The king immediately trumped Bismarck's actions.

With the Chamber still remaining at odds, the nearly fifty-year old Bismarck knew he had only to bide his time until the King relented and agreed to Bismarck's terms. "I shall declare war on

Austria, dissolve the German confederation, subjugate the middle and smaller states and give Germany national unity under the control of Prussia," he asserted.

Unable to persuade the Chamber to resolve their dispute but determined that relinquishing total foreign policy to the feckless hand of Bismarck was not a reasonable solution, the King prepared two letters, one of which was a bluff. He prepared a statement to be read to Bismarck outlining the King's demands and a dupe letter of abdication.

He summoned Bismarck to him. Before the King could read his letters to Bismarck, Bismarck silenced the desperate King with his *own* interpretation of the situation and *his* intended course of action: Royal government or the supremacy of parliament. Bismarck would bring the former to victory.

That the king tore up his own letters of abdication and his unread statement, then overrode both his and his wife's apprehension about the man is a tribute to Bismarck's presentation, stateliness and gift of persuasion. After convincing the King that in the event that the two disagreed Bismarck would submit his will to that of the King's, the King announced Bismarck the new Prime Minister.

Bismarck would see to it, though, that the King reflected Bismarck's will.

Bismarck ended the stalemate of the Chamber – the deputies were sent home for a recess. In a committee meeting, Bismarck set the mood of his regime and earned him the nickname by which he has been known throughout history: *"The great questions of the time will be decided, not by speeches and resolutions of majorities* (that was the mistake of 1848 and 1849) *but by iron and blood."* With these words, the name Iron Chancellor was forged.

When the King read of 'iron and blood' in the newspaper, certain of his wife's apprehension about the new prime minister he dashed from Baden-Baden to Berlin to revoke Bismarck's new position.

Wiley Bismarck tried to convince the king that it was to royalty he referred with the words 'iron and blood,' and not to fighting. Unconvinced, the king lamented where Bismarck's attitude could lead them – to the gallows.

Bismarck skillfully appealed to the king's majestic dignity. "Better that than surrender."

Then the king, according to Bismarck's account, puffed himself up like an officer responding to the command of a superior and the issue was settled.

It was inevitable that the two outspoken and powerful men, Virchow and Bismarck, would clash. Virchow embodied all that Bismarck detested – a liberal, well educated physician who, worse, had a tongue that could slice an opponent in half. Virchow detested Bismarck's disregard for his countrymen's individual welfare and represented a threat to Virchow's dreams of common wealth for all.

From his role in the democratic German Progress Party that he co-founded, Virchow commenced the fight of the constitutional forces against Bismarck.

Virchow submitted an address to the King that was deliberated at the 1863 session. He appealed to the king against the government's unconstitutional stance, and persecution of the opposition that rendered ineffective Prussia's promotion of German unity. Bismarck trounced Virchow with his response that conflicts were questions of power and the one with the power uses it. After Virchow and most of the house learned through foreign newspapers of one of Bismarck's military maneuvers, Virchow appealed to the King as to the unconstitutionality of Bismarck's deed, again raising the ire of Iron Chancellor. Bismarck accused Virchow of possessing more insolence than fact. Virchow responded with an opinion as to the grade level of Bismarck's speeches.

Virchow demanded smaller expenditures for the military and advocated for the development of public social welfare. As Bismarck's military actions grew more and more bold, Virchow sounded an alarm with strong warnings against Bismarck's political disarray and his opinion of the evil nature of his opponent:

"The king must be informed of the imminent danger. The minister present has within a comparatively short time adopted so many different standpoints...that nobody can define his policy. He is speeding without a compass into the sea of foreign complications...; he has no guiding principle;... no understanding for the essence of our nation, for what issues from the heart of the people...He is given over to the evil one from those whose clutches he will never escape..."

To which Bismarck responded:

Rudolf Virchow

"Virchow might be a famous anatomist but the honorable member charges me with a lack of understanding of national politics. To me it seems that the honorable member has no understanding of politics of any kind."

This to a man exiled from Berlin due to his political stand.

In 1863, Rudolf gained advantages in his corner: brother-in-law Karl Theodor Seydel was elected mayor of Berlin and Dr. Paul Langerhans, Sr., President of Council.

While skirmishing with military matters, Virchow began work to improve the citizen's living conditions. His target: Public health. His weapon: A quiver full of politically influential friends.

Virchow's summarized his findings about trichinosis in a book published in 1863 and began a vigorous campaign for meat inspection. Outbreaks were so rampant that at he ordered mandatory 'trichinoscopy' which was micro-inspection of every pig carcass sold in the marketplace as even the tiniest portion of infected meat contained lethal doses of trichinellae.

"It is possible to find thousands, even hundreds of thousands, of larvae per gram of infected meat. As a first course, the meat must not be in the market. As a second course, should the meat bypass the inspectors, all citizens whose intention is remain free of the worm shall properly heat the meat so that after appetizer and wine, as a third course the unhealthy meat is not consumed."

Strict fines, even prison sentences, were handed out to offenders. In a little German village nineteen percent of the villagers contracted Trichinella spiralis and of those, one in four died. The unscrupulous village butcher recognized the tainted pork but blended it with healthy appearing meat. He made this confession upon his deathbed after he had inadvertently consumed some of his blended meat.

Virchow also began to deal with the atrocious sewerage system in Berlin as well as school hygiene, the latter beginning his first political conflict with the church.

Although Virchow's accomplishments were far from over and his spurring with Bismarck increased in intensity, his father would never learn of their outcome. Rudolf lost his eighty year old father in 1865.

Virchow and Bismarck crossed swords often enough that around each swirled his own supporters. Bismarck implemented military reforms and declared that Prussia would use its military force for achieving national unification, at Austria's expense. A war broke out between Prussia and Denmark. The outcome of that war determined, by the Convention of Gastein, that Prussia would govern Schleswig and that Austria would govern Holstein. As an outcome to this outcome, however, was Bismarck's dogged negotiations with Austria to give up dominance in Germany. As snarling an opponent as he represented, though, Bismarck was not a warmonger. Despite his antagonistic feelings toward Austria, only since becoming Prime Minister did he truly desire unification of Germany.

In 1865, the chamber unbelievably still had not changed its views concerning the military budget. During the session's discussion about the naval budget, Virchow publicly confronted Bismarck concerning what Virchow believed were lies uttered by

Bismarck. The enraged Bismarck challenged Virchow to a duel. As the one challenged, Virchow had his choice of weapons.

Two versions of the outcome have filtered through time.

In one, Virchow accepts the duel with the condition that it be fought with inspected and uninspected sausages as weapons, and he offered Bismarck the first choice of weapon. The second version also has Virchow accepting Bismarck's challenge but the weapons of choice - scalpels.

That Bismarck challenged Virchow to a duel is fact. That Virchow wisely deflected the opportunity is fact. How Virchow managed to do so remains under debate.

Bismarck's campaign to intimidate the opposition intensified after this, even imprisoning members for statements he deemed 'treasonable.'

Virchow retaliated: *"It is clear that absolutism has been reestablished in Prussia...There is no control of public finances, no budget law anymore; instead of laws, we have decrees; the control court is without subject; treasury and property of the state are at the free disposal of the government."*

Although Bismarck's efforts to silence the opposition were not successful, his influential links to powerful foreign policy makers, especially France, were. For fear of France's repercussions, the German liberals toned down. The lifestyle of the bourgeoisie had improved through Bismarck's successful trading with France. Even though Bismarck's interests conflicted with the working class, because the German people danced with this devil, Virchow and others dared no longer to depend on the support of the bourgeoisie to go against Bismarck.

Leslie Dunn

In 1866, after a war lasting only a month, Bismarck's Prussia defeated Austria at Sadova, known in Germany as Königgrätz. From 1866 until the end of his political life, Virchow represented only a small group of unswayed bourgeoisie.

As had happened with the excavations caused by the railroads at Neanderthal Valley, prehistoric discoveries in Scandinavia, France and Switzerland filled the news and seized Virchow's interest. He conquered the living cell and for years studied those on whom death recently descended. His previous studies of skulls naturally enticed him to the field of archeology.

In 1865, his first fortunate discovery was at a lake near the city of his birth. At Lake Luebtow in Pomerania, he discovered ancient pile dwellings. Carefully studying the wave pattern of pictures on the pottery he found he showed these to be Slavic, not Germanic, in origin, and became one of the first to date ancient remains by pottery. Within a few years, this new interest of Rudolf's would play a major role in his life adding a third persona to this vibrant man – doctor, politician and now archeologist.

A year later, forty-five year old Virchow and thirty-five year old Rose had their fifth child, a daughter they named Marie. Carl was now fifteen years old, Hans fourteen, Adele eleven and Ernst eight. Their sixth and last child, Hanna, would be born in 1873, three years after the outbreak of the war which would activate her forty-nine year old patriotic father as well as two of her brothers. Before the war, though, Berlin faced a dilemma brought on by the human condition that mushroomed into a total health crisis.

Rudolf Virchow

No Berliner could escape the effect of sewerage. The number of cases of filth-related diseases continued to rise at Charité, infants were dying and citizens complained relentlessly to the city council about the putrid smell in the streets.

Since 1812, gutters formed the repository for rainwater, kitchen waste, and fecal matter. The gutters, one and a half feet wide by two feet deep were positioned between the sidewalk and the street and flowed into cesspools. Gutter contents were shoveled into oxcarts then emptied into dung pits. After a torrential rain, feces washed onto the streets. None of the collecting system – gutters or dung pits – was sealed causing the ground water to contaminate the wells from which citizens collected water. Diseases and death flowed from the foul water.

In 1862, a water treatment facility was built and flushing of the gutters was approved as well as the introduction of the toilet. Despite these advances, the problem of removing waste from the ever growing population remained unresolved.

After investigating the sewerage system of Hamburg, Paris and London, in 1867 the City Council was presented with a working plan to remove the cesspools, eliminate gutters, avoid water contamination within the city and prevent flooding of the streets. However, the plan directed the untreated sewerage into the Spree River. The City Council wisely abandoned the plan.

Virchow's background in studying health-related issues for the masses and his penchant for detailed solutions, as well as his influential standing on the Council made him the delegations choice to lead a special bureau. Applying the scientific method, Virchow first observed the problem, dissected it into individual

264

components, studied each component, and with the help of other professionals, made recommendations. In a comprehensive spirit, Virchow included the sewerage system of inner city schools as well as two new hospitals, the latter for which he designed the architectural blueprints. Five years after being selected to manage the problem, in late 1872, Virchow submitted to the Council a summary of his recommendations.

In May 1873, construction of the new sewers began. According to Virchow's architectural schemata the city would be divided into grids, each with an independent drainage area and canal system. By dividing the city in this manner, should one of the canals fail the others would continue to function. Drains consisting of glazed ceramic pipes would direct the steam-powered sewerage to the Rieselfelder (Riesel fields) outside the city. He devised emergency outlets in case of heavy rainfall. In the Rieselfelder, the sewerage was purified through the soil and used as manure.

After completion of the work, Virchow wrote, *"Thus Berlin has become not only one of the cleanest and most beautiful cities, but also one of the healthiest."*

Since its conception with his deceased friend, Benno Reinhardt, *Virchow Archiv* continued to thrive through the years. By 1869, Virchow helped found the Collection of Popular Scientific Lectures to bring science to nonmedical people as well as the Periodical for Ethnology, both of which he would edit for the next thirty years. In 1869, also, he founded the German Anthropological Society as well as the Berlin Society of

Anthropology, Ethnology and Prehistory over which he presided until his death.

In 1870, again in Pomerania, Virchow expanded his archeological research and found bronze objects and fifteen hundred year old urns decorated with human faces, findings such as those found only in Etruia and Egypt. One artifact, an urn shaped like a house, captivated Virchow. Would the style of old homes, then, reveal an approximation of the home's age?

Also during the 1870's, driven by his interest in anthropology and in defense of Germany against Frenchman Armand de Quatrefage, Virchow conducted a study of over six million school children to determine Germany's race of origin. Teachers performed counts of the number of blonde haired, blue eyed children versus brown haired, brown eyed children.

Virchow determined that while various sections of Germany contained their own majority, there existed no overall predominance of one over the other. Less than one third of Germans were blonde with blue eyes, Jewish children were predominantly blonde and Prussian children were predominantly brunette with brown eyes. Germany's roots, he concluded, were a mixture of varying races with none of them constituting a master race.

Of note, this massive, inquisitive and informative study of Virchow's would later be used in propaganda against this great man and may explain why his name has become lost in time. After analyzing the results of his study of the children, Virchow called the concept of a master race "Nordic mysticism" yet years after his death, the most heinous man in history is said to have used Virchow's study for his evil plan to cleanse Germany of all but the Aryan race. In addition to his hideous deeds, he turned around the reputation of a man who lived his life, devoted great energy and sacrificed so much for the benefit of others.

Eight years later, in 1878, fifty-seven year old Virchow would meet someone unlike anyone else he'd ever known, someone with no connection to the medical field, someone whose distinct flair for exaggeration should have dismayed Virchow but instead charmed him. Virchow met Heinrich Schliemann.

Rudolf Virchow

VIRCHOW AND SCHLIEMANN

"Have you heard what is being said about you?" Schliemann asked Virchow in an amused tone as Schliemann twirled his black thick trademark moustache and pulled its points downward.

Virchow's pen hovered over the notebook in which he kept daily logs. "No. Who? What?" he asked made curious by the eccentric Schliemann's amusement.

They were sitting around a campfire. Just a couple months after first being introduced the year before, Schliemann and Virchow had done a successful archeological dig together in Hissarlik and now, in 1879, were excavating at Troy.

"The natives here ...they say the great Medicine Man has bestowed special healing powers into that spring from which you always draw your water." Schliemann wickedly arched an eyebrow. "So, great Medicine Man, what do you say to that?"

Virchow threw back his head and laughed. "It will make a great story to write home about." Virchow turned his head over his shoulder and called loudly to his twenty-seven year old son, "Hans, come here."

Heinrich Schliemann - archeologist, multilingual and never at a loss for self-advertising – nearly two years previous had approached Virchow with an urn decorated with a face. W. E. Gladstone learned that Virchow had unearthed a similar urn and directed Schliemann toward Virchow. Virchow's life would never be the same.

Heinrich Schliemann was born January 1822, three months after Rudolf. Their pasts were remarkably similar. Both were raised in tiny villages, reared in religious homes, excelled in school at an early age, fluent in multiple languages, and both had financially irresponsible fathers. Both were chosen to attend the prestigious Gymnasium in their respective cities, but while Rudolf's father successfully found ways to keep Rudolf in the Gymnasium, a scandal swirled around Schliemann's father that terminated his ability to continue payment for his brilliant son's education. Schliemann's father was a pastor accused of embezzling church funds. The financial whirlpool continued until Schliemann's father could no longer even support his son. At age fourteen, young Heinrich left home to fend for himself.

At his first job, Schliemann befriended a youth capable of reciting lines from Homer in ancient Greek. Two fires were lit in Heinrich – one for foreign languages and one for Greek mythology.

Rudolf Virchow

Nothing about Schliemann was vanilla bland. His was a spirit of excess. By the age of twenty, he taught himself six languages. His second job in a counting house beaconed the prospect of great earning. Utilizing his linguistic skills and powerful drive for wealth, at his third job he garnered outrageous success with a large import and export business.

In this business, he traveled throughout Europe but lived frugally spending nothing on extravagances, of which he considered women. He vowed his wealth would eventually get him any woman he desired.

When Schliemann was thirty years old, he acquired enough wealth to finally permit him to enjoy what money could buy. In Russia, he allowed himself a grand apartment, show quality horses and his own carriage, expensive wines – yet all the comforts intensified his misery.

His wealth finally got him 'any woman he desired' – Ekaterina Lishin, the attractive niece of a wealthy friend. Schliemann expected that within time, Ekaterina's desires for him would grow. Instead, the young woman's desire was to become a widow.

Returning his focus to earning money and away from his disastrous marriage, the boost to the family's income heated up his wife's passion and soon they had a child. The woman's passions were short-lived and it would be years before their second child.

To escape his miserable living conditions, Schliemann visited Greece for the first time. He was as enamored with the country as he had been with its language he'd heard as a youth.

Gloriously successful at no matter what business he focused his energies, Schliemann retired at age forty-one. He settled in Paris but his wife and children refused to join him.

He began the process of divorcing Ekaterina. During the divorce he began looking for her replacement but this time his wish list included more than good looks. The woman must be a poor, beautiful, dark haired, educated Greek. Within two months of meeting Sophia Engastromenos, divorced Schliemann had a new wife.

He also began his dream of unearthing ancient 'mythical' cities. Returning to Greece in 1868, he uncovered twenty ash-filled vases using nothing more than the ancient story of Homer as his guide. Schliemann's natural instincts as a businessmen transposed themselves into an instinct for archeology.

Believing the story of Troy to be a factual account, on faith alone Schliemann next set his sight on digging at Troy. His faith paid off. He unearthed seven cities, one built on top of another. Professional jealousy, the amateur!, fueled by Schliemann's self-aggrandizing and embellished publications of his findings brought him fame splattered with mockery. Some well deserved criticism included a regard more for showcasing his findings rather than cataloging the artifacts and leaving them in place for more detailed study.

It was nothing to which he would admit or even acknowledge, but Schliemann needed someone whose name equaled integrity, a name that would lend credibility by virtue of association. Once again smiled on by the gods, in 1878 Schliemann was led to Virchow.

271

Forming a team the two men traveled to Hissarlik in Greece in September. One month later, they amassed a small treasury of gold earrings, rings, bracelets and beads.

Although his association with Schliemann discredited Virchow's name in some circles, he maintained a loyal friendship and one year later the entire city of Berlin benefited. Schliemann donated his collections to the Berlin Museum of Ethnology. Without Virchow's influence the vast treasure collection would have been housed at England. For the next sixty-five years, this collection remained the largest and finest anthropological museum on earth. In 1881, Berlin made Schliemann an honorary citizen, an honor bestowed previously only on two men, Bismarck and Moltke.

Leslie Dunn

ANTHROPOLOGIST

From 1880 to 1893, Virchow served as a Liberal in the newly formed German Reichstag and in that role continued to vigorously oppose the policies of Otto Bismarck, German Chancellor and Prince.

Having established the Institute of Pathology, the construction of which was a condition of his return to Berlin, Virchow originally used it to house his pathological specimen collection that began early in his career. Late in his life, in 1899, he contributed and opened to the public his collection of almost twenty-one thousand specimens of both healthy and diseased anatomical specimens for the Pathological Museum in Berlin. (The Institute remains to this day with only 10% of the collection that survived the wars). If possible, the collection represented every conceivable illness and disease process, each specimen chosen and presented by Virchow.

Throughout these last years of his life, he would speak at International Congresses throughout the world, set policies and continue to be the counterbalance to new theories that threatened to overshadow the medical world before the new theories could be thoroughly tested and confirmed as fact – Darwinism, bacteriology. For these he has posthumously continued to be attacked. Regarding Darwinism, Virchow stated that should a sample be found confirming the existence of a creature he would most certainly become a believer. It was not that he was for or against Darwinism. What he was against was the time spent trying to prove or disprove a theory; time that he felt could be best spent moving forward proven medical advancements.

In 1882, Rudolf became the president of the Berlin Medical Society and wrote *Trojan Graves and Skulls*. A year later the Reichstag would pass the final draft of a bill that guaranteed health insurance to the working class and, as such, the earliest development of a comprehensive social welfare system in Germany.

In 1883 he was named a member of the board of Governors of the Roman-Germanic Central Museum in Mainz and remained on the board until his death in 1902. To Virchow, inaccessible knowledge was as useless as the accumulation and non-application of knowledge. As a member of this board, Rudolf regularly disseminated to the public results of his studies. Because of his influence, multiple disciplines – physical anthropology, zoology, botany, geology and chemistry – gained permanent places in the field of archeological research.

In 1886, Virchow influenced the building of the splendid Berlin Ethnological Museum.

In 1887, at age sixty-six, when most would slow down and enjoy the dawning of their twilight years, he began his own vigorous field studies of the different types of German houses. Because of the house urns he'd found seventeen years previous he believed that the house type would generate clues as to the earliest immigrants who settled Germany. Always one to enjoy a good hike, he followed the immigrants original trails and found the oldest standing wooden house in the German language area. The house was dated 1346 with Arabic numerals.

In 1888, Virchow established yet another museum – the Folklore Museum. Its aim was to present the cultural achievements of the German people as well as those of neighboring European countries which had been excluded until then. Since 1990 the vision of one common museum, a combination of both museums established by Virchow with a European emphasis, led to the establishment of the Museum of European Cultures on June 24, 1999. Millions today enjoy this legacy of Virchow.

His unconventional friend, Schliemann, died on December 26, 1890. At a tribute, Virchow stated that he "surveyed once more the life and work of the man whom he had 'recaptured for Germany.'" As intensely as the Germans disliked the man on whom they bequeathed citizenship, without Virchow's friendship with Schliemann there is a great probability that Schliemann's death may have passed unnoticed.

In 1892 Virchow received the Royal Society of London's prestigious Copley Medal award.

In 1893, nearly forty five years after being exiled from Berlin, the revolutionary turned reformer, most notorious doctor at

Rudolf Virchow

Charité was selected as Rector of the University of Berlin. A year later he lectured at the International Congress in Rome. Within the next seven years, he would lecture also at the International Congress in Moscow and Paris. Although offered the privileged honor of adding 'von' to his name, the farthest Rudolf would allow himself to be honored was as "Geheimrath," or Private Councilor. No matter how old he grew, Rudolf stayed close to his humble roots and believed that 'von' would distance him from the working class. Throughout his life, he stayed close to the middle class from which he sprang – of all his multitude of accomplishments his Working Men Association was the one of which he was most proud.

For Virchow's 80th birthday, international authorities such as Lord Lister, Stokvis, Armauer Hansen and Guido Baccelli, arrived in Berlin for the celebration of the "Pope of Medicine's" celebration in 1901. That he opened and encouraged the minds of students who then built on his, and others, discoveries was his was his greatest contribution in life. By inspiring other great minds he cleaved a rung in the ladder of progress on which others stepped.

Three months after international celebrations of his eightieth birthday, Rudolf energetically jumped from a street car. Although not instantly fatal, the resultant hip fracture he incurred finally stopped the legend. The bed in which he never slept for more than five hours at a time now housed Rudolf for nine months.

While Wilbur and Orville Wright developed their first successful glider, the Republic of Cuba was established and Pomp and Circumstance became the number one song in America, in

1902 the life of Rudolf Virchow quietly slipped away as the result of complications from his hip fracture. He remained coherent until the end. He was survived by his Röschen, six children and nineteen grandchildren. And the world mourned.

Today in Berlin there are four hospitals named for him as well as streets, schools and lecture halls. Statues of him were erected, national awards and foundations continue in his name. Credit is given to him, too many instances to count as they are worldwide and associated with disciplines as far removed from pathology as cosmetology and veterinary medicine. His name appears in lectures and discussions on studies from Darwinism to archeology. His publications, especially Virchow Archiv begun during his turbulent barricade fighting year continues and is available on-line. It is said without Virchow's work, chemotherapy and even AIDS research would not exist as we know it.

Just as his 'cells arise from cells' theory is taken for granted today, as is his application of the scientific method and fact-based medicine for which he absorbed many daggers and published jabs. It was his belief that hypotheses did worse than waste the time of doctors; that it risked setting medicine behind. His chants at his students: "Observation, observation, observation," "Think microscopically," and "Fact, not theory, based medicine" were bricks he laid upon which medicine built a new road.

Conclusion

My subject was a multi-faceted, complex human being with so many simultaneous activities and achievements one can only shake their head in wonder. In the end I am led to speculate - what drove him, what kept Virchow afire decade after decade? The result of my living with his presence for over ten years is my belief that the following quote is the underpinning from which sprang all of Virchow's beliefs and actions: "The body is a cell state in which each cell is a citizen."

Let me explain. A body easily maintains health if only a few of its cells are unhealthy. They are easily repaired at no cost to one's overall health. Extrapolate that thought to cities in the State of Vermont. The State will experience little impact if citizens in one city become ill. However, if multiple cells in a body become ill or diseased, now the whole body feels the effect. Extrapolating once again, if several cities become ill, the overall effectiveness of the State becomes compromised. Switching back to Virchow's analogy of the body, should the illness or disease progress to the point of a system shutting down, the body is in danger of dying. Extrapolating once more to the analogy, should many of its cities become afflicted, the entire State of Vermont is at risk.

Viewed in this way, Virchow's "cell state" takes new meaning. I believe that he literally intended a double meaning with the word 'state.' Reversing his statement from, "The body is a cell state in which each cell is a citizen," to, "The State is a body in which each citizen is a cell" holds identical meaning. There is a medical and political implication in each of these phrases.

That he deemed with equal importance each person as he did a cell, and a state collectively as one body, explains his adament insistence of education, democracy and wealth for each citizen in order to maintain the overall health of the state.

To Virchow's point of view, health must be maintained on an individual basis to ensure the health of the many. Further, he believed that if the number of sick citizens rises, it is an indication of a social cause – overcrowding, poor food quality, exposure to a causative agent. That is when a physician must cloak himself in a politician's jacket, per Virchow, to make a stand against what one identifies that is afflicting a large number of patients.

Virchow had several consistent character traits throughout his life. His daughter noted that even his handwriting did not change in over forty years. To this writer, the following were his finest character traits:

- Virchow's relentless pursuit for factual information, whether of a historical nature or a biological one, together with his resolve that those associated with him stay within the realm of facts. With the magnitude of his reputation had he joined in with the throng courting the Darwin theory, medicine itself would have been derailed for years. Through his influence the theory did not sweep medicine off its feet.

Rudolf Virchow

- Although he was a cold and demanding teacher to the unintelligent or bored, many references exist of him making himself available to a genuinely struggling student. A gentle arm around the shoulders, time spent one on one in his private study, joining in for an afternooon beer at the local pub – he could not afford to be warm and giving at all time but when called on, most certainly a loving human being according to historical references.

- Without fail, and even when there were great price tags attached, Rudolf's actions were consistent with his beliefs. He was a man of integrity.

- When Virchow involved himself in an organization he became its leader, thus indelibly fingerprinting whatever he joined. If no organization or publication existed to fulfill a need, he either helped to create one or did it himself. He did not purposefully seek fame, it happened as a result of the great breadth of his activities, his leadership and who he was.

- Like Ghandi, another formidable man of courage, no matter how shaky Virchow's world became, he held his ground with almost supernatural calm against physically larger, older and/or influential men and never backed down.

- How much greater and nobler his courage that the battles he fought were on behalf of others beginning with that first and greatest battle that influenced him for the rest of his life – the despair he witnessed in Upper Silesia. Many of his over two thousand published writings were defenses on behalf of his students. When German citizens and colleagues publicly attacked Schliemann, Virchow suffered their criticism and mocking when he made the trip to Troy to defend his friend. Among his colleagues he advocated for a patient's right to knowledge and he practiced it - disseminating knowledge to the public, standing in the trenches of a sewerage system or painstakingly studying minute details of an afflicted village. When others lives were at stake, Virchow's courage had no limit. That is the definition of a hero.

Rudolf Virchow

Bibliography

Ackerknecht, E. *Rudolf Virchow: Doctor, Statesman, Anthropologist.* New York: Stratford Press, 1953

Artès, P., and G. Duby. *History of Private Life IV: From the Fires of Revolution to the Great War.* (Duby, George, Ed.) Cambridge : Harvard University 1990

Hamerow, T. *Restoration, Revolution, Reaction: Economics and Politics in Germany 1815-1871.* Princeton: Princeton University 1958

Holborn, H. *History of Modern Germany 1840-1945.* New York: Alfred A. Knopf, Inc.

Laforgue, J. *Berlin: The City and the Court.* (W. J. Smith Trans.) New York: Turtle Point Press. 2000

Novotny, A. and C. Smith. *Images of Healing.* New York: Macmillan Publishing. 1980

Paret, P. *Art as History: Episodes in the Culture and Politics of Nineteenth Century Germany.* Princetown: Princeton University. 1988

Rather, L. *Rudolf Virchow.* San Francisco: Norman Publishing. 1990

Sperber, J. *European Revolutions: 1848-1851.* New York: University of Cambridge. 1994

Taylor, A. *Bismarck: The Man and the Statesman.* New York: Random House. 1955

Virchow, R. (Rabl, M, Ed.) *Letters to His Parents 1839-1864.* (L. J. Rather Trans.) San Francisco: (Original work published 1902

Leslie Dunn

Walsh, J. *Makers of Modern Medicine.* New York: Fordham University. 1907

High Museum of Art. *Art in Berlin: 1815-1989.* Atlanta: High Museum of Art. 1989

German Worker: Working Class Autobiographies from the Age of Industrialization. (Kelly, A. Trans.) Los Angeles: University of California. 1987

Rudolf Virchow

Photo Acknowledgements

http://www.annclinlabsci.org/cgi/content/full/35/2/203

http://commons.wikimedia.org/wiki/File:Die_Gartenlaube_%281862%2
9_b_749.jpg

http://www.creationism.org/books/TaylorInMindsMen/TaylorIMMh08.
htm http://commons.wikimedia.org/wiki/File:RudolfVirchow.jpg
http://upload.wikimedia.org/wikipedia/commons/8/83/Rudolf_Virchow
%2C_painted_by_Hans_Schadow_1896.jpg

http://numismatics.org/collection/1980.165.40:
Artist: Abram Belskie (1907-1988)

http://www.britannica.com/bps/media-view/136805/1/0/0

http://www.google.com/imgres?q=rudolf+virchow&hl=en&client=firefo
x-a&rls=org.mozilla:en-
US:official&biw=1350&bih=583&gbv=2&tbm=isch&tbnid=vm09JJVX6
Ov_9M:&imgrefurl=http://www.medarus.org/Medecins/MedecinsTexte
s/virchow_rudolf.htm&docid=9wgghX2kxAJvKM&imgurl=http://www.
medarus.org/Medecins/MedecinsImages/MedecinsPortraits/Virchow/Vi
rchow_3.jpg&w=360&h=501&ei=pDc4T_vnBYTyogHt-
cXPAg&zoom=1&iact=hc&vpx=577&vpy=45&dur=70&hovh=265&hovw
=190&tx=108&ty=166&sig=117050191290730966218&page=2&tbnh=12
3&tbnw=91&start=16&ndsp=37&ved=1t:429,r:22,s:16

http://clendening.kumc.edu/dc/pc/GroupPortrait.html

http://www.aspergillus.org.uk/indexhome.htm?secure/historical_paper
s/hall_of_fame/virchow.htm~main

ABOUT THE AUTHOR

Leslie Dunn has published numerous articles in newspapers and magazines about Quiet Heroes – normal people doing inspirational things. She has also published parenting and 'Slice of Life' articles. She lives in Nashville, Tennessee, is an American Canoe Association Certified Kayak Instructor and wrote the book, "Quiet Water Kayaking - A Beginner's Guide to Kayaking" available on Amazon, Lulu Press and at NashvilleKayakLessons.com.

Made in the USA
Middletown, DE
03 December 2023

44248813R00182